The WITCH'S LENS

The WITCH'S LENS

a novel

LUANNE G. SMITH

AUTHOR OF *THE RAVEN SPELL*

47NORTH

Published by 47North, Seattle

www.apub.com

Amazon, the Amazon logo, and 47North are trademarks of Amazon.com, Inc., or its affiliates.

ISBN-13: 9781662510403 (paperback)
ISBN-13: 9781662510397 (digital)

Cover design by Kimberly Glyder
Cover image: © mammuth / Getty; © bgfoto / Getty

Printed in the United States of America

The WITCH'S LENS

CHAPTER ONE

Petra turned the last card over on the table to reveal the devil sitting on his throne. She had to tighten the muscles in her cheek to keep her mouth from giving away her amusement at paní Novaková, who'd sucked in a startled breath at the sight of the card. Everyone knew her landlady as the hoarder of lesser town. The war had put an uncomfortable strain on everyone's pocketbooks, but paní Novaková's shelves were still full of tins of food, bars of soap, imported tea, and whatever else was impossible for others to buy in the shops. The woman either kept the goods all for herself and her overstuffed husband or charged twice as much to anyone who could persuade her to part with a slightly dented, slightly suspicious can of boiled beef. With her pettiness and greed, it should have been paní Novaková's face on the card instead of the horned one, but Petra couldn't complain too much about her landlady, since the woman paid every week to hear her future foretold in the cards. A paltry sum, really, but the money was enough for Petra to buy flour and potatoes for dumplings and squeeze out a few hellers to put toward her savings for a new roll of film. At the thought of dumplings, Petra's stomach groaned under the weight of her hunger.

"The card in this position tells us that you are holding back," Petra said, tapping her finger on the Devil card while meeting her landlady's eye. "You aren't allowing your better self to shine through."

"What better self?" The woman straightened her back defiantly in the kitchen chair. Even the thought of redeeming her reputation as a stingy-hearted woman made paní Novaková's proud nose rise even higher. "I am who I am."

And I am who I am, Petra thought. *A woman left alone to survive in an attic apartment after her husband ran off to enlist in the army.* And why? Because the feckless archduke had gotten himself and his wife assassinated in the back of their car while parading through the farthest reaches of his uncle's kingdom. There was no option but for the Empire to declare war after such a humiliation. But when you rule over the center of an entire continent, the enemies come with the territory.

Marek had promised to send home his wages, but Petra suspected she might die an old woman waiting for that promise to come true. They called it the Great War, but all that meant was the conflict was bigger and better at eating the young men each nation, bound by ironclad alliances, fed into it. And, by extension, the families who depended on those men. Soldiers sent to fight in trenches that cut through western farm fields, and in frozen mountain passes in the east that proved vulnerable back doors into the castles of empire. Six months of fighting and no end in sight as hundreds of thousands of young men had already been sacrificed to the cause. All to determine the fate of a handful of old men wearing crowns in an increasingly proletariat world.

Petra knew not to push paní Novaková, and yet she had to dig the knife in just a little deeper. "The cards are very clear," she said, staring at the layout of the tarot deck with mock innocence. "When paired with the Temperance card here, you run the risk of unbalancing your luck. Any good part you cherish might topple into the bucket of slop if there isn't some leavening of"—Petra reached for the diplomatic way to put it—"personality. One must always strive for balance to attract the most abundance into their lives."

The glint in paní Novaková's eyes hardened. "You think yourself a sly one, don't you." The woman dug in her pocketbook, pulled out a coin purse, and unwound the tight string holding the leather together. She slid one of the two korunas she owed for the reading across the table. "If not for your other predictions coming true, I'd have my husband slap you around the ears for your impertinence."

Your husband, who sits at home filling his face with pork and potatoes while my husband fights in faraway fields, feeding the ground with his blood, for all I know.

"I merely share what I see unfolding in the cards." Petra held the woman's gaze, knowing her golden eyes had an uncanny effect on those who believed she was spirit-touched. "None of us is above self-improvement in the grand scheme."

The woman's lip quivered briefly, like a stray dog about to show its teeth. She wound the string back around the coin purse in an exaggerated motion. "Someone said they saw a young man leaving the fourth floor late yesterday evening." Petra's landlady sneaked a quick glance at the bed against the far wall. "It's one thing to earn a little money telling fortunes, but a woman ought to be careful about the rumors that money changing hands with a man after dark might stir up," she said.

Petra couldn't control the deep sweep of red that flushed her cheeks. Her and Marek's apartment was the only one on the fourth floor. A space so small their "bedroom" was merely a corner of the apartment they'd walled off with a blanket suspended from an exposed oak beam. Magic swelled dangerously high in her veins, but she'd learned long ago how to tamp the impulse before it was too late. No, she wouldn't let the magic rise, even if the old woman had just accused her of dabbling in the sex trade.

"Someone has nothing better to do than invent stories," Petra said, knowing she ought to respond in her own defense. Her neighbor hadn't really seen any man, but Petra couldn't confess the truth either, knowing the questions it would raise.

Paní Nováková lifted a skeptical brow, but then her eye roamed over the meager apartment that she and her husband had only ever used for storage before Marek convinced them a young couple could make a go of the unused space as an apartment—if the rent were reasonable for the conditions. Paní Novaková didn't say anything more on the subject of strange men as she fished a tin of beans out of her shopping bag and set it on the table with a thud. "They're about to go bad anyway," she said before standing to leave.

Petra's stomach answered with a grumble. Her landlady walked to the door, still defiant in her righteousness, but nothing had been permanently broken between the women. She would be back to hear more of her future. Paní Novaková didn't have enough faith in this world, or her position in it, not to seek answers from the cards again soon.

"See you next Thursday," Petra said.

Paní Novaková paused in the hallway. "Was that earlier part you said before the devil business true?" She was referring to the heart trouble Petra had foreseen in the first overturned cards. The trouble could be physical, but it could just as well be a matter of hardship or regret.

"I always tell the truth of what I see," she answered.

The woman studied her face and finally nodded. "I'll be by, but we'll have to do it an hour earlier next week. I'm entertaining my husband's most important client that evening." Paní Novaková made a weapon of her smile, determined to reclaim her lost degree of superiority before she reached the stairs.

Petra sighed and shut the door, knowing the woman would somehow manage to serve a roast and potatoes with fat slices of buttered bread to another corpulent city official with access to black markets. Still, the compensation for a little mild fortune-telling went better than she thought. The beans would fill her stomach for two days, and the coin would go toward her fund to buy more film for her camera. Perhaps she should always tell the truth in the cards when it came to paní Novaková.

CHAPTER TWO

After slurping down half the can of beans and storing the rest in a crock on the window ledge for tomorrow, Petra opened the door to the tiny wardrobe closet. What meager clothes she and her husband owned she'd hung on pegs on the wall, then stuffed every crack in the closet where the light might try to get in with paper and rags. The shelves where their sweaters had been neatly folded now held two bottles of development solution. Above, Petra had suspended a string from one side of the closet to the other with two nails she'd had to steal from the baseboards by prying them loose with a butter knife. Hanging from the string was a line of black-and-white photos, each secured with a clothespin.

Petra plucked one of the photos off the line and examined it. She'd half expected the image of the weeping woman might fade from the paper once it dried, and yet the film seemed to have captured the woman's ethereal likeness in a sort of permanence she'd thought otherwise impossible. The woman had shown up in the photos for the first time three days ago, manifesting only after the negatives had been through the development process. Petra had taken the photo on the Old Town Square long after dark, when the place was mostly deserted. She hadn't seen the woman on the square when she took the picture, though she'd sensed her presence. Petra could infer the woman's shape and feel the sorrow rising off the cobblestones like a breath of morning fog. And so she'd snapped the picture on instinct, hoping to capture the mood of the moment in the contrasting light between shadow and moonlight. With a little luck, she'd hoped to sell copies of her photos as postcards to tourists in the Old Town Square looking to take home a souvenir of the city. But then she'd been rewarded with so much more.

Petra had been given a peculiar glimpse into her magic when it merged with the clever little invention capable of capturing a black-and-white snapshot in time. While she'd learned to keep the core of her magic bottled up tight to prevent discovery, this interesting seepage stirred her curiosity. There had always been a world beyond the sight of most humans, one made up of supernatural energy pressing against the other side of the veil. Of course, not all of it remained in the realm of the unseen. Petra unclipped a photo she'd taken of the river just south of the old king's bridge two weeks earlier. As she had stood along the riverbank, drawn by some mysterious pull in her solar plexus, she'd spotted the unusual tail fin slicing through the current, only to see it slip out of view again the moment her shadow crossed the water.

Then, for the briefest of moments, the curious creature's head had broken through the rippled surface again, revealing a woman's face and long hair coated in algae. A cloud of mist encircled her as a pair of translucent green eyes stared up at Petra, who stood with her camera lens extended and poised for a photo. At the sound of the shutter click, their tenuous exchange was severed and the creature sank beneath the water with a tiny splash. Not one other person on the bridge above seemed to notice the water sprite swimming beneath them in the midst of the city.

Petra took her camera from the shelf and checked the counter on the back—three frames left on the current roll of film. She'd have to be choosy with her subjects, but it would be enough to explore the other end of the bridge after the sun went down. Tomorrow, when the shops reopened, she would buy a fresh roll of film from pan Dubrovak at the grocer's. If only she had enough for a supply of developer, too, she thought wistfully as she shook the nearly empty brown bottle.

Petra shut the closet door and undid the buttons on her pleated skirt. She hung the garment up carefully on the peg on the wall, then reached for her husband's trousers and frayed wool jacket. *So, someone saw a young man leaving the apartment, did they?* She shimmied out of her slip, then pulled on the black trousers. Tonight she would have to tread with featherlight steps to avoid the old busybodies who liked to sit with their ears to the doors.

Petra waited until her landlord dimmed the lights above the hallway staircase for the night before tiptoeing to the bottom vestibule. She'd learned to avoid the loudest creaks in the floorboards and to turn the front doorknob slowly enough so the mechanism didn't click when it opened, but tonight she brought a little extra luck with her to counter the meddler energy floating in the hallway before she slipped out the front door.

Once outside, Petra walked quickly down the street. Fog clung to the riverbank and the trees, making soft white halos around the streetlights. The cold stung her skin, and she cursed herself for forgetting her scarf in her eagerness to test her disguise yet again, but the thrill of the excursion soon alleviated her discomfort. As she'd hoped, escaping the apartment building unseen this time had proved as easy as carrying the right amulets in her pockets: a pig charm for luck, a bronze coin to honor the moon for stealth, and a bundle of dried linden leaves tied with thread for protection. The last one she carried because, though she was dressed like a man, she was still a woman alone on the streets at night.

After she climbed the stairs to the old king's bridge, light snow began to fall. Petra made sure her camera was tucked under her coat to keep it dry, though she hoped the gloomy conditions would hold. The light would be ideal for capturing her subjects on film. Crossing the river into the oldest part of the city, she ignored the gazes of the bronze saints lining the bridge while she slunk by like a night prowler in her husband's clothes.

Paní Nováková had been right to warn her of the danger of loose talk. Gossip could be as dangerous as bullets for a married woman left on her own. But that had been Petra's dilemma from the start. If she went out at night dressed as a woman, she risked drawing the wrong sort of attention. But being spotted and mistaken for a man as she came and went from the apartment stirred up her landlady's sense of morality, threatening to boil over into accusation. Staying home, bored and alone, wasn't an option she could live with, so after Marek bought her a camera to keep herself occupied while he was gone, she'd begun wearing the trousers and tattered wool blazer he'd left behind. She stuffed her long hair under his old flatcap and exercised the freedom her borrowed identity brought. Hers wasn't the only husband to run off to fight for the Empire's existence, though she suspected she might be the only young wife to sneak out in men's clothes to take photographs of the dead who wandered the quiet streets at night.

Petra had walked the route in disguise several times already, but she still had to remind herself to take long, confident strides instead of the usual quick steps one was accustomed to in a skirt. The more practice she got walking as a man, the more she welcomed the thrill of being out alone at night. She embraced the danger, too, as she slipped down the narrow street leading to the town square where she'd last encountered the weeping woman. The camera sat reassuringly in her breast pocket. If conditions held, she hoped to fill all of the remaining frames.

A couple strolled by in the opposite direction, perhaps after enjoying a late supper at a café or a violin concerto at the National Theatre. Only a faint shadow of envy crossed Petra's heart as she dipped her head to pass the couple, pretending to be a young man minding his own business on his way home from work as an apprentice. Her alter ego was a clockmaker, she decided, dedicated to the intricate and detailed work that required a steady hand and good eyes. She needn't have bothered with the backstory or the ruse in the end. The pair were too infatuated with their own company, laughing and clinging to each other's arms, to notice anybody else existed in the world. Yes, war had cast its sobering silhouette over the continent, but lovers still found a way to drink in their unique form of intoxication despite the pessimism that pervaded every morning newspaper.

Petra shook off an uncomfortable shiver. She didn't like to think of what might happen in the future, to Marek or herself. They lived in an era of facing each day one at a time. No future, no past. No tarot to paint a picture of what may come. For now, the present was all they had, and that meant being apart with no reunion in sight.

When she entered the Old Town Square, the astronomical clock was just finishing chiming the midnight hour. The last of the apostles made their mechanical appearance, following their circular path above the clockface. They pointed their pious fingers, brandished their weapons, and displayed their purity by clutching their books of faith to their hearts. Death, too, jingled his bones, warning the small crowd of late-night stragglers gathered below that the final hour was nigh for all. Aside from the tourists, a few solitary men walked along the cobblestones on the opposite side of the square after the last of the electric trams had returned to the depot for the night. None of the men had looked twice at Petra, so she turned the corner of the Old Town Hall tower to stand before the three arched doorways that made up the east wing. That's where she'd seen the weeping woman the last time, so she reasoned there was a good chance she would see her there again. Perhaps she wept for someone she'd once loved. Or someone she'd once been.

The energy near the square reverberated with the vibrancy of an ancient city, one that clung to the spirits of all those who'd lived and died behind its walls. Sometimes Petra thought the freezing fog itself was the collective breath of the dead exhaling at night. She didn't need to ask why the low hum of energy seemed to be more intense near the old tower. There'd been so many executions over the centuries, so many heads mounted on spikes by rulers determined to subjugate any hint of rebellion, how could the air not vibrate with the spirits of the unsettled dead?

Some souls seemed to be held motionless in the space, as if tethered to the earth by a thirst for vengeance. Or at least that's what the shapes and colors dancing in her mind's vision told her as she drew nearer to the door and sensed the presence of another being. The spirit's shape bloomed in her second sight, a shrouded figure standing before the door, yet Petra's eyes saw only physical stone and mortar surrounding solid oak. She had heard that other witches could see specters in the night, but her magic had always resided in her fingertips and what she could feel in the air around her.

Petra extended the lens on her vest pocket camera. As she did, a snowy cloud billowed at the foot of the large oak door. She held the camera steady, looked through the viewfinder, and pressed her thumb against the shutter before the mist dissipated again. The click of the camera caused a brief cessation in the humming energy before it resumed, like a cat startled by a slamming door only to trot off again when the noise proved unthreatening. The delicate cloud drifted to Petra's left to disperse in the snowy night air. She advanced the film for the next photo as she walked along the edge of the square, eyes and mind watchful for any changes. That's when she noticed the shadowy echo of a boy's spirit taunting her. She took a step closer to test the being, when the wisp of energy darted down a side street populated with small boutiques she could no longer afford to shop in. Apartments, costing double what she and Marek paid paní Nováková each month, rose three stories high on either side of the walkway, each painted a different happy color.

"Wait for me," Petra whispered, running to catch up.

The boy was new to her, so she followed hoping to see if he would manifest on film as the woman had. He moved with the quick pace of a child at play, his spirit sprinting over the cobblestones. Petra's breath came hard in the cold air as she ran after him, down one bend in the lane and then another. If only he would stop, she could focus her lens. Then, just when she thought her fingers would freeze from the cold, he slowed down to meander in front of a rustic stone church. A curtain of softly falling snow stood between them as she caught her breath.

Petra was familiar with the church, having passed it more than a few times on her way to her in-laws' apartment in the district just to the east. Small and rather plain by the city's ornate Gothic standards, the nine-hundred-year-old building stood out for its tenacity to hold on to its spot, as if it had roots that went deep into the earth, despite the more modern buildings that crowded in on all sides. Petra rubbed her hands together to get the feeling back, then readied her camera lens. She focused it on the wall at the corner nearest the narrow lane that ran beside the church. Had the boy smiled? She snapped the photo, and his spirit whooshed up to the roof on a whirlwind of snow and fallen leaves.

When the wind died down and the snow resettled into its softly drifting pattern, Petra locked on a pair of eyes watching her from the narrow passageway to the left of the church. No, he was studying her, seeing what she was about. A man this time, not a spirit. Petty thieves clung to the main square during the busiest parts of the day like lint on fine wool, picking the pockets of unwary gawkers who watched the famous clock strike the hour, but she hadn't anticipated any thieves would stalk a lonely side street at midnight. *Fool!* Who did she think inhabited the streets in the middle of the night besides stray pairs of lovers unable to say good night to each other and odd young women in men's clothes? But this thief would be sorry if he tried to take anything so precious as her camera from her, she thought, reaching for her amulet of linden leaves.

Petra quietly retracted the camera lens. The watcher knew he'd been spotted, yet he persisted in staring at her as he leaned one shoulder against the wall. He didn't even pretend nonchalance with a no-I'm-not-going-to-rob-you-so-don't-worry-about-me look in the other direction. The way he watched her with the confident glint of a predator in his eyes . . . was he sizing up his prey? The thought gave her goose bumps, but she wouldn't run and allow him to give chase. Instead, she stood her collar up and walked away, just another young man out late at night, her hand tightly gripping the charms in her pocket. If he followed, there were other defenses she could use. If she must. Something more forceful than a mere bundle of leaves meant to offer protection. But it had been so long since she'd dared summon her innate magic. She hoped he'd just walk on and she could avoid the confrontation in the open street and the scrutiny it would invite.

Another hard gust of wind blew through the lane in front of the church, sending snow skittering over her cheeks and stinging her eyes. The cap blew off her head, and her hair fell to her shoulders. In a near panic she bent to retrieve the hat and hide her hair again, but it cartwheeled away, driven by the wind. Fearful she'd been exposed, she was hurrying after the cap when the man came out of the shadows and stomped his boot on the brim to stop it from blowing farther away.

Petra stopped in her tracks, clutching the camera to her chest as a last gust of wind whipped her hair over her face. She swept her tangled hair out of her eyes as the young man, with dark hair and a mostly clean-shaven face, stood in front of her. He wore a fur *ushanka* and the long coat of the Cossacks, but his gray wool trousers and staggered black infantry boots with puttees were decidedly the issue of the Empire's army. He bore no insignias, no stars or silk embroidery on his collar, no double eagle on his belt buckle, and yet he was every bit a soldier. *A patchwork military man,* was all she could think as he towered over her.

He cast his eye on her camera before bending to retrieve the cap from beneath his boot. "I believe this belongs to you . . . *slečna*," he said, brushing the snow off with his gloved hand before presenting it to her.

"It's paní, actually," she said, having no more pretense to lie. Flustered by the exchange, Petra snatched the cap from him, then took a step back and reached again for her amulet, still hesitant to call the magic up before a stranger. Awkwardly, she remembered to say, "Thank you."

His eyes had a distinct shine to them as he watched her hand reach into her pocket. He inhaled deeply before saying, "I stand corrected." He bowed his head and touched the edge of his fur hat in a gesture of respect.

Petra squeezed her fingers around the leaves and let her magic rise to just beneath the surface. She wanted to be ready to visualize a sharp-ended spell if he made one move toward her. Instead, he glanced from her camera to the church wall where she'd sensed the boy, tightening his brows in what she took to be genuine curiosity before wishing her a good evening with another touch of the front of his hat.

The young man walked away with the irritatingly assured gait of one accustomed to prowling the streets at night without fear. Petra didn't know why, but instead of experiencing relief that he'd gone, the exchange left her feeling exhilarated and buoyant. As if she'd just been sniffed over by a rabid dog and found to be too wild and unpredictable to attack. The thought thrilled her, filling her with the confidence of a night stalker herself as she lifted her camera to take one last photo of the church and the boy before tucking her hair under her cap and following the side lanes to the bridge to go home.

Back at her apartment building, she crept up the three flights of stairs as quiet as a thief. A good one who doesn't get caught, she mused, turning the key in the lock to her apartment without making a sound. Inside, she shook off the snow and closed the door, exhaling in relief that she'd made it back home undetected. And with new photos to develop. The prospect of seeing the boy's figure on the film excited her, enough that she was tempted to develop the frames now, while the rest of the city slept. All but the night prowlers, that was, like the striking young man in the fur hat.

Not wanting to turn on the harsh electric lights at that late hour, Petra struck a match and lit the candle on the small side table next to the door where she set her key down. The glow from the flame was bright enough to spark her intuition. A sense that someone else was there. That's when she saw him just outside the reach of the candle's glow. The patchwork soldier from the street. He sat at her kitchen table, shuffling the tarot cards in his hands where paní Nováková and she had sat only hours earlier. He'd removed his heavy fur hat, leaving it to drip on the windowsill as the snowflakes melted. He smiled, knowing he'd surprised her.

"You do readings for old women during the day, and at night you go into the streets to take photos of bare walls." He casually set the deck of cards aside. "Do I have that right?"

"How did you get in here?" Petra couldn't remember now if she'd truly locked the door when she'd left. The latch had turned so quietly when she'd returned. Nevertheless, this man, with his mismatched great-coat and infantry boots, had let himself into her home. "I'll scream," she said, reaching for the amulet in her pocket. "The building is full of busybodies who have nothing better to do than listen for trouble."

"Sit," he said, and slid the empty chair out with his foot.

Petra ran for the door, but he matched her steps, pinning his body against hers so she couldn't open the door. How could a man move so fast? He clasped his hand over her mouth, shushing her with a whisper in her ear. His fingers dug into the soft flesh of her cheek. She struggled against him, his weight nearly smothering her, until she knew it was futile to rely on physical strength.

"Please, do not scream," he said. "I only want to talk." He seemed to understand he might be hurting her, so he eased his body away from hers, removing his hand slowly from her mouth.

Petra had no intention of screaming, despite her earlier threat. That would only give the other tenants the opportunity to form more false stories in their heads of what they'd seen—her in men's clothes and a strange man in her apartment after midnight. It would not matter what the truth was. Rumor would fly from mouth to ear quicker than a match to flame. No, she must deal with this intrusion the only way she could without stirring the entire building awake, despite what it might cost her later.

Petra let her body go still and called on her craft for the second time that night on account of this man. This time, however, she followed through. She rarely summoned the old magic to rise within her, but she found it still answered when she called. Giving way to the infusion of power, heat tingled at her fingertips, and her pupils dilated so that the room appeared bathed in strong light even though only one candle burned. Concentrating, she held the pig amulet in her pocket and envisioned the shape of a bludgeon in her mind. The spell connected, sparking to life on her fingertips as the amulet changed shape. She brought the weapon out of her pocket and jammed it in the soldier's ribs behind her, throwing him off long enough for her to escape his hold. She spun around with her arm cocked, ready to summon another spell if she must, something pointy and sharp she could throw. The man stumbled back a step, but he didn't cower or question the odd energy that had freed her. Instead, he held his hands up, palms out, as if to say he understood she could do him greater harm.

"What do you want?" Petra asked, though she already suspected. She'd known the minute she saw him sitting at her table. He knew about her magic and what it could do for him. Her breath came quickly. Had it been ten years since she'd conjured a proper spell? She'd forgotten the exhilaration she experienced deep in her chest after so much time away from magic.

The man was not put off. He sat again and drummed his fingers on the table as he took in the sight of her husband's tattered wool jacket. "Why didn't you use the other amulet in your pocket? Linden leaves, if I'm not mistaken. You use them for protection, correct?"

Petra froze. It was one thing to suspect she was a witch, but how did this man know about the contents of her pockets? She reached in and produced the bundle of leaves to show him he'd guessed right. "I suppose I could have used the strong scent to render you unconscious, but then I'd have to explain the loud thud hitting the floor in the middle of the night." She squeezed the bundle of leaves with all her strength until their soft citrusy smell rose from her palm. Remarkably, she saw the exact moment he caught the sharp increase in scent.

"You work with herbal spells?" he asked.

Curious how he could know such things, Petra scanned the skin around his collar, employing a sharper perception than she'd used in the street earlier. She narrowed her eyes at the man but detected no hint that he carried the same magic in his veins that she did in hers. He was plainly a mortal. And yet what did a mortal know of amulets? What suspicion did a mortal carry about a woman who sensed those on the other side of the veil? Was he one of *them*? Was she talking to a shadow? Or was he merely what he appeared to be: a soldier out witch hunting.

"How did you know what was in my pocket?" she asked, fighting the urge to reach out and grab hold of his Cossack's coat to see if he was truly there or merely an apparition playing tricks on her vision.

His manner changed subtly. He relaxed his shoulders, slouching in the chair and propping his elbow atop the back as if he were waiting to be served in a beer garden. "I mean you no harm, paní Kurková, but I do have some idea of what you're about," he said with a brief smile, betraying a hint that he was capable of charm when it suited him. "Also, it's obvious you cling to something in your pocket every time you feel threatened."

"How do you know my name?" Petra's initial fear transformed into stunned disbelief as her head buzzed with impossible questions: How had he found where she lived? How did he get inside her apartment? How could this stranger know who and what she was?

He tapped his finger on a letter addressed to her that she'd left on the counter by the sink earlier to show he'd read the name. Not the mundane response she'd expected. "Now," he said, "tell me why you risk going out in the snow dressed as you are to take photos of nothing in the dark."

"I don't—"

His face tightened, reminding her of the man who had pinned her against the door. The look was that of a soldier who did not tolerate lies or insubordination. "You ran until you were out of breath, only to stop and take a picture of the church wall?"

Petra glanced over her shoulder to the door. "Keep your voice down."

He held out his hand to direct her toward the chair opposite him, indicating she should sit if she wanted things civil. "What were you trying to capture with your lens?"

So many questions! It was dizzying.

"The camera is mine. I do what I want with it," Petra said. She held one hand protectively over the camera in her pocket as she sat in the chair. With the other she removed her husband's cap, letting her hair fall free.

She didn't think a man could scowl any harder, but he forced his brows tighter together, forgetting all his earlier attempts at nonchalance aimed at gaining her trust. "So, you commonly waste precious film taking photos of bricks and stone?" He crossed his arms as if waiting for her to admit she was a dolt of the highest order. "I ask again: What was your purpose in taking the photos?"

Petra thought back to her stroll through the Old Town Square, and afterward to the church at the spot where the vague sense of something supernatural had drifted before her lens. Did he think her some sort of spy because of her disguise? Yes, she could see how it might look a tad suspicious to see a woman taking a photo of little more than snow and stone while dressed in her husband's clothes, but this man couldn't be any soldier for the Empire the way he was dressed. He had no jurisdiction over her and no authority to confront her. If he thought her a spy with a mission to take pictures of a quiet corner church, perhaps *he* was the dolt.

"I don't know who you are or why you think I need to explain anything to you," she said, testing his air of authority. "But it's quite late and my husband will be home any moment. It's time for you to leave."

"Except you and I both know your husband won't be home, because he's off fighting a useless war in some godforsaken patch of snow for the Empire's supposed glory. Isn't that right?"

She wanted him gone, but his sarcastic tone about the Empire struck a sympathetic chord in her. How many fights had she had with Marek over that very subject before he left? War, should it tilt in the right direction toward defeat, could mean independence. A chance for their people to become self-determined. To make their own choices, their own laws, their own fortunes. *If* men were willing to fight for the cause of independence instead of kowtowing to the imperialists, giving their lives for a diseased dynasty that ruled over them from not one but two corrupt capital cities hundreds of kilometers away.

"I thought I saw something move through the snow," she finally admitted.

"Something?" The man reached in his pocket and tossed down one of her photos of the weeping woman. One taken from her wardrobe development room.

"You went through my things!"

He ignored her objection. "Do you see the dead walking among us?"

Petra had only just admitted the uncanny ability to herself. She might never have known she had the gift if her husband hadn't bought her the camera. Marek couldn't have known then how the small device would upend her life. Once she'd been made aware of the manifestations, she had become obsessed with finding more.

"The camera sees them," she said, uncertain why she was confiding her deepest secret to this man who'd broken into her apartment. "I only feel their presence like a cloud passing or maybe a cold shiver down the neck." He nodded, as if to say her version of the truth aligned with his own understanding of such things. "I click the shutter to take the photo, but I never know who or what I'll find until I get home and develop the negatives." She nudged her chin toward the photo he'd tossed on the table. "I call her the weeping woman because she cries at the wall every night. I don't know why."

He studied the photo again, seeming to appreciate better what he was seeing.

"But enough of your questions," she said. "Who are you? What do you want? How did you find me?" Petra tapped her finger against the table, determined to get her way. "You answer *me* this time."

His lips tensed as he held in a smile. Not because he was laughing at her, no. Instead, she thought it was because he was pleased to see her unafraid to turn the tables on him.

"Very well," he said. "My name is Josef Svoboda. I've been tasked with putting together a coalition of men to take back to the eastern front." He leaned forward as if speaking in confidence, and she caught the animal scent of his wool coat. "Not just any men, though. Men of magic."

So, he'd come to collect witches after all. Did that mean the war had finally caught up with her like all the rest of her kind?

The veil of pretense fell away between Petra and the man sitting before her. Josef knew exactly what she was, though she couldn't yet say the same about him, other than he was a soldier with far too much knowledge about the supernatural.

Petra's husband, also a mortal, didn't know about her bloodline. For nearly half her life now, she'd kept her magic hidden. At times, even from herself. She knew, of course, that entire covens of witches had been recruited to fight in the war. Individuals, too, like the composer Benjamin Laska, who could conjure up a tune on his clarinet to make the stars weep with the way his magic adhered emotion to sound in a cascade of stirring sonatas, or Julius Belinsky, the jeweler who used his skill to channel healing energy into the garnet gemstones he set in rings and brooches. Their influence was meant to alter the course of the battles so that hostilities might end quickly. Or so everyone had hoped, until all sides engaged in the same practice, transforming the western front into a stalemate of trenches, barbed wire, and deadly hexes. And the east? It was a frozen hellscape rumored to be overrun with the cursed undead. Both Laska and Belinsky had been forced to travel to the nearest capital city to serve the emperor's sorceress four months earlier. Neither had been heard from since.

"Why do you need to recruit more witches?" she asked, surprised to find herself excited to speak of magic in the open again. "What's changed?"

"There are developments happening in the east, in the mountains, that require the skills of those who understand a battlefield is made up of more than blood and bullets. I'm told there have always been supernatural forces in the world. Things only understood by those who carry the blood of the witch. This has proven true in war as well, and so we must gather even the most reluctant sorcerers to join the fight. There are"—he paused, as though evaluating how she might react to what he was about to say—"there's a type of magic that has been awakened by the bloodshed of war."

"What kind of magic?" she asked, though she already had a notion.

"The kind that requires a balancing force to countermand it."

"Navi?"

He nodded. "Men are dying in the mountain forests. That's not unusual. They die by the thousands following orders given by unskilled officers. But this is different. There is a curse, a spell, a hex. Whatever you want to call it that lingers near the battlefield, waiting for the next round of killing. Indiscriminate at times." He leaned forward until his long torso overtook half the table. "Have you ever seen the aftermath of direct battle?" He didn't wait for her to answer. He knew she hadn't. "The bloodletting is its own curse in war. Believe me when I tell you there were enough wasted lives in the name of territory already without the interference from the supernatural world."

Guilt wormed around Petra's heart, knowing she'd deliberately avoided volunteering when war was declared. Of course, she often wondered if some small effort she might make could help protect Marek or some other woman's husband. To think those mortal men were out there in the mountains being subjected to magic they had no idea how to defend themselves against was almost unimaginable on top of the other abuses they suffered. But could she expose herself to the risk?

"The group who sent me here thinks we can curb the abuses." Josef crossed his arms, circumspect. "Can you imagine what would happen if the effects of these curses were to escape the confines of battle and roam the hillside villages? It would be mayhem, extending the war for years."

"What can be done?" she asked.

Josef shook his head. "There are ways. But the navi are as elusive as your ghosts. Seen and then unseen." He tapped the photo of the weeping woman, then slid it across the table. The navi weren't ghosts, but their spirits danced in the same realm of the dead. "It's like trying to put a nail through a puff of breath without the ability to know where they are. So, when I saw you tonight, it gave me an idea."

The gravity of what he was about to say hit her, and she looked up at him in alarm. "You can't mean to recruit *me* for this." She stood, hitting the chair with the back of her legs so that it sprawled across the floor. "To the front? Are you mad?"

"No doubt there will be some who'll think me a fool for asking a woman to join the fight at the front, yes."

"But I couldn't possibly go."

"Why not? Because you're too busy sneaking around at night in your husband's clothes taking pictures of dead people? Men from both armies are dying in the forests. And not all of them from grenades and bullets. This curse is spreading. Killing as if it's an army unto itself. I believe your skills can help us in the battle to stop them." Josef stood and grabbed his fur hat. "You can make a difference, paní Kurková."

"Me?" While Petra gawked at him in disbelief, he produced a leaflet from his inside breast pocket.

"Where is your husband stationed?" Josef asked.

"I'm not sure. He isn't allowed to share his whereabouts." Petra took the leaflet from him and scanned it briefly.

"So, it is possible he, too, fights in the infected mountains."

The leaflet appeared to be a written call to service for those witches not yet engaged in the turmoil of war. Crudely printed, it stated that Josef Svoboda had the express authority to conscript any man of necessary skill and temperament to join his newly formed band of sorcerers.

"But who do you fight for? It doesn't say which side you're on."

Josef slipped his ushanka on his head and buttoned his long coat. "I entered the fight, like your husband, on the side of the Empire. Later I was captured by the tsar's army after I was, well, injured and left to die in the snow. They held me prisoner for a time before offering me a chance to fight with them against the Empire. I did so for one month before it proved an impossible task to continue. By then I was tapped for a different purpose by those outside the scope of either side's mortal leadership."

"Who?"

"Show up tomorrow and find out," he said, pointing to the location listed on the letter where she was to report in the morning. "Though I can't force you, as a woman, to join us, I hope you'll do the right thing."

"But I can't do this," Petra said as her voice rose in pitch, no longer caring if she aroused her neighbors' attention. "I'm not qualified. I'm not trained for war."

"None of us were," he said. "Tomorrow morning. This address. Do not be late." He left the apartment and closed the door behind him with a silent click.

The man was mistaken. A fool. He'd come to the wrong place. She might be a witch by birth, but she'd long ago set aside her magic. The consequences of her spells had proved too caustic. And she certainly didn't run off with ragtag soldiers who claimed to be fighting an invisible war against the supernatural.

This Josef Svoboda would find himself waiting in vain if he expected to see her in the morning. Or ever again.

CHAPTER THREE

Petra woke to the sound of heavy knocking on her door. Had that fool come back? He'd wake the entire building with his pounding. She threw off the covers, prepared for a fight, when the man on the other side ordered her to open up, punctuated by a second round of his fist thumping against the door. Not the soldier then but pan Novak, her landlord.

But it wasn't the first of the month. The rent wasn't late. Not yet, anyway. Petra sat up and covered herself in her blue wool coat as a shiver of dread threaded its way through her body. She opened the door, smoothing her hair away from her face.

"What is it, pan Novak?" Petra shielded herself with the door, still in a state of waking after only five hours sleep. Her landlord, dressed in a black suit but no tie yet, and with just the hint of shaving cream still visible on his jawline, bore the mottled red color of an undercooked sausage. Paní Nováková, already in her gray dress with the black buttons and white lace collar, stood behind her husband with her arms crossed. The woman beamed like a cat savoring the taste of blood from the mouse she'd just devoured.

Pan Novak didn't wait to be invited in. He pushed the door open and marched into the kitchen area, peering from side to side. He swept back the blanket that divided the bed from the rest of the apartment and huffed out a disappointed breath when it seemed not to reveal what he was looking for.

"What are you doing?" Petra asked, clutching her coat tight under her chin. "You can't just come into my room and start shoving things aside."

"Oh, can't I?" The man deliberately flung open the door to the wardrobe while paní Nováková continued smirking above her lace collar. He scrunched up his nose when he saw the line of negatives hanging from the string and the bottles of solution she used for developing the film. "What've you done to my closet?"

Petra reached out with one hand. "Those are mine. Leave them alone."

He squinted at the string of negatives with his mouth twisted into preemptive disgust, as though bracing for some scene that might damage his upstanding sensibilities. More confused than alarmed by the images, he swung around, finger pointing. "There was a man in here last night." And while pan Novak was normally not the sort to argue with, his accusation lacked the confidence of someone who knows definitively what he's talking about. He'd been given a morsel of gossipy information from one of the nosy neighbors and decided to act on it. At least that's what Petra deduced from the way he kept making inquisitive eye contact with his wife to make sure he had the accusatory details right.

And yet what could Petra say? There had been a man in her apartment last night. Whoever the nosy nuisance was on a lower floor, they obviously kept cat's hours, prowling in their apartment at night with their eye pressed to the keyhole.

"I was told there were *two* men, pan Novak." The wife shook her head at Petra. "In one night. I warned you I'd not have that sort of business going on under this roof," she said.

"I can explain." Petra grabbed the teakettle and filled it with water, hoping they might sit at the table and discuss this rationally. "It isn't what you think. That was me last night. I'm the man someone saw." She pointed out her husband's wool jacket and cap on the wall as evidence, but the information might as well have sailed over their heads and flown out the window.

Her landlord yanked down her photos from the line and tossed them on the floor. "We have a reputation to protect. This is a respectable house, and I want you out," he said, stomping over the pictures as he made his way to the door. "Today!"

Paní Nováková followed her husband into the hallway, sparing a brief backward glance to let her gaze travel from the men's clothing to the photos. "I did warn you," she said.

Had they willingly jumped to their flimsy conclusions so they could throw her out in exchange for some prospective tenant willing to pay twice as much for the shabby apartment? Anger welled up in her core, rising like tears, until she feared she'd be unable to keep her magic and emotions separate. Still stinging from the accusation, she let the anger and magic mingle. Just a little. She caught paní Nováková's eye with a withering stare. "As did I," Petra replied as a symbol of a flashing star winked in her mind's eyes and a tiny spark of energy snapped in the air.

Paní Nováková flinched as though she'd heard the crackle of static electricity. Petra knew the woman believed in the predictive power of the tarot. She accepted that the fate Petra had laid out for her in the cards was more than mere folly. Concern registered on the landlady's face as she clutched at the buttons on her dress just above her heart before retreating down the stairs to catch up with her husband.

The spell Petra had set loose in the room would only give paní Nováková a case of worrisome indigestion, but hopefully it would be enough to make her think twice about the consequences of false accusations—the universal sort of consequences that could alter the path of one's life for good or ill. The kind Petra had had to live with every day for the past ten years.

Petra shouldn't have been surprised, given how little she owned, that the entire process of cleaning out her apartment had taken her less than an hour. She'd packed her three dresses, her second pair of shoes, her only tablecloth, a deck of cards, her husband's sparse clothing, and a silver vanity set—a reluctant wedding present from her mother-in-law. Oh, Marek was going to be furious if and when he found out she'd been evicted from their apartment. But how to tell him? She'd sent a handful of letters soon after the war had begun, writing dutifully to her husband every week, but after months of separation from him, she had received only one response, a letter in which he complained he was too busy to write. There was no way of knowing if he'd even received the other letters she'd sent, so mailing one more carefully worded missive to describe the horrible way she'd been thrown out of their home felt like one effort too many. She knew what he would say, though. It's what he always said: if ever things got too difficult, they could just go live at his parents' home on the other side of the river. Such a gift to know you always had somewhere to land if life tossed you into the dung pile, Petra thought. It gave Marek the sort of confidence she had lacked in her own life. She could see that now. Never having anywhere solid to put down roots had led her to hold on to the safe and reliable Marek. And now he, too, was gone.

Petra stuffed her nightgown inside her bursting valise, along with her battered photos. She tried to wedge the bottles of developing equipment in, but a mouse couldn't have stowed away in the space left in her bag. With no room left in her bag, she slipped her camera inside her coat pocket, swallowed the last of the cold beans she'd saved from the night before, and then left the dirty dishes in the sink alongside the pile of used bed linens on the counter. It was freeing, really, to not have a single responsibility other than getting oneself out the front door and onto the pavement, she thought, taking a last look around.

Petra dropped the key to the attic room through the mail slot outside the Novaks' apartment, then shut the door to the building behind her for the last time. Outside, the late winter chill suspended her frosty breath midair. The frigid temperature seeped through the loose stitching of her coat and down her legs as tiny, jagged ice crystals disguised as snow stung her nose and eyelashes. She walked away from the building quickly with her head down to avoid both the snow and the prying eyes of her neighbors. She'd known the shame of having to escape with everything she owned in a small case before, but this was not that. No, she'd done nothing wrong other than having to scrounge for the rent money every month when Marek's army pay hadn't arrived as promised. She hadn't even invited the man in last night. He'd burgled her apartment, made ludicrous assertions, and then not had the decency to make a quiet escape when she rebuffed him. And his offer? Run off to battle the undead in a mortal war? The notion was absurd.

Uncertain of where to go next, Petra wandered down one icy lane and then another, hoping for a revelation, until her fingers ached from lugging her heavy valise. She could go to her in-laws. Marek's mother would screw up her face and fuss about the inconvenience, but Petra believed she would ultimately be allowed to stay. She was their only son's wife, after all. And yet her feet would not move in that direction. Even if she did want to go there, the air was too cold to walk all the way to the other side of the Old Town Square.

Petra saw her mother-in-law's disapproving face loom before her. The woman would eventually sniff out the circumstances of the eviction through a chain of gossip and gentle inquiries. Petra would argue, of course, that it was all a misunderstanding, but the truth already faced a headwind against a woman primed to believe the worst of her. She'd never been quite respectable enough for Marek in her mother-in-law's eyes.

The weight of Petra's predicament forced her to sink onto a bench where an elderly man sat waiting for the tram, still clearing the morning phlegm from his lungs.

"It's running late this morning," he said with a nod toward the track. "Ice slows everything down."

Petra glanced in both directions and nodded. "The snow will clear by afternoon," she said, knowing she was right based on an instinct born somewhere deep inside her.

The old man did a deep clearing of his throat again, so she turned away and closed her eyes against the silver clouds, letting the snow fall on her face. Snow, when it fell in sharp little crystals, provided the most exquisite gift—the scent, the chill, the sting against the skin. Others didn't know its power, but she'd been raised by a father whose head had been full of both the old ways and the new, and snow carried its own pure magic.

Petra opened her eyes and stuck her gloved hand out to catch the flakes in her palm. She knew if you could count all the snowflakes that hit before the crystals melted, your wish would come true. The way she saw her future unfolding, she could either go to her in-laws or search out a charitable home like those open to refugees. Petra knew how to cook and sew and scrub to earn her keep—all things her mother-in-law would make her do as well, though with an added dose of grief thrown in.

"Twenty-three is all I see. Is it enough to rescue me?" Petra whispered.

"What's that you're doing?" The old man leaned forward to see what she held in her hand.

"I'm making a wish about my future," Petra replied as the last snowflake—the twenty-third—melted on her upturned glove. "You see, I have two possible options about what to do once I leave this bench, and neither of them are very good."

The man looked from her disheveled, wet appearance to her valise and seemed to surmise her predicament. "It's terrible weather for indecision," he said as the squeal of metal wheels complaining in the cold signaled the tram's impending arrival. The man stood as the streetcar stopped and the doors opened. "Probably best to get on, at least until you warm up."

Wishes never did materialize right away. With nowhere else to go, Petra stepped on the tram. She thanked the man when he paid the few coins for her to ride before sliding into one of the wooden seats. She paid little attention to where the tram went until they'd crossed the river and headed toward the Old Town's center. Just as well, she thought, resigned to the notion that the fates who rule over wishes had decided her in-laws' home was the respectable and safe place for her to await her husband's return from war. If he returned. That, too, was up to the fates.

But what if she could make a difference? With her magic. Not the deep-down magic that was rooted to the earth. That she had to keep hidden, but this new expression that traveled through her camera lens could be of use to save men's lives, if the stories of the undead were true. Perhaps. At least the witch-hunter soldier had thought so. Helene Kurková would call her daughter-in-law foolish for even thinking she had anything of value to offer. Then again, the woman would call Petra a number of unflattering things regardless.

After crossing the bridge to the opposite riverbank, Petra waited for the tram to make the left turn and veer toward her in-laws' neighborhood. When it hit a bump and went in another direction, she wondered if she'd hopped on a different tramcar than she'd first thought. But no, everyone strained to look out the window, apparently wondering the same thing.

"The switch," said the man from the bench. "It must have frozen." He threw up his hands. "Sent us east instead of north."

The tram rolled forward another fifty meters before slowing to a stop. Petra rubbed her coat sleeve against the fogged-over window to see where they were, when she spotted the *pekařství* across the road. The bakery Josef Svoboda had pointed out on his flyer. The shiver in her blood told her it was no coincidence. It just couldn't be.

Petra stared through the glass, letting her intuition rise. Hadn't it felt good to talk about spells again? To spend a little time in her authentic skin after so long? Wasn't that why she'd let herself continue to risk everything to take photos at midnight after the spirits showed up? And now here was an opportunity staring her in the face. A chance to balance the scales for past wrongs. One that would let her work with other witches and use that power to save someone's life. Maybe even her husband's.

"Everyone, remain in your seats," said the conductor. "We'll get moving again in a moment."

"No, no, no." Petra grabbed her valise and rushed toward the door. "I have to get off here," she said. "This is my stop."

"Just have a seat, *slečna*. We'll get the ice broken up and be on our way."

But she couldn't wait. She might not practice magic regularly anymore, but if one didn't have the sense to listen to the intuition floating in the ether around them, they might as well proclaim themselves as dull as a mortal. Especially when young men's lives were at stake. Petra let the shape of a green triangle form in her mind, then aimed the pointed end at the door. With a puff of breath, the double doors split open, and Petra jumped off the steps and onto the snowy pavement. She stood on the sidewalk, her valise gripped tight in front of her with both hands, as she watched a young man with fair hair and glasses, and carrying a heavy pack on his back, enter the very bakery she'd been eyeing. Was this truly the place?

And then she saw the tall mismatched soldier from the night before and knew she was where she was meant to be. Josef had stepped outside in his long coat and fur hat, blowing on his bare fingers and rubbing his hands together to get warm. He greeted the young man with the fair hair with an eager handshake and a gleaming smile that transformed his features into a face that made her forget she was cold. Josef pointed the man inside, assuring him he'd be along in a minute with a brotherly clap on the shoulder. Blowing on his hands again, Josef scanned the road as though watching for someone. That's when he spotted Petra across the road. After a quick I-knew-you'd-show-up smirk, he called her over with a tilt of his head.

"Welcome, paní Kurková," he said when she'd crossed and approached him on the snowy sidewalk. "Are you sure?"

Petra clutched her valise tighter, summoning her courage. "I'm sure."

"In that case, I hope you are enjoying the weather, because snow is all you'll see for the next several weeks, once you enter that door. It will not be easy. We have a long drive ahead of us, and you'll be the only woman among the men."

No resistance, no doubt, no fear, no anger. Petra entered the building and felt nothing but relief when the door closed behind her.

CHAPTER FOUR

Four witches, including herself, had answered the call to show up at the bakery. The small group of strangers huddled near the bakehouse fire that fueled the ovens. The fair-haired man built up the flame with a soft-spoken spell, drawing an impressed nod from all as they thawed out. Besides Josef, herself, and the fire-starter, there was a middle-aged man with graying sideburns who proudly stated he carved the decorative details on fine furniture for a living, and a young man not much older than Petra who claimed he'd been rejected by the mortal army, though he only shrugged and said he was too good for them when the fair-haired man asked why.

Josef introduced the fire-starter as Viktor Veselý. "As he just demonstrated, his specialty is flame," he said, patting the man on the back.

"I'm a glassmaker by trade," Viktor said, peering through his full-moon glasses. The lenses had the slightest tint to them to protect his eyes from too much heat and light. Petra knew already she would prefer to keep her distance from anyone who loved to play with fire as much as a glassmaker.

"And this is Karl Unger," Josef said, indicating the furniture maker. "His talent for working with wood and enchanted tools will prove useful in our work."

The man scratched nervously at his unshaven face. He had the look of a family man who preferred to sit home by the fire, in his sweater vest with the pipestem sticking out of the waist pocket. Petra had to wonder, if he was so talented, why the Empire hadn't already conscripted him into service on behalf of the emperor. Or any of them, for that matter.

"Our young man here," Josef continued, "is Dragoș. His background is in . . . well, he's adept at using mortal weapons and spellwork that tends to go undetected by the authorities."

The young man made a noise with his mouth like he thought Josef's comment was funny.

"Just Dragoș?" Viktor asked.

Petra took in the young man's work boots, his Bolshevism-inspired vest and cap, and got the measure of him as just another quarrelsome hooligan who stirred up trouble in the street. A regular Ravachol, though one who used spells to agitate rather than mortal bricks and bottles.

Dragoș laughed. "Do you think I'm stupid enough to give anyone my full name?"

The others bristled at the implied insult, but perhaps he had a point. Petra had no idea if the undertaking was sanctioned by anyone who had any true authority. She didn't even know if she'd get paid for her contribution to the effort. But food and shelter would be enough for her immediate needs. She hoped, at least, they would be provided with bread, as the smell from the ovens was making her stomach clench from want.

"And who is this?" Dragoș asked with a leering look at Petra. "Didn't think this was the sort of venture that required a secretary." The two other men straightened, also curious to know why a woman had been invited to the meeting.

"Ah," began Josef. "May I introduce you to Petra Kurková. She, along with her camera, will be our eyes on the ground."

"A woman is going with us?" The furniture maker was apoplectic, judging by the face he pulled.

"I take photos of the dead," Petra said. When the men remained confused, she clarified her remark. "Ghosts mostly, but certainly other beings too: rusalka, vodnik, and other navi when they're in the mood to be seen." She pulled the wrinkled photo of the weeping woman from her valise and passed it to Karl on her right as proof. "I'm a witch too," she added, believing for some reason that she had to convince them she had just as much right to be there as any of the rest of them. "And I was born not far from the mountains where the fighting is."

That got Josef's attention. Had he assumed she was from the city?

"I never told you where we are going," he said with a shake of his head.

"You didn't have to," she said. "I already know where the battles are being fought. There are only two passes where an army would even consider such a foolish exercise as going up against the tsar's Imperial forces in winter. But the passes must be defended against invasion."

The men laughed nervously as they passed the photo to Josef, who slipped it in his pocket, but no one objected to her presence after seeing the ghostly image of the woman in front of the church wall.

Petra found it curious that Josef had been able to scrounge up four witches in the city who hadn't already been called to serve in the fight against the Allied front. It was understood all were expected to report, even the women, to be evaluated for service. She, of course, had never previously registered her talent with the Empire, having all but given up using her magic in her day-to-day life long before she'd arrived on the bustling city streets. Since she hadn't been born in the city, she didn't think there was any way the authorities could track her down after the war began. And so far they hadn't. Not until Josef showed up. Even then, she still believed it was only chance that he'd caught on to what she was doing in the street while she took her photos.

But the others? What were their stories? Besides Dragoş, that was. She'd already surmised he was unfit in temperament to be trusted with a rifle, let alone the sort of magic that was otherwise illegal, except in times of war. The Empire's Department of Enhanced Magical Defenses had rightly refused that one, she thought. But Viktor? Karl? Whatever they were hiding, it must be buried very deep for them to have escaped service. Something she knew a little bit about.

Josef called for their attention again as he spoke beside the fire. "I told each of you that if you showed up this morning, I would reveal the entity behind our mission." He reached in his pocket and produced a small bronze medallion adorned with stars on one side and a palm tree on the other, presenting it like an amulet he carried for protection. "This is their emblem, and it is under their authority that we travel east. And for now, that is all you need to know. The journey to the front will be dangerous. Cold. Hostile. You will want to turn back when you hear the machine guns fire and field artillery explode in the distance. We will not do that."

Petra felt the men's fleeting glances as they signaled their doubt about her resolve, but she stood like a rock that parts the stream. Not even her eyebrow quivered at the promise of danger. There was no quiver in her intuition. She had set her feet on the right path, and the eastern front was where she was going.

"There are two wars being waged in the mountains," Josef said. "One between mortal men, and one between supernatural forces. *That* is your fight. One that no one else can do."

"So, this is it?" Dragoş asked. "This is our unit? Four men and a woman? How are we supposed to have any effect with such low numbers? It takes entire covens to put up a spell wall the size you'd need in war."

Josef stepped up to the man, his eyes as hard as stone, telegraphing his ferocious devotion to duty and discipline. "I'm sure that if we are committed to bringing all our legitimate and legal talent to the effort, we will prove a force to be reckoned with. Do you not agree?"

The young man flushed, taken aback, as though he'd been publicly humiliated, though none of the others quite understood what had just passed between the men. "Yes, yes, of course," Dragoş answered. He nodded quickly and didn't say another word.

"Yes, yes, of course, team leader," Josef corrected.

Karl laughed until Josef turned his fierce stare on him. The furniture maker swallowed and averted his eyes, telegraphing he was not a man who sat easy with conflict. Viktor nervously adjusted his glasses and straightened his back while Petra wondered at the extremes on display in Josef's demeanor, from smiling and genial greeter to taskmaster with the gravitas to make a grown man weep. She dared not smile at the revelation.

"You all read and signed your papers when you agreed to join," Josef said, though Petra knew she hadn't done any such thing. "Do not doubt that we will endeavor to function just like any other disciplined military unit. Only we have a very specific and narrow mission that only we can do. And one that cannot wait." He held his hand out to direct them toward the back door. "This way."

He ordered the glassmaker to reduce the fire in the oven to a comfortable blaze, and the rest followed their new leader to the alley behind the bakery. A delivery truck, renovated with a canvas top secured over the rear bed, awaited. Two wooden benches had been installed perpendicular to the cab of the truck to transport at least a half dozen people. After gawking at the rudimentary level of comfort for their transportation, the group was ordered to get in. All except Petra.

Josef looked her over, inhaling deeply as he shifted his glance to her valise. "You still carry your husband's clothes with you," he said as a matter of fact. When she nodded, not knowing how he could have reasonably deduced as much, he told her to go inside and put them on. "It will be for the best," he said, and pointed her to a storage closet where she could change.

Last to climb inside the back of the truck, Petra sat on the bench opposite Viktor in her trousers, flatcap, and overcoat and slid her valise under her feet. The canvas smelled like wet sheep and wood rot, and it dripped overhead from the weight of new-fallen snow trapped between the bowed strips of pine propping it up. Just when she began to regret her decision, Josef appeared at the back of the truck and offered a small sack to the group. Inside were several perfectly browned *houska* rolls and salted pretzels still slightly warm from the oven, a small chunk of cheese, and four bottles of beer.

"Eat," he said. "It will make the journey easier if you have something in your stomachs." He watched them divvy up the rolls and pretzels, then reached in his satchel and handed out medical armbands to everyone. "And this is for you," he said to Petra. He produced two full rolls of unused film. Two! That was sixteen photos she could take. "Keep it protected. There's no telling when we'll get our hands on more. When we get to camp, we'll figure out a developing room."

"Thank you, team leader," she said, stupefied by the sudden wealth within her possession. The men, too, thanked him, though their words were muddied with the inflection of confusion more than gratitude.

Josef slammed the tailgate shut, and a moment later the truck engine revved up. With bread in one hand and film in the other, Petra already felt vindicated in her choice to jump off the tram when she did. Later she would need to send a letter to her in-laws to explain, but for now she stuffed her precious film in her coat pocket and grabbed hold of the bread in the other as Josef drove them out of the city. The snow swirled behind them as they gained speed, wiping out everything in their wake in a vortex of white—the Novaks, her brief life with Marek in an attic apartment before the war, and, praise the stars, her rumbling belly.

The food made for a silent ride for the first few kilometers while everyone ate. After that, the novelty of the ride wore off and awkwardness set in. They were four strangers riding together in the back of a flatbed truck rigged purely to accommodate the rigors of moving in wartime. There was no heat, no padding, and no privacy. Soon the silence between the recruits swelled, like their bellies and their bladders, to the point of discomfort.

It was Dragoş who belched first, followed by a whispered question aimed at stirring the pot. "Why do you think he really got thrown out?" The young man folded his arms over his stomach and spread his knees wide to get comfortable as the truck rumbled over a rut in the road. He nudged his head toward Josef up front in the cab when no one took the bait. "Are you buying that story that he was captured, then injured, and now he somehow gets picked to lead a unit of magical misfits? No offense, but you know as well as I do we'd all be enlisted by the Empire already if there weren't something off about our magic. But him? He's a mortal. What gives?"

Petra looked up from the last crust of bread she'd been saving. She'd wondered the same thing herself, of course. She glanced at the back of Josef's head through the cab window for the hundredth time. No aura. "Maybe they thought it was more important to have someone with fighting experience in charge of us," she said.

Viktor pushed his tinted glasses up his nose and gave a maybe-yes-maybe-no nod of his head, but Dragoş made a dismissive noise through his lips. "Would make more sense to have a master sorcerer in charge, if these battle curses are as bad as he says they are." He looked at Petra out of the side of his eye. "Did you get the talk before you signed your contract?"

"No," she said, glancing from one man to another. "I didn't sign anything."

Karl gave an authoritative grunt as he took a chunk of wood and a knife from his bag. "You're a woman. You're not allowed to join the regular military," the woodworker said with a shrug. "He's probably taken you on under some regulation that allows female nurses and secretaries to travel near the front."

Dragoş nodded, but he also saw an opportunity to add some devilry into the mix. "That means you don't know about the real mission."

"Know what?"

"What we'll be up against." The young man eyed her trousers and jacket. "At any rate, it's no place for any decent woman."

"I was told there were curses and hexes that needed to be countered," Petra said. "What's complicated about that?"

"This is war," Karl said, guiding his knife along the surface of the wood grain. "The normal rules don't apply." He pursed his lips and shook his head, as if such consolations were a thing that couldn't be avoided. "We won't necessarily fight them with spells."

"Curses have called up all sorts of undead creatures," Dragoş said. "Upíri. Strzygi. The drekavac." He downed the last of his beer. "Fire will kill them, though," he said, acknowledging Viktor with a hooked thumb in his direction. "Or a stake through the head, which I suppose is why they dug up a woodworker. Think either of you can manage that?"

"Thought they were already dead," Viktor said, seeming eager to regain some footing against the brash young man.

"Oh, their human bodies are dead," Dragoş said. "Their skin and organs are decaying even while they walk among the living. But the soul . . . sometimes you have to get close enough to cut out that second heart and fry it in the flames to destroy them." The young man sat back once he got the satisfaction of seeing Viktor flinch. "Maybe that's why they invited a woman along," he said, getting in one more dig. "A cook to do the frying."

Petra ignored him. The young man with no last name was winding her up, trying to frighten her. Having been raised in a rural village, she knew the stories as well as anyone. She'd also heard the rumors about the mountain forests and the unnatural creatures who roamed the hillsides since the war began, resurrected by the bloodshed.

"My great-grandfather was supposedly buried with an iron blade over his throat and a brick in his mouth," Karl said as his enchanted knife made quick work of the chunk of wood until a small figure of a bird began to emerge. "He had the eyes like yours," he said to Petra, referring to the trait of amber irises as he carved two eye sockets. He turned the bird around in his hand to get perspective, and the wooden eyes blinked at Petra. "Back then they still believed witches were navi too." He resumed his whittling.

The uncomfortable mention of the sometimes-violent past silenced the conversation momentarily so that each retreated to their own thoughts again. The irony of those same institutes of mortal authority now relying on the talents of witches in the war was not lost on any of them. But apparently working for your onetime oppressor and tormentor was better than being hounded by dogs or buried with a brick in your mouth.

"Better be careful walking around with those witchy eyes of yours," Dragoș said, and snickered. "Someone might come after *you* with an iron blade."

Petra decided Dragoș had the heart of a snake. Always watching and waiting for some little movement that would give away his prey's weakness so he could coil and strike at the vulnerable points. She only hoped he was as deadly with the navi as he was with his new friends.

CHAPTER FIVE

Six hours later, at times crawling along at speeds little faster than a horse at a trot because of the muddy roads, they approached the first mountain pass. A sloppy, wet snowstorm had settled in at the higher elevation. Already the trees sagged under the weight of the falling snow, and the sky had grown gloomy as the temperature dipped into the frigid, finger-numbing zone.

Josef, in a hurry to reach the other side, kept the truck rolling at a steady pace, shifting gears as necessary, until the wheels hit a rut the size of a water trough. The jolt knocked Petra so hard she bounced off the bench, cracking her teeth together when she landed again. Across from her, Viktor's travel bag jumped across the floor. The glassmaker crashed to his knees, diving to retrieve his belongings. He managed to scoop the bag up in his arms as the truck lurched and rattled to a stop.

Dragoş had bitten his tongue and spit blood. He pounded on the cab window. "Are you trying to kill us back here?"

Josef held his right hand up, waving in acknowledgment of the rough road. He shifted the truck into first gear and revved the engine, but the vehicle only fishtailed wildly to the left the more he accelerated, sending the passengers sliding in their seats. He tried again, and Petra gripped the bench, convinced the truck was going to overturn. After one more half-hearted attempt to get the vehicle moving forward, the engine sputtered and stalled.

Josef came around the back and ordered everyone out. "We'll have to push, unless one of you sorcerers can conjure a flying truck."

Karl laughed out loud. "A pig maybe, but not this hunk of metal."

Josef did a double take at the furniture maker before lowering the tailgate. "I'm surprised we made it as far as we did. The road's as worn out as a *kurva's* . . ." He stopped midsentence when Petra's leg extended from the bed of the truck. "It's a mess out here," he amended. "Watch your step."

Once out of the back, the four men put their shoulders against the tailgate while Petra sat behind the steering wheel with instructions to simply guide the vehicle onto the good part of the road and accelerate the moment she felt their weight against the truck. Her lace-up boots were covered in mud and her toes had lost their feeling, but she held steady on the steering wheel as the men rocked the vehicle back and forth to no avail. Surely there had to be some spell that could aid their predicament. That's when Dragoş told the others to stand back. Petra watched through the rearview mirror as he pushed his sleeve up and barked, "Mud and ice, snow and frost, release the wheels or pay the cost." He'd spoken in anger, making a spark snap in the air near the sunken tires as his spell took shape. The heat of his words melted a patch of snow beside one of the tires, but otherwise all he'd done was anger Josef. "Are you trying to blow the petrol tank up and get us killed? Or worse, get us stranded in these haunted mountains after dark? I know I'd survive it, but I'm not so sure about you," he said, walking away.

Petra decided Dragoş must be a *štípnutí*, a witch whose only real talent was to spread irritation and make others miserable. Closing her eyes, she leaned her head back to think. She was so out of practice with day-to-day applied magic, she could hardly identify the elements of an effective incantation anymore. And none, as she recalled, were suited to making a car levitate, as Josef had alluded to earlier. But maybe there was something to be done.

While the men caught their breath, she took the empty paper sack from the pretzels out of her pocket and gave it a shake. Loose salt rattled inside. Yes, she thought, maybe she did know a spell that could work. It required only a spoonful of salt, something symbolic for the magic to adhere to. And weren't they all recruited to use their magic? After overcoming a moment of doubt, Petra stepped out of the truck's cab and walked to the rear, where the men stood cursing at the tires sunk in the muddy rut. Dragoş's effort to get the vehicle unstuck had only made the mess worse. Splattered mud covered the trees, rocks, and men's trousers.

Petra cleared her throat. "May I try?"

"Oh, right, that'll fix it," Dragoş said, rolling his eyes and stepping away to light a cigarette.

The others, red-faced and breathing hard from their failed effort, took the interruption as a chance to stand behind a tree and empty their bladders.

"We just need to get some traction under the wheels," Josef said, suggesting she leave it alone. "We'll get it unstuck. Get back in the cab and wait for the signal."

Petra replied with a slow nod. She was being dismissed as useless by all of them. Ignoring Josef's instructions, she surveyed the situation, making a show of examining how deep the rut was. The others casually kept an eye on her as she knelt and sprinkled the salt from the bag around the tires. She closed her eyes, and in her mind she envisioned a photograph she'd once seen in a magazine of an inland desert on a southern continent. The ground in the picture was cracked and parched, a mosaic of hard earth with the moisture sucked dry. It was a good image. Firm. Concrete. Nearly tangible. The spell ought to work.

A burst of red flooded her third-eye vision. Her face flushed with warmth and her fingertips tingled as she extended her hand to touch the mud.

"What's she doing?" Karl's voice rose in tone with excitement.

Petra opened her eyes. The earth beneath the truck made a sucking noise as the excess water was drawn out of the ground. The mud hardened, drying out in a four-meter span beneath the truck, only slightly encasing the stuck tires.

Karl knelt to inspect her work. "How did you do that?"

Petra freed the tension holding the spell together. The tingling in her fingers receded, and the cold air returned to torment her extremities. "It's an old salt spell an honored *babička* in my village used to do when she lanced people's boils," she said. "I figured it might work to drain the ground too."

Beside her she saw the smile return to Josef's face. The change was like watching a key turn a lock that freed the vulnerable, amiable man he kept hidden inside.

"But you didn't recite any incantation." Karl knelt to touch the hardened ground for himself.

"Yes I did," Petra lied. "I just don't shout my spells out like some."

"Well done, Kurková." Josef's praise was momentary, however, as the smile retreated and he flipped the collar up on his coat. "Everyone back inside. We've got ground to make up to get to the next village before dark. And you can all thank paní Kurková for her ingenuity while you're at it."

Dragoş tossed his cigarette away and brushed past Petra, knocking against her shoulder as he spoke a terse "thanks." Brushing him off, she shook hands with Viktor and Karl, who seemed to regard her with less indifference now, and then climbed into the back. This time, however, Petra chose to sit next to the glassmaker, who conjured up a ball of heat that floated in the air just a little nearer to her than to Dragoş.

By the time they reached the mountain village, five hundred kilometers east of where they'd begun the day, the sun had set and frost coated the truck's hood and windshield. After parking outside a small church, Josef ordered them to grab everything they owned and follow him down an empty backstreet. With the wind picking up, they trotted to keep up behind their long-legged leader as he turned the corner and unlocked the door to what appeared to be the rear entry to the Café Liliana.

Shivering and soaked to the knees from their journey, Petra knew a bowl of hot goulash and dumplings was just the cure she was looking for. To her great disappointment, the café was no longer in the business of providing hot meals. The space was filled instead with a printing press in the corner, stacks of unused paper piled on desktops, colorful flyers demanding independence for nations chained to the Empire, and dozens of black-and-white photographs pinned to the walls of horses and soldiers lying in the snow. And in the corner, atop a row of wooden crates, slept a man wrapped in a plain brown robe. When he didn't bother to roll over to see who had entered, Petra wondered if someone ought to check for a pulse.

Her concern was cut short when another man entered from a back room hidden behind a curtain. He wore the uniform of the hussar— blue wool dolman tunic, red trousers, black boots, and a saber and pistol at his side.

"I begin wonder if you make it," he said, attempting to greet them in their mother tongue. The hussar, bearing a thick black mustache and a hardened expression to rival Josef's, carried a small cup and saucer with a spoon sticking out. He stirred the contents and tapped the spoon once against the rim. The aroma of coffee nearly made Petra drool.

"We hit a small delay," Josef said.

"Trouble?" The man's eyes darted to the front windows that had been obscured by a layer of whitewash, all but the lower panes, where one could presumably watch the sidewalk outside.

"Not that kind," said Josef. "Just the weather. The pass was heavier with snow than it had been when I ran through four days earlier."

The hussar nodded, then looked over the new arrivals, his eyes pausing only briefly on Petra in her men's clothing. "This all that's left?"

Dragoş balled his fists, but before he could open his mouth and make a fool of himself, Josef slapped his hand on the young man's shoulder and held him back. "These are the last four," he said. "All full-blooded witches eager to join the fight we face against the undead, as you can see." He let go of Dragoş's shoulder and directed the group to the room in the back.

The hussar huffed out his skepticism. "*Lelkesedés* . . . eager . . . is overrated."

"And who are you?" Dragoş asked, earning himself a dark look from Josef.

"This is Major Bako," Josef said in a tone that said the man deserved respect. "Our liaison with the Empire's forces."

The hussar's neck flushed red as he pointed toward the door. "I'm officer whose comrades die because of . . . weetches," he said. "I'm officer forced to follow orders and rely on you to save them." He crept closer, his mustache twitching. "And I know about the spells and the hexes." He spit on the floor and left Dragoş eating his words as he marched into the next room, waving at them to follow.

And still the robed man slept on without so much as a snore.

"Help yourselves to the coffee," Josef said, pouring himself a demitasse cup from a graceful metal carafe with a long spout.

The back room, the former café's fully equipped kitchen, boasted a sturdy wooden table with four chairs around it. Viktor was first in line for the coffee, though he offered Petra his cup before pouring himself another. Bako and Josef sat on the countertop on the opposite side of the room, letting their long legs dangle nearly to the floor. Petra and the others sat in the four chairs arranged around the table, sipping their coffee in silence and growing nervous when neither Bako nor Josef said a word, yet stared at them constantly over the rims of their own cups.

To avoid the discomfort of their stares, Petra let her eyes drift until she landed on a string of teeth hanging from the edge of the stove. They were pointed like dog's teeth, only bigger. She tried not to flinch at the sight, wondering instead why they were there. Curious, she looked closer at the other side of the kitchen, where the men sat on the counter, and there she spotted two femurs nailed together like an X on the cupboard behind them. Below on the counter were a mallet, a handful of wooden stakes, a stack of dusty bricks, and a human skull with a railroad spike protruding through it with an obvious strand of bloody hair still attached. The skull had been arranged in the corner of the countertop like one might place a cookie jar.

Petra sipped her coffee and pressed her lips together, trying to make sense of the macabre objects as she waited for the others to discover what she had. Viktor was the first. He followed the line of her emphatic gaze, then uttered a minor curse when he spotted the skull. Karl and Dragoş caught on next. They tried to downplay their shock, but their furrowed foreheads and aggressively tensed jaws gave them away. Dragoş, in particular, flared his nostrils and turned a flaming shade of red.

"I am pleased to learn you are not completely without observational skills," Bako said, reaching to pick up the desecrated skull. "This is Laszlo." The hussar kissed the top of the skull near the spike, while Josef shook his head like someone who'd seen it all before. "Come morning, this little beauty will be your new best friend."

CHAPTER SIX

After a day of sitting on a hard bench in the back of a truck in the freezing cold, Petra didn't need to be ordered twice to turn in at lights out. The men had tried to give her as much privacy as possible, letting her bed down alone behind an overturned desk below the window. She'd been so tired she'd barely put her head on her valise when she sank into sleep.

Sometime in the middle of the night, while dreaming of wolves running in the snow, Petra was roused by the wind battering the trees that lined the street outside. She rolled onto her back and winced. The pain in her hip from sleeping on the hard floor had her second-guessing her choice not to go to her mother-in-law's apartment after all. Then again, Major Bako was not nearly as intimidating as Helene Kurková could be, once you'd earned her disapproval. The wind slammed into the side of the building, rattling the window above her head. She felt a pinch of worry in her chest then, wondering if Marek was sleeping out in such blustery weather. What if he were fighting in the next valley? Would she be able to see him? Would he be glad to see her?

Petra turned over on her side again when the wind whipped itself into a fury. Shadows of tree branches swept past the window, rocking back and forth as they were blown about. Something tapped lightly against the glass. She sat up, worried a blizzard had hit and they'd be snowed in come morning. Yet outside, the sky had a blue cast to it. The clouds had cleared, and there was no snow. The waxing moon hung in full view like a woman turning her veiled face away.

"She's in a restless mood," a voice whispered.

Petra lifted her head and saw Viktor staring out the second window. He cupped an ornate glass-and-metal vase in his hands. He held the vessel up before him almost like an offering.

"What are you doing?" she whispered back.

"That's why she won't come down."

"Who?"

Viktor looked at Petra then. "The moon," he said. "She's not herself tonight. In this phase she usually sends a strong glimmer of light to fill the vase."

Petra blinked at him, wondering if he was sleepwalking. "Go back to bed, Viktor."

"Probably for the best," he agreed. "I don't think she's going to come down."

He wrapped the vase in cloth and stuffed it back in his bag before settling under his blanket again. Petra put her head down, unwilling to let Viktor's odd behavior invade her thoughts and ruin what little sleep she might salvage. Whatever mad games he played with the moon in the middle of the night were his business, just as taking photos of the dead was hers.

The glassmaker had just started snoring when something softly pelted the window again. Petra got to her knees this time to investigate the source of the noise, rubbing her sleeve against the pane to clear the sheen of frost that had collected on the inside. Through the small hole she'd made, she saw a gray moth hitting its wings against the window. The incongruity of an insect in winter made her blink in confusion. She smudged more frost away, and when she lowered her arm, a soldier stared at her from across the street, mouthing the words *help me*.

Petra's body flooded with adrenaline at the sight. She cursed under her breath and leaned forward to see him better, bumping her head on the glass. Dressed in only his uniform coat and trousers, the soldier stood motionless in contrast to the freezing wind that thrashed around him. Young, pale, and sickly looking, he made a sorry sight. He'd surely die if he didn't get in from the cold. And yet what was he doing there alone in the middle of the night?

Was he really there at all?

Petra reached for her camera and extended the lens. A part of her brain was working hard to assure her the young man truly needed help. Another part was eager to convince her the ghosts she'd only felt up until that moment were, at last, becoming fully visible to her. The camera would tell her for sure, and so she went to the front door, tiptoeing around the others so as not to wake them. No need for them to tell her it was too dangerous. After all, she'd been capturing images of the dead in the city on her own in the middle of the night for months without incident.

She unlocked the door and turned the handle, ready to slip outside, when the door burst open and the wind howled in her face. The soldier flew at her with supernatural speed from across the snow, his mouth open and his voice shrieking to top the wind. Petra had barely sucked in a stunned breath when the door slammed shut again and the creature hit the wood so hard he cracked the frame.

"Never open the door after dark!" The robed man who'd been sleeping on crates shoved the dead bolt in place. He glared at Petra until she looked away in defeat, then yelled to Major Bako in a voice heavy with the accent of the Middle East. Words she was certain had quickly been translated from his native language *inside* her ear. "Secure the back room," he said. "There may be more."

How had she understood him? Was he a witch as well?

Karl rushed to his feet, followed by Dragoș, whose face lit up at the prospect of a fight. Viktor blinked repeatedly, as though trying to decide if he was dreaming.

"What is it?" Karl shouted. "What's happening out there?"

The soldier slammed against the door again, crying in anguish at being denied.

"He's one of the local undead." The robed man hobbled on a false leg to the crate he'd been sleeping on and threw the lid off. "Josef, we have a visitor!"

"On it," Josef replied, tossing the man a stake from the kitchen.

Petra was caught in a storm of fear and guilt, unsure what to do as the two men ran down a checklist of actions they'd obviously gone through before. Outside, the undead soldier slammed against the door and the wall, determined to get inside. Petra had retreated to her space beneath the window when the creature exerted its full weight against the glass. She screamed and covered her head as Josef threw his arms around her and swept her into the corner of the room to huddle on the floor.

"Get down," he said. "All of you, stay away from the windows!"

The brute smashed the glass and forced his wretched head through the pane in front of Petra and Josef. His flesh caught on the sharp edges, tearing the skin of his cheek away, and yet there was no blood. He inhaled, then followed the source of the smell to the floor, where Petra was practically smothered under Josef's body. The thing hissed and pushed itself onto the sill.

The stench of the creature's breath and the clammy fishlike color of his skin nauseated her even from two meters away. She'd expected a phantom when she'd opened the door. Instead, Petra had nearly let in a fully fleshed-out creature with teeth bared and bloodlust churning in its veins. She wanted to scream but the sound caught in her throat, strangled by fear and revulsion as the thing lurched closer to them, his body catching on the jagged shards of broken glass. Petra turned away, burying her face against Josef until she felt the thrumming of his heart-beat beneath his shirt.

Between the creature's fiendish wails, a commotion across the room made Petra lift her head. The robed man had limped to the center of the café, waving a branch in one hand and a lit candle in the other. He prodded Viktor with his false leg when he passed. "You," he said. "Be ready with your magic."

Viktor checked left and right, unsure what was required of him, but got to his knees and pushed up his sleeves.

The man proved a sorcerer of some foreign magic, as he held out a hawthorn branch with bright-red berries. The plant was a potent protection against harm, yet this man brandished it like a weapon. He rattled the branch in front of the creature while holding the candle firm in his other hand. The undead soldier screeched and hissed, tearing its abdomen on the glass to get inside the room. The sorcerer shook the branch again and the number of berries doubled, drawing the creature's attention. Its eyes locked on the berries, seemingly dazzled by the simple trick.

"Yes, how many do you see?" The sorcerer stepped closer, shaking the hawthorn. Again, the number of berries increased until the branch drooped in his hand from the weight. The flame on the sorcerer's candle grew slowly brighter with each step he took closer to the fiend, as if he were drawing the beast's attention with one hand and holding it back with the other. A dance to maintain control.

Josef still protected Petra with his body, exposing his side to the creature. She raised her head above his shoulder until her cheek was even with his. He smelled of sweat, and woodsmoke, and the damp leaves of a forest. The pleasant mix made for a dizzying contrast to the hideous scene before her.

The creature had stopped its thrashing, mesmerized by the increasing number of berries. It stared at the hawthorn while leaning away from the glowing candle flame. When the sorcerer got near enough he could have hit the creature in the face with the branch, he held the candle up and called to Viktor, "Now, glassmaker! Give us your fire."

Viktor stretched out his hand and a blue flame shot forward, catching the burning wick of the candle and shooting hot wax and fire at the undead soldier. The sickening creature winced and hissed, knowing he'd been tricked. He squirmed on the shards of broken window glass, twisting and writhing as he shrieked like a ghoul, but could not free his torso before he was encased in flame and molten wax. There was a quick flash, as though he had been dipped in oil, before the fiend shriveled under a steady blaze and his body disintegrated into a green puddle of smoldering ooze that slid down the wall. Karl wretched at the sight, turning away and bracing his hand against the wall to steady himself.

"Well done," the sorcerer said to Viktor as he bent down to take a closer look at the remains. Using the end of the hawthorn branch, he dug two canine teeth out of the pile and scooped them up gingerly between thumb and forefinger.

Major Bako returned to the front room, sparing only a fleeting glance at the ooze on the wall. "Nothing on my end," he said. He lit a lantern and set it on the printing press, giving the room a soft glow.

The sorcerer straightened. "For you," he said, dropping the teeth in the major's hand.

"That was incredible." Dragoş stood gaping at the remains, taking almost too much pleasure from the encounter. He checked through the window to the road outside, as though looking for more monsters to take on.

Josef eased his hold on Petra, taking the comfort of his body heat with him. "All right?" he asked her.

"Yes, of course." She wiped her eyes and blinked at the stain dripping down the wall as cold air blew in through the broken window.

"It's no coincidence that thing showed up here tonight." Major Bako wrapped the teeth in a handkerchief and stuffed them in his breast pocket. "We're one hundred and forty kilometers from the front. He didn't just wander by."

The sorcerer nodded, but his attention remained on Petra. "Why did you open the door?" he asked her.

Petra watched his lips move out of sync with the words she was hearing. "Why can I understand you?" The hussar, too, had spoken in broken sentences when she'd first arrived, but now his speech was as fluent as any man in the Old Town Square.

The others perked up at her question, noticing the irregularity themselves for the first time.

Mischief darted behind the sorcerer's eyes. "You drank the coffee, yes?" When they all nodded, he answered, "It is not my own spell, but one a friend concocted at the behest of her government. Her Lingua Franca spell was designed using the red wine she and her husband produce at their vineyard. After she shared the incantation with me, I found it perfectly adaptable to coffee too. Once you drink and the spell enters your bloodstream, your ear adapts to the sound of any language."

"You understand what I'm saying?" Karl asked, then waited to see if the man truly comprehended before smiling at the novelty of conversing with someone from halfway around the world with no more difficulty than saying hello to the butcher and asking for a pound of shaved ham.

"This is Yanis, by the way," Josef said, introducing Petra and the others to the sorcerer. "He's a priest with the Order of the Seven Stars who'll be traveling with us. That's whose banner we now operate under."

"Order of the Seven Stars?" Petra had a vague notion of who they were from talk on the wind, but everything she'd heard sounded more like a fantastical rumor than the truth. "You're saying the Order is real?"

Yanis tossed the hawthorn branch on the floor and brushed his hands clean, while Viktor cast an orange flame that hovered in the center of the room, giving off much-needed warmth against the cold air flooding in through the open window.

"The Order is very real and very ancient, I assure you," Yanis said to Petra. He knelt down so that his eyes were on an even plane with hers. "We're very well acquainted with the undead and their Old World reputation in this region. Now tell me, why would you open the door to that creature?"

The man's sincerity to know the truth overrode any accusation in his question. Petra tried not to shrink under his scrutiny. Perhaps twice her age with graying hair, he watched her with worry-worn eyes that promised understanding. "At first he appeared so normal, so vulnerable," she said. "He looked like he was lost and needed help, but then I thought he was just another ghost."

"Another?" Yanis glanced quickly at Bako in alarm. "Did you see others?"

"No, just him." She took a deep breath and held her camera up to show him. "I was going to take his picture."

When Yanis seemed confused, Josef explained. "She takes pictures of the dead. The ghosts show up in her photographs." He got to his feet and pulled the photo of the weeping woman from his uniform coat to show to the priest. "Her gift might have some use to us."

Dragoş scoffed, pointing at the mess. "War is no place for a woman. You see how she nearly got us all killed with her poor judgment."

"It is strange how the creature fixated on her," Bako said. "And how did that damnable monster pick out our group to attack out of all the village? They already suspect we're here."

Yanis agreed it was unusual. "A spell might have attracted such a creature to our location." He returned his attention to Petra. "Did you say a spell to enchant your camera before opening the door? You must learn to restrict your spells while you're here until otherwise instructed."

"No, the magic doesn't require a spell," she said. "I can sense the spirits are near like a breath of cool air against the skin." She placed her hand against her exposed neck. "It's the same sensation you get when someone is staring at you hard enough to make you look up. That's when I point the camera at the spot where I think they are. It's only later, when I develop the film, that I can see who and what I was feeling."

"You're lying." Dragoş's hand shook while he lit a cigarette. "You do your spells in your head, like you did earlier today. You drew that thing to us."

Petra shot to her feet. "I didn't."

"You see," he said, pleading his case to the others as he exhaled. "She's already a liability. Too emotional."

Before their exchange grew any hotter, Viktor tentatively raised his hand. "Actually, I think it was me," he said. "If that thing was attracted here by magic, then it might have been because I was trying to draw down the moon. It's something I usually do at home, but she wasn't herself tonight, so I gave up."

"You regularly call to the moon?" Josef asked, scrunching up his nose with a sort of curious disdain.

Viktor answered with a lovesick gleam in his eye. "She's my muse. My *bella luna*. Her patronage helped me create this," he said, digging out the ornate glass vase he kept stashed in his bag and unwrapping the cloth.

"Well, this is an interesting bunch you've brought to the front," Yanis said, picking up the hawthorn branch off the floor. The berries and leaves shrank in his grip until there was only a wooden stake left with a sharpened point.

"It's what you asked for." Josef sank onto a crate and rubbed his hands through his hair. Without his ushanka he appeared much younger, much less invincible. A man who, a year prior, one might have spied at a theater or beer garden on a Friday night and spun romantic fantasies about for the rest of the evening.

Outside the window, the horizon was rimmed in a faint pink hue to match the one Petra knew had risen to the tips of her ears after her thoughts about Josef. There'd be no more sleep for anyone now that dawn approached. No dreams of warm summer nights in the beer garden to cushion the nightmare of what they'd seen.

"If it truly was attracted here by one of their spells, we may have overestimated one of our clearest advantages," Bako said, throwing his hands up. "We just lost the element of surprise."

Dragoş yawned and stretched. "I don't understand. What surprise? He's already dead, isn't he? What more harm can he do?"

Bako, Yanis, and Josef exchanged an awkward look between them.

Yanis limped forward on his wooden leg into the lantern light. His robe was dirty, his hair a tangled mess, and dark circles sagged beneath his tired eyes. "He means that you were brought here—the four of you—because you all have one thing in common," he said. "Something we thought we could use to our advantage in the war to help save lives."

Petra looked at her fellow recruits; none of them keyed into the commonality they seemed to share. "Why would we need an element of surprise to counteract hexes?"

Josef sighed. "I'm afraid that was only part of the truth of what you were brought here to do."

Karl crossed his arms as if bracing himself for bad news. "What's the rest?"

Josef nudged his chin toward the mess on the windowsill. "Perhaps as little as a week ago, that thing was a soldier fighting for the Empire. Now? An upír. A flesh-eater. A bloodsucker intent on attacking the living, jealous of the life that was taken from him."

Petra added up the teeth on a string, the spike through the skull, and the convenient branch of hawthorn at the sorcerer's fingertips. "You want us to kill the upíri?"

"Told you so," Dragoş said.

"Nearly two hundred thousand men were sent to this valley to serve in the emperor's army last fall," Josef explained. "Ten thousand have since died in battle, soaking the ground with their blood. Tens of thousands more have died from sickness and cold."

Bako grunted. "Sent to fight in the mountains in winter with cardboard for boot soles and wool puttees that do nothing but soak up the cold and freeze a man's legs off."

Josef nodded. "Those are the official deaths. But then there are the others. The unaccounted for. The missing that also number in the thousands."

"What happened to them?" Viktor's face was pale as his beloved moon.

"Some deserted, some died and were never identified, but the others . . ." Their young leader put his ushanka back on and rubbed his heavily stubbled chin. "When the attacks first happened, we thought it was just superstition and nerves playing tricks on us. You hear things at night in the forest when you're on patrol. Strange sounds that play on your fear—ice cracking between stones, a deer stepping on a stick, a growl behind shining eyes watching you in the distance." Josef shook his head the way a man does when he wants to empty it of unpleasant memories. "Later, when you're awakened in the middle of the night with a primeval urge to hide to save your life, it can be hard to tell if the sound that woke you was a scream, an animal calling out in the night, or simply the wind shrieking through the trees. But in the morning, after the sun rises, you find your fellow soldier is gone, and in his place is a streak of blood three meters long where he last stood guard."

"An ambush? Or raiders crossing lines?" Viktor said with a note of optimistic ignorance.

"Is that what you saw attack paní Kurková?" Josef stood, rising to his full height. "Because these creatures aren't like the bogeyman from the stories you were told as a child," he said.

"These things rise from the heaps of bodies in open graves." Bako's fists were clenched, and his knuckles had turned white as a statue's. "Soldiers are being resurrected after they've died in hospital or been killed on the battlefield. Bones and flesh of good men snatched from the earth to make those fiends, who seem to have no other purpose but to kill soldiers to satisfy some craving for savagery."

Yanis tapped his chest. "The upíri rise with two hearts. Their human heart shrivels to dry bark, and the other twists into a torsion, a pulsating knot that lusts for blood. As you saw, they appear as human as you or I, until the bloodlust overtakes them and their teeth come out. Once sated, they blend in again. I daresay, if that creature were still intact, you might find the blood and flesh of his last victim still under the fingernails."

"But they do eventually begin to smell," Bako added. "That's one way to sniff them out."

"Like rotten garbage," Dragoş confirmed, waving his hand in front of his nose while standing near the mess.

Yanis tapped the hawthorn stake against his graying temple. "There's some speculation the full moon's light drives their urge to kill, as they do appear more active then, but they're just as likely to strike under a gibbous moon, as you saw tonight."

"She cannot help how others react to her," Viktor said. "The moon," he clarified with all sincerity when the others gawped at him. "She intends no harm to those on earth. It's merely our eyes and brains that get mesmerized by her aura."

"She's certainly harmed you, you lunatic." Dragoş kicked the crate next to Viktor.

"Leave him alone." Petra emulated Josef's steely stare to make sure she got her point across. "Don't forget it was Viktor's fire that saved us tonight."

"She's right," said Yanis. "We're lucky to have someone so proficient with fire. Only the jinn could have outmatched his quick skill."

"Which makes me wonder why you've brought us all here," she said. "There's nothing special about my talent with fire." She checked with Dragoş and Karl, who both shook their heads as if to say they could call up fire the same as any witch, but not like Viktor. "And yet you said we possess some common element you hoped to use against the upíri. So what is it?"

Bako made sure the door was securely locked, while Yanis scanned the street outside the broken window.

"Glassmaker, can you fix this window first?" Josef asked.

"It won't be pretty, but I could probably patch it up." Viktor muttered a barely audible spell under his breath, words of fire and earth, heat and viscosity. The window glass heated up, then oozed and softened into a malleable form. The glassmaker shaped the molten glass into a solid plane by alternating the heat from his hands with the coolness of his breath until it patched itself together. When he was finished, a swirl of green and black from the upír had been embedded in the pane near the bottom like a bad rendition of art nouveau stained glass. Yanis gave Josef the all clear to speak.

"Now to answer your question," Josef said. "The number of upír attacks has been increasing over the winter. From a handful when I first arrived to three or four a week now."

"In the last century, our Order had only been called on to hunt down two rogue navi in these mountains." The sorcerer shook his head. "This young soldier was the third I've encountered since getting off the train."

"Their aggressive behavior suggests something fundamental has changed beyond the bloodshed of battle," Josef said. "There's a good chance a sorcerer or witch or whatever you call yourselves is involved."

"One of us?" Viktor was as confused as the rest of them.

"We haven't been in touch with the enemy forces in the north to know if they suffer the same casualties," Major Bako said. "We simply don't have a reliable contact in the tsar's army anymore. But all of the victims we've found so far have fought on the side of the Empire, which leads us to believe the war has entered a new and dangerous phase beyond hexed trenches and cursed canteens."

"Someone is deliberately calling up the undead?" Dragoș whistled low.

"A strategy that cannot be allowed to spread beyond the theater of battle for obvious reasons," Yanis said.

Petra had heard the rumors. She knew the undead had always been attracted to the bloodshed of war. It was a common-enough tale to hear of one or two upíri stalking the perimeter of where men slept in camps. But a host of undead being summoned by a sorcerer to attack one side only? That raised the specter of a supernatural war crimes tribunal.

"But what are we supposed to do against a witch with that kind of power?" Petra asked, rightfully flummoxed.

"We've recruited witches before," Yanis said. "And you're right. Most proved not to have the temperament to deal with an uprising of this magnitude. We tried having them band together in covens to strike with a single powerful spell, but something always thwarted their intentions."

The hussar lit a cigar. "Ego," he said, squinting through the smoke. "Every damn one of them thought they could out-conjure the other. They wouldn't work as a team. Each of them thought if they could shine individually in battle, they could move into the ranks of the royal court."

"The generals had hailed their talents prematurely," Josef said. "They thought the intervention would bring a quick end to the war, and so they encouraged the witches to do whatever it took to make the problem go away. It was a flawed strategy, and unfortunately, many of those same witches were quickly targeted by the upíri, once their spells failed to do anything more than dazzle their peers."

"Killed?" Viktor asked.

"Yes." Josef crossed his arms. "Which is why we've adopted a new approach. You all specialize in a different type of magic, yet there is one quality you all have in common." Again, Petra had no idea what trait they could possibly share. "Each of you has successfully evaded the effort to be drafted into the army," he continued. "Even after every other witch within five hundred kilometers of the fight has already been summoned. And why is that?"

Petra's stomach dropped. *They couldn't know. Nobody did.*

"You've hidden so well, in fact, none of you even show up on the registry for witches," Yanis said. "Something I'd be very curious to learn more about. But for now, that is the one thing we have in our favor. No one knows you're here. No one knows you're witches. But, more importantly, none of you appear to be overly ambitious when it comes to magic."

"Which is exactly what we need," Bako added. "Recruits who won't try to override our instructions with their own stupid ideas about how to fight this upír curse." He grinned and pointed his cigar at the group. "That's the main advantage we think we have with all of you. You're too apathetic about spellcasting to go rogue and fight them on your own like the others did. Which means maybe we can solidify our efforts for once. Because when it comes to killing the undead, the old, proven ways work best. *If* you can get the jump on them."

Yanis and Josef diverted their eyes to check the street outside the window again, once the truth of why they'd been brought there was out in the open so plainly. Frustration colored both their faces. How long had they planned this? How much did they really know about each of their new recruits? About her, her past, her capabilities? Of course Petra wasn't on any register. She'd taken every precaution she could to keep from being identified. Not because of the war or because she was incapable of magic but because she didn't want to spend the rest of her life in prison.

"But he's really dead, right?" Petra walked up to the edge of the upír's remains. A faint wisp of steam rose from the center, where spellfire hadn't completely incinerated a knot of twisted muscle. They thought she would turn away in disgust. Instead she integrated the odd bruise-like shade of green into her third eye memory. Usually green represented life, abundance, lushness, but there was a place in spellwork for the repulsive too. "There were no others with him," she reminded Major Bako. "You said so yourself. It was just a fluke he showed up here. A rogue attack. And judging by the state of him, he won't be telling anyone about us anytime soon, so our advantage hasn't changed."

"She has a point," Josef said. "We're only a few kilometers from a field hospital. He could simply have wandered over from there."

Yanis kept his eyes on the dawn. "Yet there's the risk he wasn't act-ing on his own. That whoever or whatever is coordinating the attacks already knows what we're up to."

"Everything we do is a risk," Josef countered. "We don't stop now."

Easy for him to say, Petra thought. Witches were the ones targeted after their last plan failed. She understood why her predecessors had reached beyond the scope of the mission. For a witch to make a name for themselves through some feat of spellmaking—like the witch who'd devised a way for everyone to understand each other through her enchanted wine—was ingrained in their psyche. Everyone wanted to be remembered for their ingenuity. Recognized and rewarded by the crowned heads of the continent. Her own father had been the talk of the upper echelons of society for a brief time. Before he'd married her mother and abandoned city life. She never knew what had happened to make him leave, only that it was too painful to talk about with his young daughter.

The priest of the Order turned from the window as the sound of heavy artillery echoed in the distance. "Naturally, there is an element of uncertainty in everything we do. Danger, hesitation, doubt, fear," he said, addressing the recruits. "I've received word the escalation in mali-cious curses has prompted the need for talks between magical factions. A preliminary treaty negotiation that may negate the need for our unit in the end. But until then, *we* take up this fight so that mortals don't have to." Yanis let his eyes drag over each one of them. "We'll start training right away. Bako, Josef, let's proceed."

The major lit a fresh cigar and held it in his teeth until the match flamed out. "In that case, welcome to the war, witches. Do as we tell you and maybe, just maybe, you'll stay alive."

CHAPTER SEVEN

Petra had reason yet again to be grateful she'd packed Marek's clothes in her valise. Josef had been right. Wearing them made her feel less self-conscious about being female in a room full of men resting on their masculinity in the face of looming danger. They were all scared—it wasn't just her—but she noticed the men had a way of carrying their fear not in their hearts and stomachs but in their anger. It swelled their fists and transformed their faces into masks of aggression. Like them, she stood in her boots and trousers with her feet apart and her arms crossed as she watched the major prepare to demonstrate how to pound a stake into the heart of an upír.

The major removed a wooden box from one of the heavy crates, explaining that the antique had been in his family for well over a hundred years. Made of deceptively simple walnut on the outside, the box, when opened, revealed an interior lined in royal-blue velvet. It held three hawthorn stakes, a mallet, two candleholders, two pistols with corresponding silver bullets, and a dagger with the symbol of the Empire on its decorative pommel. The hussar removed a stake and the mallet and positioned them over the dummy upír he'd assembled on the upturned desk, complete with Laszlo's skull wired on.

"One hard blow like this." Bako slammed the mallet down, driving the stake into a burlap sack filled with mud and sticks, the contents of the garbage can, and not a small helping of pig shit. "The smell is part of it," he said. "If you're lucky enough to get in this position, you have to learn to ignore everything but the effort of driving the wood through the ribs to get to the heart. It won't always kill them. Hell, most of the time it won't, but it will give us the time we need to either remove the head or incinerate the body properly, which are the only ways to fully destroy them with the tools we have. Unless you have the stomach for removing the heart and singeing it over a fire."

"Our bodies are designed to protect the vital organs," Josef said. "Physical combat requires you to find ways to overcome nature's intent. But to strike home with the stake, first you have to survive getting close enough to try."

Bako looked at Petra, extending the mallet to her first. "Your turn."

Josef pried the stake loose from the sack and set the dummy aside. He passed the hawthorn stake to Petra, then stepped back, wiping his hands on a moist washcloth before signaling her to charge at him. "Let's see what you've got. Try to get near enough to have a reasonable chance to plunge the stake in me."

Was she supposed to just ram straight into him? Could she use magic? There were no instructions, so there must not have been any rules.

Petra gripped the stake in one hand, the mallet in the other. In her mind she visualized a storm cloud billowing up before the rain, ready to give the mortal a metaphysical shove. She wanted to feel her power, if only to reconnect with that piece of her that had been missing for so long. She channeled enough force from her vision to reasonably push Josef to the wall without hurting him, and then she attacked. Keeping her shoulders low, she charged, ready to take advantage of the force from the spell. But when she got within arm's reach, he hadn't moved. Not a foot off-balance. The mortal easily grabbed her and twisted her around as if her spell had no effect on him, locking one arm over her chest and pretending to take a bite out of her.

"You're dead," he said.

For a moment Petra was too confused to react. Not only had her spell not worked to knock him off-balance, but the strength of his body as he held her against him aroused something else nearly forgotten inside her core. The few seconds she'd been caught in his embrace had made her flush with want, a feeling she quickly dismissed.

"I don't understand," she said, spinning loose from his grip once he dropped his arm. "How are you still standing? You should have been knocked off-balance. How did you block my spell?"

Josef stood with his hands casually on his hips. "Perhaps your spell wasn't strong enough." The comment elicited a conspiratorial smile from Yanis, though she had no idea why. She might be out of practice, but there was nothing wrong with the way she'd delivered the spell. To prove it to herself, she sent the same spell energy toward the grain-sack dummy. It flew into the wall with a thud, spilling a small pile of pig shit onto the floor.

"Excellent," said Viktor, giving her a thumbs-up.

She thought so, too, so why didn't it work on this mortal soldier? Unless Yanis had somehow protected him. But she would sense the aura of a spell on a mortal, wouldn't she? Or had she really become as inept as they'd insinuated?

"If I hadn't been expecting it, you might have made me stumble a step or two," Josef said to Petra. Then to the group he said, "But you'll all have to get more creative with your magic. A mere shove isn't going to be enough to stop an upír once it decides to attack."

Yanis concurred. "For being the undead, their strength is deceptively well developed. Upíri don't feel pain, and they'll never shrink from their bloodlust because of fear." The priest held up a finger. "However, this does not mean they cannot be stopped. Their brain suffers from a type of atrophy that limits their concentration. As the old tales remind us, they are easily confused and distracted by small objects. They become mesmerized by the compulsion to count every seed or berry, as our friend demonstrated earlier with the hawthorn bush. The creature was bewildered by the changing number of berries. The more there were to count, the more he lost track of his purpose, and that's when you strike. It sounds unbelievable, but done right, their focus can be easily manipulated by simple illusion spells. Use seeds, berries, even rocks or pine cones."

"Village idiots," Dragoş said with a laugh. "So dumb even a woman could outsmart them."

Josef eyed the mouthy young man. He threw off his greatcoat and told Petra, "Why don't you go practice driving a stake into the dummy over there and let me have a turn with this one." He kept his eyes on Dragoş while he rolled up his shirtsleeves.

"This should prove interesting," Bako said, chewing on the butt end of a fresh unlit cigar.

As the men faced off, Yanis led Petra to the other side of the room and helped her stand the grain sack up. They both winced at the unpleasant task of stuffing it again with the manure. "Believe me, the smell isn't half as bad as the real thing can be. That one tonight was fresh. Poor man must have died only a few days ago."

Reminded that the soldier in the yard had once been a vibrant young man, Petra was struck by how fiendish it was for him and others to be exploited so horribly after death. The young men had come to the mountains to fight for the glory of the Empire, arm in arm with their comrades, only to freeze to death, or bleed out after a bullet or piece of shrapnel severed an artery, or, more likely, succumb to a sickness that would ravage their intestines until they no longer had the strength to sit up. Their bodies not given decent burial; their families denied a proper service to mourn their passing. Then to be cursed to rise as the undead to attack others seemed beyond cruel.

"I understand your husband fights for the emperor," Yanis said. "Do you know where?"

Petra shook her head. "Communication has been understandably sparse," she said, leaving out the willful omission on Marek's part to stay in touch. "I suppose that's one reason I decided to come." She positioned the stake over the center of the upír dummy. "I want to find out if my husband is here in the mountains, but it's just as likely that he's somewhere else." *If he's still alive.* She brought the mallet down, and the stake skittered off the wooden "bones" inside the grain sack.

"The technique can be harder than it looks," Yanis said. He positioned the stake in her hand and told her to aim for an opening on the right side of the breastbone. "You want to hit the second heart. The one with the knot. It will kill them if you hit it at the right angle, but you have to be in close contact. Fire and decapitation are the only foolproof ways we know that can destroy them for good once they've reanimated."

Petra shrank internally at the notion of burning the creatures, but she gripped the stake and concentrated on the spot beneath the dummy's rib cage. How had she gone from reading tarot cards for nosy neighbors at her kitchen table to preparing to kill the undead in only two days' time? With a shake of her head, she brought the mallet down, and the pointed end of the stake rammed through the gap between the "bones," hitting the soft manure filling. The successful strike was surprisingly gratifying.

"With the right stake in your arsenal, you can also go for the head, but that takes an enormous amount of luck and skill. Not for the beginner," Yanis cautioned, with a nod toward the hussar.

This sorcerer had an easy way about him. Not like Bako and Josef, who seemed to relish the physical part of being soldiers, with their sabers and pistols proudly hanging from their belts. The priest of the Order of the Seven Stars instead carried his confidence as his weapon, and yet there was humility on display, too, from his modest wool robe lined with fox fur to the *bashlyk* on his head trimmed in goat hide. His wooden leg would seem to disqualify him from such a dangerous occupation, but she'd yet to see his affliction slow him down.

"Have you faced a great many monsters?" she asked, wanting to know more about him.

The man laughed in a way that told her he had been in many scrapes already. "A few," he said. "But killing them isn't always the objective. Not outside of the war, anyway. Sometimes we just need them to go back to being the shy creatures they normally are."

Petra thought about her experiences of photographing the spirits in the city. "Most of the ghosts I take pictures of are oblivious to those around them. I often think they're trapped in their own era, even from a hundred or five hundred years ago, still standing on the street corner they once knew, but their energy somehow seeps through an ethereal veil, unconcerned with the constraints of time."

The priest of the Order smiled, appreciating her conclusions. "Is it true you don't require spoken words to implement your spells?"

The question reminded Petra she needed to be careful around people she'd only just met and not reveal too much. "My magic has always come through in shapes and colors in my mind's eye first before invoking incantations." *The best lies always shear closest to the truth.*

Across the room, Dragoş grunted after being thrown to the floor for the third time. His face was flushed with the rush of blood under his skin as steam rose off his sweaty head in the chilly room. He hurled a curse at Josef, but their team leader scoffed, unharmed, and told him to sit down and give someone else a turn.

"What about working with herbs and other ingredients?" Yanis asked. "Do you also rely on the images in your head for those spells as well?"

Petra paused, pretending to be interested in the conflict between Dragoş and Josef. "Yes," she said at last. "It works the same way, though I rarely have cause to do complicated spells anymore, which I suppose is why you recruited me."

Yanis removed the stake from the dummy, wiping the wood and muck off with a sheet of newspaper. "But you can defend yourself with fire, correct?"

At the mention of spellfire, Petra did what she always did. She turned away, denying she had much skill calling fire into her hands. Most believed her. Yanis merely tightened his skeptical brows together and seemed to make a mental note to himself before suggesting she report to Major Bako to get instruction on how to properly bury a suspected upír. And then he called Karl over without another word to her.

That night, while the men drank the last of the beer Josef had brought from the city, Petra took advantage of a few minutes of privacy in the kitchen to clean herself up. She leaned over the sink with a washcloth and bar of soap from her valise and scrubbed her face, taking care not to rub too hard on the skin of her right cheek. After patting her face dry using a clean blouse for a towel, she checked on the men in the other room by pressing an ear to the door. They laughed about Viktor nearly gagging on the smell of the dummy when it had been his turn to practice driving the stake in. He'd hammered it so hard his fist broke through the ribs and sank into the manure. With the men drinking and recounting the highs and lows of the day, she stole a last private minute for herself.

Taking care not to make too much noise, Petra removed a small handheld mirror from her valise and checked her reflection. Her skin still looked smooth and natural, but she needed a short break. The energy required to maintain an illusion day and night was almost too much after such a rigorous day of exercises. Her concentration at times had nearly slipped, jolting her back to the first days all those years ago, when she'd had to constantly remind herself to renew the spell. Closing her eyes, she let the illusion fall away. A bright-pink scar, shaped like two winding tree branches spread out over her skin, from chin to cheek. She exhaled, feeling the last tingle of the self-induced illusion spell fade. She'd read there were doctors who could transform the skin with surgery, but not for someone who could barely afford a roll of film as a luxury.

On the other side of the door, the men continued to laugh and insult each other with horrible nicknames. Dragoş called out to Petra as if he were just on the other side of the door. Worried the men would come looking for her, she took a last peek at the scar before envisioning a sheer veil over her face. The image of smooth skin returned as moonlight reflected in the mirror beside her.

CHAPTER EIGHT

"On your feet, you lazy bastards!" Major Bako circled the recruits as they stretched and yawned in the gray morning light, eating a small breakfast of hard bread and dried fruit. His bootheels pounded the hardwood floor like a drumbeat. "The undead do not wait for you to fill your bellies and comb your hair. They strike day or night like hungry animals who smell the scent of blood." To drive his point home, he thrust his saber in the air, narrowly missing Viktor by a few centimeters when he stood to button his coat. "Now line up," he ordered, pointing his weapon toward the wall.

Alarmed at being yelled at when the call of dreams still clung like spiderwebs to the insides of her tired eyelids, Petra jolted up from the table, banging her head on a low beam. "*Sakra.*" The minor curse said under her breath drew mild expressions of disapproval from her fellow recruits. Once the men relaxed their eyebrows again, they lined up against the wall. They beat Petra there by the extra two seconds it took to make sure her illusion spell hadn't been broken. She resisted the urge to rub the sore spot on the back of her head while the hussar looked them over, eager to intimidate them with a disapproving scowl.

"All right, time to load up," Bako said, seemingly pleased with their quick response. "Grab your gear and meet us at the truck."

Leaving? Petra scrambled to tie her hair up and stuff it under her flatcap, while the men packed their canvas grips with their loose personal items. "Where are we going now?" she asked, thinking they'd be staying in the café a little longer. At least until they were proficient at stabbing bags of manure with their stakes.

"Off to join the fighting, I imagine." Viktor looked as lost as she was as he carefully wrapped his glass vase for travel.

The front door opened, bringing in a gust of wind and snow. Josef stepped in from the cold and stomped his boots on the threshold as he leaned a shovel against the wall.

"Of course we're going to the front line," Dragoş said. "We can't fight the undead from here."

"But we've only had a few hours of training," Petra argued. Her hands suddenly fumbled at her half-empty pockets, wondering why they weren't filled with more amulets and protection charms.

"You've been instructed in the basics," Josef said, dusting snow off his coat and ushanka. "You know how to kill an upír. The rest is learned through experience."

So we're being thrown in the river to swim to shore or drown in the current. Not a very reassuring prospect, given how much emphasis they'd put on this Order of the Seven Stars being their last-ditch effort to defeat the undead. Rather than argue further in front of the others, she stewed in her misgivings. What had she been thinking, traveling to a battle zone? Dragoş was right—this was no place for a woman who should be home waiting for her husband to return from war. At least not this woman, she thought. Men's clothing couldn't disguise her inexperience or make her fit into a world she knew little about.

Major Bako hefted a heavy crate in his arms and nudged his head toward the door. "Time to move."

The men began filing outside as a whirlwind of snowflakes gusted in their wake. Petra felt the chill travel to the core of her veins, freezing her to the floorboards. "I can't do this," she said.

"It's just nerves." Josef handed Dragoş a crate to carry to the truck. "You'll be fine once we get there."

"You lied to me," she snapped. "You brought me here under false pretenses."

Josef's brow tightened in annoyance. "Tell them to give us a minute," he said, handing the last crate to Viktor before facing Petra again. "Yes, you were lied to. As were most of the young men called to fight in this tragic excuse for a war. You're right—you're no different in that regard." Viktor closed the door behind him, leaving them alone. "But where you are different," Josef said, taking a step closer so he towered over her, "is how you can actually do something to change the outcome. Save lives. You. Using this magic you were born with."

Petra stood with her coat hanging off her shoulders after she'd lost the will to pull it all the way on. "What if I'm not ready? What if I can't do this? What if I get someone killed?" *What if I get killed?*

"Frankly, I'd be a lot more concerned about you if you weren't worried about those things."

When she didn't move, Josef put his hands firmly on her shoulders. "You won't be the only woman there, if that's what you're worried about. There are others in camps all around the front. Nurses, as well as healers, who work for the Empire."

Her doubt receded a notch. "What kind of healers?"

He smiled and tugged the lapels of her coat forward so it hung on her properly. "For a mere mortal who hails from a small apartment above a bakery, I have witnessed a great many unusual undertakings since I joined the army. Things even you would not believe with your eyes, paní Kurková. But I will tell you this." He paused, still holding the edge of her coat. "Do you recall from school the old map the teachers liked to show us? The one where all the countries of the continent were drawn so they formed the shape of a queen?"

Petra nodded, remembering the young university man from the city who'd taught the children in her village their letters. He'd shown them a copy of the map with pins in all the capital cities, offering it up like a poppet with needles protruding from the body, as if demonstrating an advanced form of sympathetic magic, only on a larger scale. "Europa regina," Petra said, looking into Josef's eyes.

Josef nodded. "It is our homeland that represents the map's heart, yes?" His face was close enough to hers she could smell the warmth of his skin under his collar as his voice carried the cool conviction of a philosopher. "Aside from the skewed geography, I believe the mapmaker was correct in this. Our homeland is a place of beauty, mystery, and contradiction. The same qualities that often reside in a woman's heart." Petra's cheeks flushed to hear him speak like that. "In the same way," he said, pulling her coat closed in front with a final gentle tug, "I'm told women are the beating heart of magic, which we need more than ever in this forsaken place. And despite what was said earlier about recruiting you all for your lack of interest in magic, I believe you may be an exception to that. So please, paní Kurková, get on the truck."

Petra blinked back at the curious mortal with a dizzy desire to take his face in her hands and kiss him for his strange logic. Worried she might actually follow through on the impulse, she grabbed her valise and stepped outside with her camera secure in her coat pocket.

Outside, the men had gathered in a semicircle in front of the truck to wait for Petra as snow piled up on the road. All except for Dragoş, who threw bread crumbs at a pigeon before scaring it away by flapping his coat. Yanis and Bako looked to Josef for confirmation when he ducked his head and came out. Once he gave them the nod, the recruits were ordered to get in the back of the truck. Before they climbed in, Petra begged for one more small delay.

"A picture to commemorate our first mission for the Order of the Seven Stars," she said.

Josef tried to protest, saying they needed to get on the road, but Yanis didn't think a photo would do any harm. Instead he thought it might help bond them in a way, and so the men lined up against the side of the truck, their arms around each other, cigarettes dangling out of their mouths, and the unripened confidence brimming in their eyes that all young men new to war seemed to wear. All but Bako, Yanis, and Josef. Their faces were tired with eyes that betrayed a lack of sleep, yet their demeanor remained focused on the daunting task ahead. Petra snapped the photo before she missed the glint of determination in their eyes.

Surprisingly, Yanis stepped into the back of the truck with the recruits after the photo. He sat next to Karl opposite Petra. She didn't know why, but his presence made her uneasy. No, that was a lie. She knew exactly why she was afraid of being in such close proximity to this priest of the Order. She was terrified he could see right through her, through her illusion, and that would only raise questions she wasn't prepared to answer.

Dragoş sat with his arms crossed over his chest and his legs out-stretched in the cramped space, made even tighter by three anonymous crates they'd been forced to share the truck bed with. He remained oblivious to his own insolence as he asked the priest, "How'd you lose your leg?"

Yanis watched the snow swirl in their wake as the truck revved into third gear. "An angry ghoul," he answered, then pivoted in his seat to offer a meaningful glance at the young man's blatant violation of leg space. "One swipe from her powerful reach and I am limping on one leg for the rest of my life."

Dragoş, perhaps feeling exposed, perhaps catching the hint, casu-ally bent his knees and drew his legs in closer to his seat. "You didn't have a strong-enough amulet with you," he said with a shrug.

"I thought I did. Pride let me believe my position as an acolyte with the Order was the only authority I needed to overpower the creature. It wasn't. She taught me that."

"She?" Petra asked.

"Mother Ghulah. A creature not unlike those we deal with now."

"She took your leg off?" Viktor was aghast.

"It is not such an inconvenience, considering it could have been my life she carried away in her teeth." Yanis knocked on the wooden leg. "And luckily wood does not feel the cold in winter," he said, blowing on his hands and rubbing them together. "Where I come from, the sand and sun work in harmony to fry a man's brains. I don't know which extreme I dislike more."

"How are a handful of us supposed to stop these things if they're as bloodthirsty as you say?" Karl rubbed his palms against his trousers as though his fingers itched to work with his knife. "There can't be that many upíri, could there?"

So it wasn't just Petra. The men were feeling the same crisis of confidence the nearer they got to the site of the conflict as she was.

Yanis kept his body relaxed and his eyes steady as he leaned forward slightly. "Their number grows every day in relation to the dead. It is a terrifying prospect. But imagine being a mortal and discovering these creatures are not only real but they cannot be destroyed by the only weapons at your disposal. Bullets and bayonets are useless against the undead. And while I do not agree with this war and the killing of young men, we will summon the courage to protect them, on all sides of the conflict, from this threat from our world. Because that is the task that no one else can do."

The four recruits, recognizing the desperate state of a mortal army thrust into the storm of a supernatural hell, all straightened their spines at the same time. Perhaps Yanis had joined them in the back of the truck for a reason, Petra thought, sitting up a little taller.

Two hours later, the truck bounced to a stop on a stretch of rutted ice pretending to be a road. Through a tear in the canvas, Petra could just see a makeshift gate fashioned from two felled trees and a pair of barrels. Two soldiers approached the truck cradling rifles in their arms. They demanded identification papers from Major Bako while Josef let the engine idle. Each soldier's head was draped with a wool scarf with the ends tucked inside their turned-up coat collars. Their field caps sat at angles atop their scarves, and their heavy mustaches drooped with ice. One of the soldiers reached for the papers with bare fingers bound in a strip of cloth. The other's body appeared bloated like a weevil beneath the extra layers of garments he'd put on under his coat. In the distance, the sound of gunfire ricocheted through the pine trees, though neither soldier paid it any attention.

After the first guard scanned the paperwork, he ordered two other soldiers huddling beside a fire to check the back of the truck. They pushed the flap open with the noses of their rifles. Petra fought the urge to raise her hands like a criminal as she kept her head down under her flatcap. The soldiers' expressions were grim as they studied the fresh faces being allowed inside their camp. One guard elbowed the other two and told them to get inside and unload the crates. Karl offered to help but was ordered to remain seated. When the guards finished removing the last crate, they jumped out and closed the flap, banging on the back of the truck two times. Josef lurched the truck forward, bouncing over the frozen ground.

"A bribe," Yanis said when they were gone. "Tinned meat, candles, soap. So that we may enter the camp without questions. Command knows why we're here, but they prefer the enlisted men to believe we are a medical envoy sent to assess the spread of disease among soldiers."

The truck chugged forward, changing gears as it crept down the road. If Petra thought the ride before had been rough, it became downright dangerous as the wheels rolled hard over a hole, rattling their teeth as they bounced on the benches, hands reaching for something to hold on to. Thankfully, their destination was only a short distance away. Five minutes later another soldier cocooned in wool waved them to a rutted track on the right. There, they pulled ahead to a small cluster of buildings surrounded by a rocky, forested area. At least a hundred trees had recently been felled, their stumps littering the snowy ground like headstones. A wave of foreboding ruffled Petra's intuition at the sight.

Petra stepped out of the truck, catching wind of something that had gone off. A sour odor permeated the ground, the air, and even the frost itself where a suspicious mound of earth on the far side of a clearing stood out unnaturally against the rest of the surroundings. "What is that?" she asked, covering her nose with the back of her hand.

"Consider yourself lucky," Josef said, getting out of the truck's cab. "There's been heavy, fresh snow. You don't want to be here when the weather warms and the frost melts." He gave the enormous mound in the distance a meaningful glare. Petra took a harder look at the swollen ground and saw a pair of desiccated horse hooves sticking out through the shroud of snow. At the same moment, a battery of artillery shells exploded beyond the ridge. Behind her a line of enlisted men with bloody rags tied around their heads stumbled by, carrying more injured men on stretchers. A pair of ravens cawed in chorus at the sight of fresh blood.

"This is the front?" Petra asked, confused by the seemingly lax urgency at the explosion of gunfire.

Dragoş lit a cigarette and inhaled. "This is just the rear, *princezna*." He grinned and made an obvious glance at her body. "This is where they keep the supplies. The field hospital. Oh, and the officers sitting in tents drinking hot coffee while their men freeze their balls off."

He thought he'd offended her with his rough language and leering looks, but she'd seen his kind before: A crude exterior with a hollow center. A bonbon.

"I think the real fighting is over on the ridge," Karl said, pointing in the direction of where the shells had exploded. His eyes had the sheen of unshed tears. Like a man homesick for the comfort of his tedious life.

"Boys are taking a pounding, by the sound of it, which means we may see a rise in upír activity." Josef ordered the group to gather their gear from the truck and follow him through the trees.

Yanis and Bako took up the rear as they trailed behind a half dozen injured soldiers on a path of trampled pink snow. They walked in silence until they came to a collection of old farmhouses with barns, a small wooden church, and a rough outbuilding tucked away in a sheltered clearing between rock outcroppings. Two huge piles of hay had been stacked up beside the first barn. What once must have been huge heaps were now so heavily carved away that Petra doubted there'd be enough to last through spring. If any animals remained to feed it to.

"This way," Bako said, leading them around the first farmhouse to the back, where men suffering from blood loss and missing limbs swarmed the area in various states of consciousness. Many wore wool blankets strapped around their bodies with twine for coats. A few of the soldiers weakly saluted Major Bako when they saw him coming, but the rest sat hunched over their cigarettes, pretending he wasn't there.

"The largest house is used as the hospital where they take in the wounded," Josef said. "They've got a pair of nurses in there and a doctor who's more of a butcher than a miracle worker." He glanced at the windows of the attic, and Petra swore he shivered at the sight. Josef cleared his throat and tilted his head toward the barn behind the farmhouse. "They house the injured in there on a bed of hay to recover." He looked back at his recruits. "To soak up the blood."

"Until someone comes to haul them back to the line again the minute they get on their feet," Bako said. "And sometimes before."

Josef pointed farther down. "We'll be staying there, in the barn that looks like it's held together with two rusty nails and a prayer. Leadership didn't think it was safe enough for the injured, so they've been using it for storage and animals."

At the back of the barn, beyond the depleted haystacks, Petra saw an open horse shed, a trough, and a wagon missing its wheels. "Welcome to your new home," Major Bako said, taking pleasure once again in his recruits' horrified reactions to their new reality.

Shortly after midday, once they'd secured their sleeping quarters in the squalid conditions by propping the broken wagon at an angle against the back wall and piling a thick layer of pine boughs on the ground for their bedding, Yanis prepared a spell to protect the space from the overly curious. The sorcerer used a stick to draw a circle around the perimeter of the barn, then sprinkled a fistful of herbs inside—rosemary, bay leaf, and marjoram, if Petra's senses had detected correctly. At least that's what she would have used if it were her spell. A few of the wounded soldiers looked on with eyes narrowed in confusion, but no one interfered as Yanis recited a spell in his native language.

When he had finished securing the space, the novice monster hunters were given their first assignments. Karl and Dragoş were sent with Bako to the eastern end of the camp with knapsacks full of rolled bandages on their backs and crosses on their armbands, while Petra and Viktor were paired with Yanis to inventory the most recent burial sites. When Petra asked why the dead needed counting, Yanis merely smiled and walked on without comment.

"How will we know if something's been disturbed?" Viktor asked, watching his every step through the snow and muck. The glassmaker's face was flushed from the cold, and his icy blue eyes glittered inquisitively, like a Siamese cat's, behind his tinted glasses.

Yanis lumbered through a patch of knee-deep snow, using for a staff the stick he'd marked the perimeter of the barn with. "It can be difficult," he answered. "Wolves often leave behind the same sort of . . . disarray as the upíri. But with the new snow, it should be easy to spot any fresh disturbance."

"Our team leader isn't coming with us, then?" Viktor's second question saved Petra from asking about Josef. She'd been dying to ask where he'd run off to after the protection spell was finished, but the wrong question from the wrong mouth could ignite a rumor like the one that had seen her thrown out of her apartment.

"While we begin our work here," Yanis said, "Josef has gone to see if our counterparts to the north are also being preyed upon by the undead. As Major Bako pointed out, we've had little communication with anyone on the other side of the fighting for months now, but we need to define the scope of the attacks so we have a better idea of the epicenter of the uprising."

Petra shook her head like she hadn't heard right. "He went north? Alone? Isn't that incredibly dangerous?"

Yanis showed little concern, paying more attention to where he placed his feet than any discussion of Josef's welfare. "He knows where he's going."

"But shouldn't we watch out for him or, I don't know, send someone with him? What if something happens? What if he's captured or injured?"

Yanis and Viktor exchanged a quick glance of concern. Not for Josef, she presumed, but for her overly concerned outburst.

"He knows the territory. He'll be fine." Yanis punctuated his terse answer with a flat smile that indicated he'd said all he was going to on the matter.

Walking on, the sorcerer directed Petra and Viktor to an inner ring of the camp, where they were asked to present their papers once again. Petra presumed their documents were forged via an illusion to get them past yet another pair of guards who looked like they'd sell their grandmothers at a discount to be home by a warm fire.

"Keep that camera tucked inside your jacket," the first guard told Petra. "Command doesn't allow photos in camp."

"In case you actually take a photo of something that shows how badly we're losing," the second guard said.

The first young man slid his own vest pocket camera out of his coat in a show of camaraderie. "Keep it warm under your coat so the parts don't freeze up. Journalists aren't allowed near the fighting, but personal photos are tolerated when the commanders aren't looking. But no selling photos to the papers later," the guard said.

Petra nodded the way she'd seen Marek do with his friends, nudging her chin up to show she would comply. She opened the top button on her coat and slid the camera inside as the guard folded up their papers and pointed to the areas they were allowed to explore.

Cleared to continue, Yanis tucked the papers away and cut through a cluster of soldiers in the center of the encampment sleeping and eating in the open air. As the trio walked past them, inquisitive stares grazed Petra's silhouette, searching for clues as to what was hidden underneath the baggy clothes. She'd fooled some with her blazer and overcoat, but others let their looks linger, suspicious of her slight build and smooth cheeks. Calling up an image in her mind, she altered her walk slightly. Just as she'd done in the city alone at night while ghost hunting, she let her steps fill with the swagger of a boar safe in his forest territory.

With the change, her attitude shifted. Nervousness transformed into curiosity, driving her need to understand the look that registered on the rest of the men's faces—those who huddled under blankets with red, swollen eyes that begged for sleep but would not close, or the young men whose faces cringed in terror when the ice cracked and a branch snapped in the forest.

Along the perimeter of the camp, beyond the glow of cookfires, where the snow clung to boughs of juniper and golden eagles hunted smaller birds from above, Yanis pointed out their first suspected mass grave. The ground was slightly mounded in a ten-meter-long shape that sat at odds with the natural lines of their environment. The sorcerer inspected the area, deliberately dragging his wooden staff to leave a track in the snow as he walked around the site.

"Here," he said, pausing and pointing. "Do you see the indentation?"

Petra squinted at the depression. There was a saggy area in the middle, but nothing struck her as being tampered with. She raised her camera and took a photo anyway when she felt a wisp of breath across her neck that told her *something* was there.

"I see it," Viktor said, adjusting his colored glasses to inspect the snow.

"This is a new site since I was here a month ago," Yanis said, checking his bearings to make certain. "The grave has been hastily dug and isn't very deep. It wouldn't be in this cold. But look at the depression in the side," he said, pointing. "It may have already become a location of reanimation."

Viktor scanned the ground, flipping his glasses up and down on his nose to change perspective. "There are footprints too," he said. "They've been snowed over, but the dark glasses reveal them. Just there." He pointed to a trail of sunken snow leading west. "And over there too."

The sorcerer dug in his satchel and handed Petra and Viktor a small cloth sack each. "Poppy seeds," he said. "Scatter them on the ground. Go all the way around. If any more of the undead arise from this mound, it will stall them, just like the fellow we encountered in the café."

"Hey," a soldier shouted from the trees. "What are you doing there? Leave that area alone."

"We have permission," Yanis yelled back, waving his papers.

"No, get away," the soldier said. "You don't want to be messing about out there." The man urgently waved them in. "Come back this way. Come, come."

Petra and Viktor made a mad dash of tossing the seeds around the grave site, then joined the sorcerer when he decided to approach the young soldier yelling at them.

"Why shouldn't we be out there?" Yanis asked, encouraging the man to speak freely.

"You're here about *them*, aren't you." The soldier spit on the ground and crossed himself. "Evil things."

"We're a medical crew assigned to assess the rate of disease," Yanis lied. "Have you seen something out here?"

The soldier looked over his shoulder. "They don't want me talking about them. Some deny it's happening, but I've lost my best friend and I don't know what to do. Teodor was attacked three nights ago by something in the dark." The man paled as he scrutinized the overhead branches of the trees. Petra followed his gaze, wondering what he'd seen up there to make his hand shake so badly.

"Who doesn't want you talking about them?" Yanis asked.

The soldier stomped his feet in the snow, rubbing his arms against the chill. "What do you have on you? Food? Cigarettes? I'm happy to tell you, but nothing is free anymore."

Behind him, three men who'd been huddled around a small fire lifted their heads and looked in their direction.

Yanis held his empty hands out. "I'm afraid I have nothing to offer but my condolences."

The soldier stopped rubbing his arms and frowned. He turned his attention to Petra, then Viktor. "You brought crates in the truck. I saw. You have something. Please, I'll tell you all about the wolves and the wind. What I have seen."

Wolves and wind?

The soldier's three friends got to their feet. Their faces were gaunt and dirty with black mustaches that drooped over their lips, limp with damp and grime.

"Please, we are hungry and cold," the soldier pleaded. "Even a cigarette to take away the boredom."

"Yes, of course." Viktor reached in his jacket and gave the man the cigarette he craved, but before he could light it for him, the three men marched over and grabbed their comrade by the arms.

"Best leave him be," the first one said. "He's not right in the head. The cold and the empty stomach. They work together to make a man delirious. Do not pay any attention to his ramblings." Before Yanis could protest, they dragged the soldier back to their fire and forced him down on his knees, slapping the back of his head for good measure.

"What did he mean by wolves and wind?" Petra asked.

Yanis shook his head. "I'm not sure." He glanced at the trees as though trying to divine some meaning in the man's words, but turned away none the wiser. "Come, we have more work to do," he said.

Petra watched the highest tree branches sway in the breeze, silent as ghosts. She resisted the impulse to snap a quick photo, mindful of her limited riches, before they left to inspect more resting places of the dead. It occurred to her only after they'd walked away that she hadn't thought to ask any of the soldiers if they knew her husband and whether he was still alive.

CHAPTER NINE

The cold was tolerable enough during the day, if one kept moving and had other things to think about besides how numb their toes were. Nightfall in the mountain pass, however, brought with it an altogether different level of misery. Petra had seen men in and around the hospital with blackened fingers, ears, toes, and noses—the deep tissue killed by frost, only to be lopped off, thrown in the medical trash heap, and the victim left limping or disfigured but alive.

Petra pulled her blanket up to her chin as she lay on her side atop the pine boughs, thinking of the tiny campfires that burned along the ridgeline where soldiers desperately fought against the elements to stay alive. Those same cruel conditions afflicted the tsar's men to the north—the enemy of the men fighting and dying on this side of the ridge. It wasn't lost on her that should those same northern men turn the tide of war to their favor, a defeat for the emperor and his allies could prove the salvation for her homeland's hopes of attaining independence from the dual monarchy. The collapse of the eastern front would expose the weakness of a bloated sovereignty past its prime. The emperor would be on the defensive against invasion from the east, while forced to sacrifice men and fortune to protect the western borders. It was an unsustainable prospect for the Empire, but a fortuitous one for those with dreams of independence. Losing the war would break the tenuous bonds holding a cobbled kingdom together. For her homeland to no longer be shackled to a sinking empire and instead rise to become a self-governing nation free to make its own laws—that's what was worth dying for. Marek could never see the value of such self-determination, but why be a soldier for a failing empire when there was so much more to be gained in the fight for liberation?

And yet she knew her desire to see the enemy win could mean her husband's demise and the deaths of those soldiers around her. A chilling prospect, yet one she could not banish from her mind no matter how many times she turned under her blanket.

Petra struggled with her discordant thoughts as she rolled over on her back. With little room for privacy, she'd settled in beside her fellow recruits in an empty stall that still smelled of horses. Their snores were oddly comforting. A reminder she was no longer on her own in the upstairs apartment, wondering where her next meal would come from. The warmth from Viktor's fire spell, conjured before he'd been tasked with first watch on guard duty, finally began to reach her fingers and toes. It felt unfair—unkind even—that they should enjoy the privilege of magic when misery lay mere meters away. Poor men suffered all around her, summoned to a fight under the false pretense of a quick victory. Was that what had drawn Josef to the war in the beginning too? A chance to prove his valor? His honor? Heroism? Was that why he risked his life today for a scrap of intelligence from the other side of the mountain that wouldn't change anything anyway?

What if he didn't return by morning? The thought made her grind her teeth with worry as she rolled over again, turning her back against the others should her fear turn to tears. She blinked at the strangeness of sleeping just beyond the reach of a hundred thousand men when something moved through the slats inside the barn, coming toward her. She lifted her head slightly to get a better look, reaching for the wooden stake beneath her valise. And then the outline of a solitary figure—a man in a long coat and furry ushanka—formed before her. He walked toward the horse stall, his long stride making quick work of the gap between them. His eyes shone in the dark through the fog. His breath rose like a cloud in the moonlight. She slid over and made a space for him on the pine boughs.

"How did it go?" she whispered.

"In the morning," he said, putting a finger to his lips.

He crawled under his blanket and stretched out on his back with his hands tucked behind his head. The smell of the forest clung to his clothes. Animallike. Feral. Bristling with scents of wild things. Petra rested her head against her valise and watched as his eyes closed almost instantly. With his body beside hers, safe within the camp again, she let sleep come, where dreams took her to fields of mist and moonlight.

It wasn't quite dawn when the first scream shook the camp awake. An alarm whistle blew. A gun discharged. Men ran and shouted in a panic. Petra opened her eyes expecting to see the oak beams of her apartment but was quickly transported back to the barn and her new reality by more shouting.

"It's them," Josef said, urging her to get up. "All of you, prepare yourselves. Fire. Stakes. Now!"

Yanis had slept with his false leg on but struggled to stand quickly without help. Karl scrambled for his weapons, dropping his stakes on the ground before stumbling over his own boots. Viktor, who'd been scheduled for relief from guard duty at two in the morning, groggily searched for his glasses. Bako yelled at them all to move their asses, but he reserved his harshest vitriol for Dragoş, who'd fallen asleep on his watch.

Petra stuffed her hair under her hat, grabbed the stake and mallet she'd been assigned, and followed Josef toward the sound of the disturbance. Roughly three hundred meters away, a group of twenty men stood in a circle, pulling their hair and screaming in wounded-animal anguish while others strapped on their rifles, swearing to kill the beast.

On the ground, a man's body lay in a pool of steaming blood. His uniform had been torn open, his neck gashed to the bone.

"Which way did it go?" Josef shouted. "Which way?"

"That way." A young man pointed, still holding his other hand over his mouth as though he might be sick. "Toward the ravine."

"I'd just turned over when that awful smell woke me up," said another soldier. "That's when it jumped on him. Took a bite right out of him."

"It?" Petra asked, too shocked to lower her voice.

"Had to be an animal. It was huge. A wolf maybe." The soldier stifled a sob. "No man could have done that."

Yanis, Bako, and the rest of the crew caught up, and together they headed toward the ravine, spreading out in a line. A pale-pink rim of light rose above the ridge in the east as they chased the creature into an abyss of rocks and fog. There was no trail, no track to follow that Petra could see, only the scent of death. Predictably, the creature had flown into the deepest darkness it could find after the attack. Josef led the way, curiously without aid of a flashlight, as if he had the eyes of a witch, pushing back tree limbs while following some unmarked trajectory. Snow and mud clung to their trousers, and bitter cold filled their lungs. Men shouted behind them at a distance, giving warning.

Then, in the mouth of a crevice between stones, they found the thing hissing at them—fangs bared and eyes engorged with rage.

It was no wolf. Nor a man, in its current state. Yet the creature wore the uniform of the Empire, stained now with both fresh blood and old from a giant hole through the trouser leg on his right.

"Got him." Bako grinned at their quick luck. "Who wants to finish him off? Kurková?"

The upír's hair was blond like Marek's, cut tight on the sides in the style her husband had always preferred. The resemblance caught Petra off guard, and she hesitated when she should have stepped forward. She wasn't prepared to stab the thing through the heart with the stake, not while the upír still had its full strength. The creature was trapped, certainly, but still deadly. She knew she should call up fire and cast it at the wretched thing, but her magic froze up on her. It wasn't Marek, she knew it wasn't, but the resemblance played tricks on her heart. Petra offered a feeble excuse as her hands began to shake. "I have no hawthorn to distract it."

The creature laughed at her weakness before lunging at Yanis, who struck it swiftly with his mallet. The fiend stumbled over a rock and Bako attacked, driving a half-meter-long stake into the beast's heart. It screamed and shook, struggling to be free, but the upír did not die while pinned to the earth, not until Viktor formed a ball of fire in his hands and hurled it at the ungodly thing.

The fire consumed the creature as though the body had been coated in petrol. The sickening result was a burst of warmth that hit their faces and melted the snow from the rocks to the lowest tree limbs. Petra reached for her camera in her coat pocket, thinking she ought to document what had happened, but she'd forgotten to bring it with her in the mad rush to hunt the thing down. A failure on two counts.

Dragoş knelt next to the corpse as the initial flames shrank in intensity. His eyes were lit from the fire as much as from the rush of adrenaline. "Should I knock the head off for good measure?" he asked a little too enthusiastically.

"No need." Yanis swept his robe back and removed a carefully tied-up pouch of seeds. "Verbena," he said. "We bury the body and plant the seeds on top. The plant's roots are poison and will destroy any chance the revenant can return, however unlikely in its present state."

"But it's winter," Karl said, reminding everyone he was there when he spoke up. "Will that work? Won't the seeds freeze?"

Yanis looked at Petra and waited for her to answer and redeem herself.

"It will work," she said. "We just need to protect the seeds with an incubation spell until spring."

"How'd you know that?" Dragoș asked, though his question sounded more like an accusation coming out of his mouth.

"Just do," she said. "Anyone raised in the countryside knows about verbena."

Josef had kept his eye on her from the moment Bako had suggested it was her turn to kill the upír. He'd watched her refuse, watched her grow nervous about calling fire into her hands, something any witch ought to be able to do, and then watched her casually recover with her knowledge of folk magic. All with a look of *knowing* that left her perplexed and wary. Thrown by his scrutiny, she reached for the comfort of her camera, only to be reminded once again she'd left it behind. Her fingers fumbled against her coat buttons in its absence.

An audience of officers in plumed caps, bright-blue uniforms, and heavy wool overcoats appeared on the high ground above the ravine. They kept the line of curious soldiers contained at a distance while rocks were piled over the burned body and the seeds spread around the grave. Come summer there would be a cluster of purple verbena stretching toward the sun above the ravine, but there would be no upír to rise again from that patch of earth once the roots sent their poison into the soil.

"The commanders here know the truth," Josef said as he, Viktor, and Petra walked back up the steep slope to camp while the others remained behind to hunt for traces of more upír activity.

Petra had noticed the enlisted men craning their necks behind the officers, despite the threat of cut rations if they didn't back away. "The men thought a wolf had attacked," she said, recalling their shouts in the midst of bloodshed.

Josef acknowledged the mismatch of information. "The officers won't confirm any rumors of undead to them. As it is, there are factions of soldiers willing to give up, calling the war a misguided suicide mission. If they knew the truth of what's out there, the Empire would have a full-scale mutiny on its hands. So the commanders are usually the first to blame the wolves when an incident happens. Of course, sometimes they're right."

Viktor walked on Josef's other side. "They can't afford a morale failure. If they lose the pass, they lose the war. That's what the newspapers said."

Josef agreed. "There are two passes where the army must hold the line. Sixteen hundred kilometers of territory to defend. If the tsar's army breaks through at either point, I'm afraid they will be like the houseguest that never leaves. Their boots will always be under our table."

"Did you really make it to their camp yesterday?" Viktor asked.

When Josef said that he had, the glassmaker reacted the same way Petra had. *How?*

"We'll talk about it when the others return, but first we should check on the victim," he said.

Back in camp, the initial panic had subsided. Men stoked their meager fires and warmed their tinned rations of meat and cans of water to make a weak swill of coffee. They barely looked up as Petra returned alongside the mismatched soldier in the fur hat and long coat, almost as if they didn't want the evil eye to fall on them by showing any interest in anything outside the reach of their fire. The trio made a quick sweep to see if anyone else was hurt, even a scratch, then made for the small cluster of farmhouses to check on the dead soldier.

The victim, a young man from a village south of the dual monarchy's western capital, had been put on a stretcher and taken to the field hospital, where he'd died instantly from the blood loss. "Carotid," the doctor explained, pointing to his neck. "Severed clean through."

Josef asked permission to check the man's eyes. The doctor scoffed, but had no real objection. Petra suspected he'd merely wanted to assert his professional claim over the body's care and disposition. He frowned before asking a captain, who'd also come to check on the dead man, who this group of civilians was and what they were doing in his hospital. But the officer brushed off the concern, saying they were there to chronicle the heroic effort of the Empire's learned doctors in their epic struggle against the aggressors in the north, not to mention the extreme challenges of fighting disease and frostbite in these cursed mountain passes. The doctor gave a wan smile and left them to it.

"Petra, come take a look," Josef said. He held the dead man's eyelids open. "What do you see?"

Petra leaned in, not sure what she was looking for. Viktor held an oil lamp overhead to provide stronger light. The pupils were slightly dilated. Naturally they did not react to the lantern light, and yet something moved in the eye, left to right. *There!* A dark spot under the white membrane.

"There's a fleck of shadow," she whispered. "Already?"

Viktor swallowed. "What does that mean?"

Josef leaned in but didn't see the shadow as she had. "If there is such a mark, it means he'll become—" He pointed toward the slash in the man's throat to avoid saying it out loud within earshot of the other patients. "He'll need to be burned and buried with verbena like the other."

Behind them the door to the surgery burst open. Two more soldiers were carried in on stretchers and laid out on the last remaining tables. Their skin was as pale as dumplings from the twin gashes in their throats.

"Attacked," said a soldier whose coat was so stuffed with crumpled newspaper it poked out between his front buttons. Steam rose around his head from the effort of carrying his comrade through the snow. Possibly from as far as a kilometer away. "They were walking the perimeter on guard duty. The wolves, or whatever they want to call those things, got them both." He saw the other body laid out and wiped his face with his coat sleeve. "God damn this place," he said as he and his comrades left without another glance back.

CHAPTER TEN

Midday, after all three bodies had been ritually buried with fire and verbena so their corpses would never reanimate, the crew gathered in the barn for a debriefing. Viktor did the honor of lighting a central cookfire in a stone pit while the others fought off the cold by bundling up in blankets swaddled around their shoulders.

"It's not as rare as it used to be to see multiple attacks in one day," Bako said. The lack of sleep showed in the lines around his eyes. He nervously bit his lip and shook his head. "The incidents are escalating. You kill one, but two more rise up."

"Our team caught a second fiend before he crossed the ridgeline," Dragoş said. "Who knows how many lives we saved by roasting his hide too." He spoke as if it were the most heroic thing a man had ever done in the midst of war.

"Or," Josef said, opening a package of *erbswurst*. He dumped a chunk of the compressed meat-and-pea paste into a pot of water. "Instead of simply increasing, what if the attacks are being organized?"

The others looked up, curious to know where he was going with his thinking. "You suspect the upíri are coordinating with each other before they attack?" Bako asked, rubbing his chin. "Or someone else is doing it for them."

"I think it's something we need to consider." Josef set the pot over the fire. He dug in his coat for a wooden spoon and gave the pea paste a stir. "Not only has the number of attacks gone up, they are also curiously concentrated here in the mountains. In *this* camp."

"Weren't they always here?" Viktor asked as he stared at the cookfire through his tinted glasses.

Yanis opened a tin of olives by peeling back the lid with a metal key and offered them to the group. "You're all aware of upíri because of tales you've heard growing up, but before being recruited, when was the last time you can recall a bona fide attack in the mountains or anywhere else?"

They all shook their heads, but then Petra raised her hand. "There was a man in our village when I was a child who they dug up and reburied upside down because they said he haunted people in their sleep."

"Oh? Which village was that?" Dragoş asked while biting a fingernail rimmed with dirt.

The question put Petra on guard. She'd said too much. Not enough to reveal anything important, she didn't think, but she went silent after that, ignoring Dragoş and his nosy question.

"The point is," Yanis said, "upíri do appear semiregularly in this region, according to the transcripts we maintain on the subject at the Order, but the occurrence is closer to once a decade at most. And, as paní Kurková mentioned, the attacks are often of the mind rather than the body. Yet there have been more than a dozen attacks in these mountains in the last six weeks, including our friend from the other night. It's as if they have an agenda."

"It's not enough they're just bloodthirsty fiends hungry for more?" Bako struck a match to a fresh cigar.

"They are that." Josef stirred the chunk of erbswurst, helping it dissolve in the boiling water. An aroma of greasy pork rose from the pot. "And yet, I spoke with a Cossack acquaintance in the north last night who swears they've not seen such horrors on their side of the battle. Other curses, yes, but not upíri."

"If only the Empire's troops are being attacked, isn't that the evidence we need that this is coming from someone on the other side? A witch's curse?" Bako rubbed his stomach like a man who suffered from ulcers, refusing the olives when they were passed his way.

Yanis cautioned against hasty conclusions. "Some in the Order believe the blood from the dead soldiers was so thick after the first battle in these mountains it called to the undead, seeping through the liminal space to wake them from their graves. Like sharks getting the scent of blood in the water. If someone has figured out a way to control the revenants to use in war, we have an altogether different problem."

"Why would someone do that?" Karl asked, aghast at the idea. He fiddled with a piece of wood he'd picked up on his way back to camp, claiming it would make a good horse for his son, if he could figure out how to enchant the legs to move in rhythm.

"Why?" Dragoş pulled a face of disbelief as he spit out an olive pit. "Are you affected in the head? Have you seen the terror in the men's eyes out there? There might have been only a dozen attacks, but eighty thousand men have been infected. In here." He tapped his index finger against his temple. "Hard to win with an army that's too scared to even take a shit after dark."

Josef banged the spoon against the side of the pot to get the drippings off. "Exactly." He drew his coat sleeve down over his palm and used it to protect his hand as he lifted the pot off the fire and poured a serving in each person's cup. "So, any ideas about how someone could gain control of our undead friends?"

Yanis unwrapped a stack of stale flatbread, enough for each person to take half a piece. "It's possible there could be a spell for such things, but it would take a master of unusual skill to control so many bloodthirsty creatures."

Everyone drank their soup—some in small sips to make it last and others in one long gulp to get it over and done with before gagging on the greasy, pasty concoction.

"The wind," Petra said, tearing off a piece of flatbread. "There was a soldier yesterday who talked about the 'evil things.' Said he'd tell us about the wind and wolves, but his friends pulled him away before he could explain. No idea what he meant, but the wind blew through the trees this morning as the first attack happened."

"The wind blows here all the time," Dragoş said, unimpressed. "He likely just wanted to trade you a story for a—"

"Careful," Josef said, cutting him off.

Dragoş gave a derisive laugh and tossed the last greasy drippings of his soup into the fire. "Just saying what's on everyone's mind."

"Not everyone." Yanis looked up at the eaves and squinted. "The beams aren't creaking from the wind now. And it wasn't noticeably windy on the ground when the attack occurred this morning, but I, too, saw the highest treetops moving."

"You think there could be something to it?" Bako blew on his erbswurst before downing the whole cup.

It had to be a strange conversation for him and Josef, each mortal-born yet called to this fight against supernatural creatures. Liaisons between the emperor's army and a corps of witches. Petra wondered what intrinsic quality each possessed to be selected for such a mission.

"There are witches who are certainly capable of manipulating the weather under the right circumstances," Yanis said. "And we know we have entities on both sides of the war using hexes and spells to interfere with the conflict. I've not experienced a spell carried on the wind before, but such a thing might be possible."

Josef's and Bako's eyes met, and they came to a silent agreement. "All right," Josef said. "We'll keep an eye on the wind. See if a pattern emerges. Well spotted, Kurková."

Petra stuffed the last of her flatbread in her mouth, chewing to distract her from spitting curses at Dragoş. Apparently he'd gone off and killed a second upír after she'd faltered with the first, but it wasn't for lack of courage on her part that she'd restrained herself. He might not see it that way. None of them might. But they knew nothing about her. Wind was a trifling plaything compared to what she could call up in her hands—before she'd sealed off that part of her life.

With their midday meal eaten, the group broke into teams again. Karl was asked to show Yanis how he might use his talent to enchant their supply of wooden stakes to help them strike true, while Dragoş and Viktor were sent with Bako to explore more of the camp and elicit statements from witnesses about what they'd seen.

"What about me?" Petra asked when the others had gone.

Josef wrapped the cook pot in a cloth and shoved it in his knapsack. "You and I have work to do in the attic above the hospital."

Menial work in a storage attic? Petra worried she really had fallen out of favor after she'd been unable to kill the upír earlier in the day. She knew how it must have looked to the others, but the thought of losing Josef's support wounded her in a way that was difficult for her to reconcile after knowing him for only a handful of days.

Petra walked with her head down as they crossed the rutted track to the big farmhouse, eager to prove herself again. The doctor and two nurses barely paid any attention as she followed Josef up the fold-down ladder leading to the attic. They were too busy extracting a bullet from a man's chest, while another young soldier, no more than a teen, sat on a chair cradling his left hand in his lap. Three of the fingers had already turned black.

"So, what do you think?" Josef asked when they'd reached the top of the steps and entered an attic cluttered with crates.

"Are we supposed to move all this stuff?" Petra scanned the room, wondering what he'd meant bringing her up there. Boxes of supplies had been stacked up on both sides of the room, creating a sort of maze one had to enter to get to a space in the back. There was a broken stretcher propped against the wall, an IV stand and bottle that still contained a brown liquid, helmets and armbands stacked atop boxes, and a set of restraints bolted to the wall beside a bloodied straitjacket.

"No," he said, amused by her assumption. "I thought it might make a suitable workspace for your photography."

If she looked up at him in confused disappointment, as she suspected she had, he didn't let on. Sidestepping the boxes, he led her to the back corner of the attic, where a kitchen hutch took up a small space beside the chimney. There she found three bottles displayed on the shelf—developing solution, stop bath, and fixer. All brand new and filled to the top.

"Where did you get these?" she asked, already thinking of how they might build an enclosure around the space and seal up the cracks to make a darkroom.

"Yours were nearly gone, so a photographer in the city gave me a good price on a start-up kit before we left. Paper is in short supply, though, so you'll have to be careful."

Petra spun around, catching him with a relaxed, carefree glint in his eye—a look she suspected he'd worn most days before war made a mask of his emotions. "You knew I'd come with you even before I did." He had to have bought the items before she'd hopped on the tram that led her to the rendezvous spot.

"I didn't have the option of letting you say no," he said, opening a box containing paper, a pair of tongs, and a funnel.

Petra wrestled with the implication of what he'd said. Did he have a plan to kidnap her and force her to come to the front if she'd said no? Or had he somehow made sure she'd have no choice but to say yes? Perhaps he'd made too much noise on the steps on purpose when he'd left the apartment that first night, hoping to get her kicked out. She ought to be upset by his confession, but she was so flattered by the idea that someone needed or wanted her enough that they would buy her the supplies she needed to develop her photos.

"I'll need some string," she said. "And a handful of clips to hang the negatives. If we use the hutch for a base, we can build around it. Seal up the chinks so the light doesn't get in. I'll bring my developing box up, and it will be perfect."

"You'd used cloth and newspaper before to make it dark." He studied the small space again. "What about a light? You didn't have one in your wardrobe at home."

Again she cringed at the idea of him being in her apartment alone before she'd got there. She still didn't know how he'd found her, but she suspected their encounter in the square at midnight hadn't been random. "I don't need a red light for developing the photographs. My eyesight—we witches can see well enough in the dark."

"Ah, yes, of course. Like cats." He nodded as if he'd heard such a thing before, but it was clear, too, that he was out of his depth. Whatever magic he'd witnessed in the world to make him comfortable enough to command a group of witches was still something foreign to his mortal-born sensibilities. And perhaps a little frightening too.

Their breath floated in the chilled attic air, but the cold was tolerable enough if moving around. Modest heat rising from the fireplace in the bustling surgery room below provided just enough warmth to keep the space from freezing solid. Josef shrugged off his coat and got to work piecing together the rest of the structure for the darkroom. He broke open a pair of half-empty crates and turned them on their sides to use for a work surface, flattened cardboard boxes to create an enclosure, and then began stuffing newspaper into the cracks and over the single window under the eaves.

Meanwhile, Petra took her cap off, letting her hair fall free while she organized the supplies. She took inventory of how much solvent she had, calculating the amount against the number of negatives she might be able to develop. She'd just used up the last frame on her personal roll of film that morning, but only two photos on it needed developing. The rest could wait.

Yes, she thought, in times of war everything had to be reevaluated—the need against the want.

Petra stole glimpses at Josef's long-limbed body as he worked in his shirtsleeves. She'd not seen him out of his long coat and ushanka often. The sight of his lean, muscular body reinforced something she'd suspected about him. Where Marek had grown city-soft from office work and pub food, Josef's body appeared toned from the daily demand of physical labor. She caught him glancing back at her in the same curious manner moments later while he crossed the room to gather more cardboard.

"Why have you done all this?" she asked.

Josef straightened from his work, not answering right away. His eyes roamed around the room while he thought about what to say. "Your photos capture images that aren't clear to the naked eye. They may help us better understand what has happened in the mountains to awaken the undead. Some spell moves unseen in the air, but I'm helpless to figure it out without someone who can breach that veil."

She believed him for the most part, but there was something more. "Why have you done all this for *me?*" Petra challenged him, stepping near enough to smell the light sweat building on his skin.

Something in him accepted the challenge, meeting her eye with a confident smirk. "Because a woman like you deserves whatever you need," he said.

Petra was stunned by the generosity of his words. No one in her life had ever said anything like that to her before, let alone believed it. Including herself. Her eyes watered as she fumbled for something to say in return. But by then Josef's attention had been drawn away to the straitjacket on the floor. His self-assuredness, that quality that elicited recognition in others of a man worthy of following into combat, melted into quiet reflection as he bit his lower lip and backed away as though wrestling with unpleasant thoughts. Petra was left with a mouth full of unspoken words as he picked up a piece of cardboard and went back to work in a sort of wounded silence.

It was midafternoon when they finished light-proofing the small space at the back of the attic. They stood back, making adjustments to the wadded-up newspaper here and there until they were satisfied with their work. It was a sorry affair, held together with paper and string, but it might just serve the purpose.

"I'll try developing a few of the photos tonight and see if we've managed it," Petra said with a last look at what they'd put together.

Josef slipped his coat and ushanka back on after the heat of constant labor had worn off. "First, I want you to take pictures of the camp tonight. See if there's anything out there we need to look at. I'm curious to know what moves in the dark," he said, pulling his gloves on.

"Thank you, by the way," she said, twisting her hair up and stuffing it back under her cap.

"For what?"

"For insisting I come. You saved me from a mundane life in a stuffy apartment with a mother-in-law who can't stand the sight of me."

"You call this place an improvement?"

"Well, the company very much is, at least."

"Ah, in that case you're very welcome, paní Kurková." Josef's tone had reverted to a formality he hadn't felt the need to use with her only moments ago.

"Please, call me Petra."

He bowed his head in acknowledgment, then extended his hand toward the ladder. "Also, you should know, I put in an official request this morning to learn if your husband is assigned here. If he is, the commander will let us know," he said and escorted her downstairs again. "I hope for a happy reunion for you both."

"Yes, of course, thank you." Petra, accompanied by an odd flutter of disappointment, climbed downstairs and braced herself for the outside cold again. She was wrapping her scarf around her neck when a disturbance rumbled through the camp, followed by the sound of gunfire.

"Not again." Josef rushed toward the commotion to see what had happened.

Petra chased after him, worried there'd been another attack. Instead they found a row of soldiers on their knees with their hands behind their heads. Two infantry officers stood with rifles aimed at their shoulder blades, while a captain shouted, "The next man to run will be shot in the back for the coward he is."

On the far side of a clearance, three men ran with their packs and their rifles. Their feet kicked up snow as they dodged through the trees just in time to evade being shot.

"Put a team together and go after them," the captain said to the man at his side. He chewed on the filter of an unlit cigarette as he watched the deserters disappear from range. As he drew his lighter out of his pocket, he caught sight of Josef and his eyes tightened in anger. "This is your doing," the captain said, marching up to Josef and dragging him aside. "You promised you'd remedy our little problem, and it's only gotten worse. Three men lost today," he said through gritted teeth. "And now we've got soldiers deserting in broad daylight, scared half out of their wits."

Josef pursed his lips. "I've only just returned with my team," he said. "We're making progress." He glanced toward the farmhouse. "We're burying the dead in a way they cannot rise again. It will help."

The captain glowered at Petra, his face puffy and red, then lit the cigarette and blew the smoke in Josef's face. "This is your last chance to fix this, you understand me? Or you might as well be one of those men running in the daylight with a target on his back." He gave Josef a once-over with his eyes, then walked away uttering the words "damn monstrosity" under his breath.

CHAPTER ELEVEN

Once the sun went down, the chill mountain air penetrated through to the bone like a blade. Petra had put on every layer she could the night before, but tonight she stuffed crumpled newspaper from the attic under her coat as she'd seen the soldiers do. She wrapped her scarf around her face and awaited Josef's orders.

"There are three sections of the camp," he explained, pointing to a crude map drawn on the barn wall with a piece of chalk. "If you can make it to the far side, do so. Otherwise, don't risk the exposure. Be careful but thorough with the film. Take photos of anything that raises the hairs on your neck."

"Trust your instincts," Yanis said. "Worry about what shows up on the film later."

"Viktor will go with you," Josef said. "His fire ability is unsurpassed among the team, should you encounter any upír."

Yanis agreed. "Don't provoke. Just go straight for the fire, if confronted. We'll explain later if anyone witnesses your magic."

Petra's stomach fell as Yanis slipped a small amulet in her hand as an added safeguard against her own inability. Her failure to act that morning had branded her as unreliable when it came to a fight. It was almost laughable that they thought her weak—the girl who'd once killed a man with her magic. But in a way they were right, because that girl no longer existed.

Bako checked with Viktor. "You have your stakes?"

"Here, sir." The glassmaker opened up his satchel for inspection.

"The wood is enchanted with a spell to strangle the double heart, if you're able to penetrate the chest," Karl offered, proud of his contribution. He pointed out the tiny five-petaled verbena sigils he'd carved into the shafts of all their stakes.

"Good." Bako nodded. "The rest of you are on watch tonight. Eyes sharp. If one of those things enters the camp, it's getting torched on the spot. Understand?"

Petra patted her camera, testing to make sure it was secure in her pocket, and then she and Viktor took off through the maze of small campfires to document life on the other side of the mist.

The soldiers watched them warily as they passed through, two civilians in plain clothes walking about without an escort. Petra found the camp generally quiet at night, other than the few groups of men who mustered the enthusiasm for cards despite the cold. The whispering was new, though. Rumors. Gossip. Words like "witch," "mystic," and "priest" passed their lips. No one really believed they were part of a medical team, unless they were the sort to chase down ghouls. Nevertheless, when she got the inkling something was nearby, she unfolded the camera lens and asked a few men if she could take their photo to document physical conditions for doctors in the Empire's capital. The men obliged, with some making clownish faces, others straight-faced and woeful.

A mist shimmered slightly over the shoulder of one of the somber young men, giving Petra a tingle under the collar. She raised her lens and snapped a few more photos. After advancing the film, she looked up to the treetops, but they remained still against a clear night sky with the moon resting overhead.

"All calm," she said to Viktor as they walked from one group to another.

"She's in a better mood tonight."

Petra tilted her face to look at the glassmaker. She wondered briefly if he was touched in the head. Or maybe he was under the influence of some kind of love spell gone wrong, and instead of looking at the object of his affection when the magic was cast, he'd happened to glance up at the moon—the way baby ducks are said to attach themselves to other animals or people if the mother inexplicably goes astray at the moment after they hatch.

"Does she truly speak to you?" Petra asked.

"We have an understanding," he said, smiling. "Me and my *bella luna*."

"Yes, you called her that before, but she didn't want to answer you that night."

"She goes through phases."

Petra narrowed her eyes at him. "Yes, I imagine she does." She shook her head, thinking he couldn't truly believe he talked to the moon. It was some sort of game he played. Perhaps a ruse to deflect from his magical inadequacies, aside from casting fire. But as it was just the two of them on this assignment, she didn't see the harm in playing along. "Does she see what's happening here? Could her phases have any effect on those things, do you think?"

"I can call her down, if you like. I think she would be open to meeting you."

Petra rubbed her hands together in the cold, thinking about the photos she was supposed to take and the film she needed to develop. But hadn't Yanis told her to follow her instincts? "Yes, all right," she said. "What do we need to do?"

Viktor's eyes lit with a spark of genuine infatuation. "Over here," he said, and led her away from the nearest group of soldiers to a space that edged too close to the sight of the last attack. There, nestled between three pine trees, they found a suitable granite boulder. Viktor reached in his satchel and dug beneath the wooden stakes and mallet to where he had stashed the glass vessel wrapped in cloth. When he brought it out again, Petra was struck by the exquisite beauty of the cut-glass detail.

"You truly made this?" she asked.

Viktor gave the glass a quick polish with the cloth, then set it gently on the rock. "Yes," he answered. "I needed something worthy of her light."

Petra decided that if he was a lunatic, he was the genius sort imbued with unsurpassed talent in the mortal arts. She stood back when he said he needed a few meters of space. Viktor checked over his shoulder to make sure he wouldn't be interrupted. "I usually light a candle, but I don't want to risk being seen," he said. The glassmaker cleared his throat, cast his palms up to the sky, and closed his eyes, ready to call down the moon. "Argent goddess of ethereal light, grace me with your glow tonight. Fill the vessel so I may see, the love and light you stir in me."

Seeing him go through the ritual gave Petra a chill, the sort generated from within rather than from the bitter cold. It had been so long since she'd seen the old magic done with such reverence. Something stirred alive within her, an aching to whisper words out loud and feel that power at her fingertips again, if only for a moment. But then, out of habit, she raised her hand to the cheek where the illusion spell hid her old wound. The feel of the scar's ridges through her glove doused the desire for magic again just as a glimmering beam of moonlight shone down on them.

"She's here," he said, opening his eyes.

Petra stood motionless, waiting and watching for something to happen with the vessel, even though she was sorely tempted to stomp her feet to get the feeling back in her toes. She opened her mouth to ask how much longer his goddess would take, but Viktor shushed her with a finger over his lips. She exhaled in exasperation, only to see her cold breath become illuminated by a white light. Had a soldier shined a flashlight at them? Surely Viktor hadn't actually called the moon down from the sky.

The glassmaker kept his hands poised in an open gesture. He seemed on the brink of welcoming some entity, when a gust of wind barreled through the trees, knocking snow loose from branches and stirring up debris on the ground. Artillery exploded on the ridge, filling the sky with orange flashes. The vessel tipped over on the rock. The entity called up by Viktor's ritual retreated like a bird scattering at the threat of capture. He dived for the glass vase, catching it just before it rolled off the rock and onto the ground.

"Something's here," he said, shouting over the rising pitch of the wind. "It scared her." He cradled the vessel in his arms, protecting the glass until he could get it in his satchel. His jaw tensed as he hurriedly put the vase away. Wind blew leaves and twigs in their faces, stinging their eyes with debris.

The shift from calm to storm had been too sudden, too artificial. Manipulated, even. Following her intuition, Petra used the last frames on the roll of film to snap images of the squall as it passed through the treetops before Viktor yanked her by the elbow and made her retreat back to the barn.

They made it as far as the makeshift hospital inside the farmhouse when they were overtaken by a group of soldiers dragging in wounded men on stretchers. The wind nearly toppled them over before they made it through the door. Petra and Viktor followed the wounded inside to see if they could help, but they were chased away by the nurses.

"Out, all of you," the doctor shouted when he saw them hovering over a soldier with a gash near his shoulder.

"Is it another attack?" Petra asked.

She was pushed out of the way. "Not like the others. This is shelling." The doctor blocked her view of the soldiers, but not the blood that had soaked their trousers and already gone stiff from the cold.

"We should go back," Viktor said, eyeing the deteriorating weather out the window. "The others will need a reliable fire to keep warm, if this storm gets any worse."

Petra nodded but said she was staying. She pointed upstairs and told Viktor to let Josef know she'd be working into the night. When the doctor turned his back on her to attend to his newest patients' injuries, she climbed the ladder to the attic.

Outside, the wind howled against the rafters. The wooden beams rattled and shook before creaking ominously, as though the roof might blow off completely. The windy assault only further convinced her that she needed to see exactly what was on that film.

After successfully rigging the film canister in the lightproof box and running the film through the development bath, an image of what lay beyond the veil began to emerge as she hung the negatives up to dry. In every photo she'd taken of the soldiers, a lone figure floated in the negative's background. Sometimes there were others, but one ghost seemed to follow her from scene to scene, always looking toward the camera. A soldier. But unlike the living, who huddled under blankets and rags with tree bark tied around their flimsy boots to reinforce the soggy cardboard soles, this man was filled with fresh optimism. He stood in a perfect summer uniform, back straight, hair parted to the side, and face cleanly shaven. After waiting for the negatives to dry, Petra cut the film and placed the most compelling images over individual pieces of photographic paper. After double-checking the booth to make sure no light seeped in, she stirred her finger over each of the negatives while visualizing a cloud expanding on a sunny day. The images responded to her magic by enlarging and imprinting on the paper. Soon the soldier's face came into focus. The light hair, the small scar on the right cheek, and the trademark smirk on his firm lips—she had no doubt it was Marek.

Breath caught in her throat and she covered her mouth with her hand, knowing his image appearing in the photo after she'd developed the film could mean only one thing: her husband of one year was dead.

They'd both known death was possible when he'd walked out the door to fight for the Empire, but they never believed mortality could touch anything as invincible as youth and passion combined. The war was meant to be over by Christmas, after all. A quick show of force to let their enemies and their allies know not to meddle in the deadly game between kingdoms or face certain annihilation. But just as naive as youth proved in the face of death, the gray-haired rulers behind the dual monarchy never thought failure would come for them. And yet they now found themselves one finger's grip away from ruin, with their men dying by the thousands—good, stout men from the cities and fields who had no other reason to volunteer to stand on the line with a rifle other than for hollow honor and a paltry promise of compensation.

"It wasn't supposed to end this way," she whispered, grieving for the life cut short. A single tear slid down her nose until she wiped it away. She stripped the illusion spell from her cheek in the dark to better reckon with the truth. Certainly theirs had not been a good match, the kind the old women praised as worthy of the forfeits a bride must make for long-term happiness. They'd rushed into marriage on a wave of desire, but when the lovemaking was done, they'd had very little of common interest to say to each other, so they'd eventually retreated into the side-by-side loneliness of solo pastimes inside their tiny apartment. She'd often wondered, as she lay alone on their bed, if Marek had rushed off to war just so he wouldn't have to suffer the silent humming of another person in the room with whom one does not communicate. Perhaps they'd been doomed to fail from the start, but she'd only ever imagined an amicable parting. Never this.

When or how Marek met his death she might never learn for certain, but as Petra studied each of the photographs she'd taken that day, one thing was clear: his ghost was there watching her. The bewilderment of discovering his death in the intimate setting of her darkroom was perhaps a small blessing. Would the others have judged her horribly for not grieving more deeply? For experiencing regret more than anguish at the revelation? She replaced the illusion spell over her cheek and turned back to the photographs.

Several minutes later, as the storm died down, she examined the batch of developed pictures, including the ones she'd taken of the sky just as the wind had picked up. The images were hazy. Distorted even. The clouds appeared to be backed by some sort of electrical charge or energy. But even in those photos Marek was there, though he no longer looked directly at her lens. Instead, he stared up at the clouds in anger. And there, masked beneath the mist and haze, she saw what appeared to be a pair of eyes watching from within the storm clouds.

"Oh, Marek, thank you." She kissed her fingers and pressed them to his image for the gift he'd given her before gathering up the photos and stuffing them under her jacket.

CHAPTER TWELVE

The soldier who'd tried to warn her about the "evil things" had been right. The threat to the army very possibly did fly in on the wind. Someone, somehow, was manipulating the energy of storms and conceivably the undead as well. She still had no idea how it was done, but her photos may have captured the means.

Eager to share her discovery, Petra closed up the darkroom and scrambled down the attic steps. The scent of ether hit her at the bottom along with the unusual stillness of the surgery. She nodded as she passed the doctor, who sat in the corner smoking a cigarette with his legs spread out before him. He waved her away and hunched forward, rubbing the top of his bald head in exhausted frustration. Three men lay on the tables in front of him—one breathing in rough spurts and two shrouded under bloodstained sheets.

Outside, the sky had turned goose gray, with snow rapidly covering the tracks of those who'd passed through hours earlier. Petra wrapped her scarf over her face and ran for the barn. The road was eerily quiet, and yet something hummed in the air. Her skin tingled with more than the normal shivers as she crossed in front of the church where the overflow wounded slept. Some unfortunate had likely died inside and found himself facedown on the underside of the veil, only to walk about unseen as a ghost. If not for her need to ration her film, she'd take his photo, too, to know he'd existed. But as she'd already gone through one roll of film, Petra turned her face from the church entrance and shoved her shoulder against the barn door.

Her first mission was to find Josef and report what she'd discovered, but she stopped inside the doorway at the sound of an unfamiliar woman's voice speaking softly in the corner stall, as if trying to soothe a sick child.

"You're letting the cold in." Dragoş spoke from the other side of the barn, where he and Karl played a game of cards atop an upturned horse trough. "Thanks to our visitors, we finally got some decent cookfire heat going in here." His criticism was aimed at Viktor, who leaned against the stable wall reading a book by a ball of firelight balanced on the tip of his finger. The glassmaker rolled his eyes, just visible over the top of his book, and went back to reading.

Petra closed the door and unwrapped her scarf, stealing glances at Josef and the mysterious new woman who huddled over him. Her curly hair glowed like a halo around her head in the lamplight as she held Josef's open hand in hers with his palm up while he writhed on his back on a pile of pine boughs. The image stung her, though she could have no reason to be covetous of the woman's intimacy with the young man. She quickly brushed the confusing emotion away like a bee buzzing too near her ear.

"Ah, paní Kurková, you're back." Major Bako set aside the pistol he'd been cleaning and waved Petra over to the corner stall. "I'd like to introduce you to someone."

Was she still paní Kurková? Had she ever truly been? Petra nearly got stuck in the semantics, thinking of Marek's ghost finding a way to communicate with her through the photos. But that was something she would have to dwell on later, she thought, and removed her hat so her hair fell over her shoulders.

The woman tending to Josef stood when Petra approached, straightening the folds of her skirt. She was dressed in the rural style, with an embroidered peasant shirt and a sash around her waist. A small leather pouch hung from her neck, presumably filled with herbs and amulets for warding off evil. Another witch woman. An enchantress from the east, by the look of her.

"This is Valentina Romanescu," Bako said. He rubbed his palms against his trousers like a nervous schoolboy when the woman smiled.

Petra introduced herself and slipped her gloves off to shake the woman's hand. "Call me Petra," she said. "What's happened to him?" Up close, Josef's skin appeared flushed and sweaty, and he couldn't seem to lie still. "Has anyone sent for the doctor?"

"A doctor can't do anything for him," the woman said. "He needs to sweat it out."

Valentina had spoken with the authority of learned experience. Still, Petra knelt down beside Josef and pressed the back of her hand against his cheek to check for herself. He was ice cold and yet he perspired. "What's wrong with him?" she asked. "He was fine when I left him a few hours ago."

"Oh, he gets like this from time to time," Valentina said with a shrug. *Is she being deliberately vague?* "Luckily, we arrived before the storm settled in."

Petra felt the woman's stare on her, scanning her aura with her third eye, trying to delve deeper beneath appearances as she spoke. The illusion spell had just been rejuvenated, so she didn't worry about discovery, but she couldn't be so certain about everything else.

"Valentina has a special medicine she cooks up to heal Josef when he gets like this," Bako said, also leaving the details vague.

"It's happened before?" Petra noticed a wooden bowl filled with herbs floating in oil. She took a sniff and thought she detected common self-heal and calendula.

"Now and then," Valentina said, still with an evasive tone. "He was wounded at the start of the war. He's suffered recurrent bouts of fever and fatigue ever since. Usually after he's overexerted himself."

Petra thought back to the journey Josef had taken through no-man's-land the night before. Had he run the entire way? In the mountains? If true, the only thing she could fathom was that he must have been wounded in the lung to cause such a reaction. Yet that didn't explain the pure herbal leaves Valentina had applied to his wrists, where the quickest infusion into his veins would take place.

"Once the potion circulates through his bloodstream, he'll be himself again." Valentina took her seat beside Josef on the ground once again. She lit a candle propped on a milk can and wafted the first smoke toward her, inhaling.

So, Josef and this woman have history together. He'd said there were other women here, other witches. She just hadn't considered they might be young like her and smelling of fragrant herbs.

Petra had started to stand when she felt a tug on her trouser leg.

"What did you find in the darkroom?" Josef's grasp was weak, but at least he appeared lucid and not lost to fever dreams and hallucinations.

"Get some rest first," she said, managing an encouraging smile. "We'll talk later."

He nodded and closed his eyes, releasing his grip. She would have told him about her discovery, if only to put his mind at ease while he recovered, but the woman was a stranger to her. However much the rest of them seemed to trust her, Petra's own instincts told her to bide her time a little longer before divulging anything. Her eyes met Valentina's as she rose to her feet. They parted with a nod and veiled smile.

Petra followed Major Bako back to the corner where his pistol was laid out in pieces on a white handkerchief, with springs and pins scattered around the main barrel. The scent of gun oil made a curiously intoxicating aroma when mixed with the smell of Bako's cigars. "Where's Yanis?" she asked, looking around.

"With the aunt," he said with a jerk of his head in Valentina's direction. "Evaluating a wounded soldier for what you call 'shadow.' The pair of them travel from camp to camp as healers."

Of course. Valentina had said "we" when she mentioned arriving before the storm hit.

"Did you find anything useful in your photos?" Bako asked, picking up the gun by the grip. He pumped a small wiry brush in and out of the barrel a few times.

"My husband is dead." Petra held off telling him about the face in the clouds. The major was one hundred percent invested in ridding the war of the undead, but beyond that he was just another mortal with a limited understanding of the world beyond what he could physically see.

Bako stopped what he was doing, eyeing her with a mix of doubt and compassion. "Did the commander inform you of this?"

"No, his ghost appeared to me in the photos."

"Show me," he said and set his cleaning tool aside while she dug in her coat pocket for the images.

Petra spread the six photos out, describing where each had been taken. In every picture, Marek stood in glowing contrast to the men before him. Bako squinted at the images, studying them for any information he could use. Viktor joined them, leaning over Petra's shoulder to get a glimpse. After a moment, Bako straightened, chewing hard on his cigar.

"You took all of these photos today?" he asked. When she confirmed she had, he shook his head again. "This man, Horvath," he said, tapping his finger on the man's image. "He was killed three weeks ago. Shot in the chest. I saw it happen myself. Is he a ghost as well? He looks different."

Petra looked closer at the photo. The man wasn't a ghost. He'd smiled when she took the photo.

"No, I remember speaking to him about his bad luck at cards," Viktor said. "I kept thinking if the war didn't kill him, his bad teeth would. The rot in his mouth was horrific."

"Something isn't right. Look at his eyes." Bako pointed out an anomaly she'd missed in the darkroom. "This fellow too," he said, turning the second and third photos sideways. "Your ghost is standing behind a different man in each photo, and each of them has eyes that glow."

"Eyeshine," Petra said. "Their eyes all reflect the light. But if this man is truly dead and not a ghost, then he could be—"

"A revenant," Bako finished for her. There was urgency in the way he reassembled his pistol.

"Let me see." Josef had stumbled over, clutching his stomach with one hand.

"Should you be up?" Viktor offered to help him back to his bed.

"I'm fine," he said, grabbing a photo. He blinked several times, as if he couldn't quite focus yet, but then he steadied himself and seemed to confirm what they'd seen.

"There's more," Petra said. Now that Josef was more alert, she pulled the last two photos out and spread them on the crate. Valentina sidled up beside Josef, as did Karl and Dragoş. "After what the soldier said about the wind, I took these of the clouds when the storm blew hard enough to sway the treetops."

Petra moved out of the way so the others could lean in for a better look.

"Are those eyes in the clouds?" Karl asked. "They're looking directly at the camera."

Dragoş snatched the photo from Karl, then tossed it down on the crate. "She's just messing with us. It's a photography trick. I've seen photos like this before, where they overlap the negatives to make it look like a ghost is standing behind the person."

"I didn't." Petra pleaded her case to Josef and Bako. "I wouldn't do that."

Josef slid down onto a chair, grimacing while still holding his stomach. "I know. But what else could it be? When have you ever known a cloud to have eyes? An honest mistake."

"Not necessarily," Viktor said in her defense. "After all, there's more to the heavens and earth than most of us will ever understand. Let alone mortals and witches with little experience with the cosmos."

After a bout of eye-rolling, Bako lined up three of the photos. "Be that as it may," he said, "there's one thing I understand all too well: we have at least three potential upíri out there sitting among the soldiers, and for the first time since we started this mission, we know where to find them *before* they attack." He jammed a loaded magazine in the gun's grip and strapped the weapon in its holster.

Josef cocked one eyebrow. "Hunting party?"

Bako gave him a firm nod. "I'll get the stakes."

"What?" Valentina put her hand on Josef's shoulder. "Are you sure? You've only just recovered."

Josef patted Valentina's hand to reassure her. "I'll be all right. I'm over the worst of it," he said, and grabbed his coat and ushanka.

"I didn't make a mistake." Petra repeated her denial about the photos being contaminated, but only Viktor seemed to side with her as the rest prepared to hunt down the possible upíri she'd captured in the photos.

After a mad rush of throwing on coats and gathering lanterns, Bako handed each person two stakes and a mallet—except for Petra. "Maybe it would be best if you stayed in tonight," he said.

She knew what he was about. Leaving her out of the mission was his brand of sympathy so she could mourn her husband. "No," she said. "I want to go. Please don't say anything to the others." She grabbed his sleeve. "Besides, I know where the upíri are. I took the photos."

The major twitched his mustache, evaluating.

"Is there a problem?" Josef asked, noticing the interplay between the two.

Petra stared at the major and held her hand out for a pair of stakes. After a pause, Bako relented and handed them over. She shoved the hawthorn stakes in her waistband, buttoned her coat, and stuffed her hair back under her cap.

"Should we fetch Yanis?" Viktor asked.

Josef shook his head vehemently. "He's busy with another matter. And will be for some time. We're on our own. Let's move."

Josef paced as he waited for everyone to get out the door. His body was long and lean, putting Petra in mind of a caged animal waiting to break free. His renewed energy was remarkable, considering he'd been laid out on his back in a writhing sweat only minutes earlier. Whatever potion Valentina used to cure him had done an impressively quick job of it.

Outside, the team broke into two groups, with Viktor leading Josef and Dragoş to one end of camp and Petra showing Bako and Karl the other, where she'd taken two of the photos. It was late enough that the camp had gone quiet, all but for the few rowdy pockets where men stayed up playing cards around small fires, waiting to go on duty. Petra pointed toward one of the groups as she and the others silently made their way by circling around to the other side of them.

Two of the five men were nervous and alert, keen to notice any unusual movement outside the sphere of their meager firelight. Their eyes watched every leaf kicked up by the wind, and their ears bent toward any unfamiliar sound in the forest. They were frightened. Jumpy. Petra knew they had reason to be.

Bako pointed to the man sitting between them. "That's him. Horvath."

The man in question wore no head covering, no scarf, no newspaper stuffed into his jacket. No puff of warm breath escaped his mouth as he spoke. Yet he sat at the fire, cards in hand, as if he were just another soldier passing the time until his next assignment on the ridgeline.

"He hasn't moved from his spot," Petra said. "He's exactly where he was sitting earlier." She glanced up, wondering if Marek was still hovering nearby too.

"We can't take him here," Bako said. "Too much risk he'll lunge at one of the others. We need to lure him away."

"With what?" Karl's knuckles had turned white gripping the stake he'd enchanted with the verbena sigils. The pattern reminded Petra of the embroidery her mother had added to their shirt collars and cuffs with her red thread. Small flowers to offer protection from malevolent energy and curses. Busywork to pass the long, cold nights when the goddess Morana departed, leaving bitter winds in her wake to threaten famine and death to those unprepared for winter's long reign. Petra hoped the enchantment was strong enough to bond the spell's intention to the stake's core.

"We lure him away with blood," Bako said. It was almost sinister how quickly the hussar pulled the knife from his belt. He flicked the tip of the blade against the skin above his wrist, just enough to draw a steady trickle of blood. "Pull back to that stand of trees over there," he said. "And be ready."

Bako put the knife away and approached the soldiers, who stood and saluted him when they recognized his rank. The revenant was the last to react, doing so only begrudgingly. Until he got a whiff of the hussar's blood. His eyes glazed over with craving at the sight of the red stuff, which Bako expertly let drip on the snow in full view of the revenant.

The major gestured with his injured hand toward the trees, saying he'd cut himself trying to lift a fallen tree needed for firewood and could use the man's help. Another soldier tried to volunteer first, but Horvath shooed him away. "It would be my pleasure to help, Major," he said. Petra thought the upír might wipe the saliva from his rotting mouth at any moment.

Petra and Karl shrank back as the major led Horvath toward the clump of trees. "Through here," Bako said, but the revenant stopped in his tracks just shy of their ambush site.

They were on the fringe of the camp, where the light bled into darkness, and where mortal eyes could not see much beyond the reach of their arm. The creature turned around with eyes shining in the moonlight. Whatever part of Horvath had held his human form together long enough to remain undiscovered by his former comrades began to wither. His skin paled, glistening like rancid meat, and his canine teeth grew sharp and threatening. The reek of his body made Petra want to gag until she had to cover her mouth with the crook of her elbow.

Horvath grinned so his reddened gums showed. "You think I don't know what you're up to." He inhaled deeply as the wind picked up, then looked directly at Karl. "All of you playing your hide-and-seek games in the dark. Waiting to be heroes with your sticks and stones." He squinted and found Petra in the shadow of a tree trunk. "Wearing disguises in the hope we won't find you."

How did he know? Petra stepped out of the shadow, hoping to lure the upír closer. Was he the one? The leader? He talked as though he knew more than some random dead soldier would. Petra squeezed the hawthorn stake in her hand. One well-placed blow between the ribs could end all this misery and fear. She steadied her foot against a rock, ready to lunge, but the creature leaped first.

Horvath flew at her and batted the stake and mallet out of her hands. Disarmed, she staggered backward, trying in vain to form a single image in her mind to throw him off. He moved his hand to her throat and bared his teeth. Snow swirled over them, making her vaguely aware that the wind had picked up. She heard a twig snap just as the fiend pinned her to the tree trunk by the throat. Now there was laughter. But not nearby. Farther away. In the camp. The thing screamed in her face, forcing its stench on her. She struggled to breathe. The cartilage in her neck was near the breaking point. Why didn't Karl do something?

She couldn't even call her true magic. Not against a living creature. Just when his teeth meant to tear her flesh, the thing winced and arched its back. Black bile oozed from its mouth. The upír stumbled back, hissing in pain as Major Bako stood behind it, maneuvering the stake deeper into its heart.

"Hold your fire," Bako said as the creature crumpled to its knees. "No need to make a scene just yet and alert the others."

Petra clutched her throat and watched in horror as the major drew his saber and lopped the upír's head off before the poisonous stake could work its magic. She took a breath and coughed several times, relieved to find her throat and lungs still worked.

"Hopefully the others are still none the wiser." Bako wiped his saber on the creature's coat before returning the blade to its sheath. "Let's go."

Karl gaped at the body. His eyes fixated on the teeth still protruding from the severed head. "I couldn't move," he said to Petra. "I had the stake in my hand and couldn't move. Not even to help you."

Petra swallowed, feeling a bruise forming on her neck. "We're all afraid," she said.

"I have a wife. A son." Karl begged her with his eyes. "I shouldn't have come here. I have to go home."

Petra feared he'd slip into full panic if allowed to dwell. "Come, help me spread these seeds before we go." She handed Karl a handful of verbena seeds from her pocket and told him to scatter them over the body. "For protection," she said, encouraging him. "Like the symbols on your stake. They worked, yes? We're all right." Karl seemed to float out of his stupor. When he nodded and did as she said with the seeds, she collected her dropped stakes and mallet.

Ahead, Major Bako waved at them with his saber to catch up. Even if he could no longer stomach the mission, Karl was safer traveling with them than being left alone, so Petra pulled him by the arm, urging him to hurry. As they made their way toward the others on the far side of the camp, the snow and wind intensified, sending soldiers sheltering under their blankets and in their tents.

Petra blinked through the snow as a stream of fire licked the sky ahead of them. "It's Viktor," she said. "He's found another one."

The trio moved with urgency, hoping chaos had not been unleashed. Yet the nearer they got, the more agitated the soldiers in camp became. They stirred from their blankets, shielding their eyes from the stinging snow. "Is it wolves?" a man shouted, inspiring a familiar fear in those around him.

Men ran from the source of the flame. Like earth giving way in a sinkhole, it seemed an entire infantry division retreated from the epicenter to stand their ground at the perimeter. Bayonets and rifles pointed toward the familiar fear of an unknown threat. Wind scoured the snowy ground, smothering the meager fires and extinguishing the lantern wicks one by one. At the heart of the commotion, a single soldier charged—his skin pale, his mouth stretched wide, and his eyes engorged with seething hunger. Darkness engulfed the army as the creature's howl raised the hackles of all who witnessed it.

A shot was fired. A man screamed, followed by another. A second blaze of fire ignited through the trees. A heartbeat later a dome of translucent energy surrounded Petra, Karl, and Bako. Someone had cast an illusion spell to hide what was happening from the mortal soldiers who'd scattered yet remained curious.

Bako drew his blade. Karl clenched his stake in his fist and muttered a feeble fire spell. A pale-blue light ignited in his other hand, briefly illuminating the tortured face of the fiend before sputtering. Major Bako wasted no time and struck with his saber, splitting open the revenant's thigh before it could bite. Black bile exuded from the wound but only made the creature cry out in anger. Karl fended off a second charge from the creature with his meager flame, pushing him back from the others, but it wasn't enough. He needed more than a fading blue light to drive an upír into retreat.

Snow pelted their faces, freezing their eyelashes and noses. Karl bravely tried to call a flame into his hand again. He had none of Viktor's talent, but the fire he produced was enough for Petra to take advantage of the distraction to creep closer. Could she stop this madness now, despite her vow? Use her magic to disembowel this creature? The temptation nearly outweighed the fear of being found out. In the end she did what she'd been brought there to do and stuck to her training. She gripped the stake and mallet and waited for Bako to strike with his saber again. This time she would plunge the weapon into the beast's heart.

The major went for the creature's head as he had before but only managed to slice the collarbone when it evaded the swing of the blade. Enraged, the revenant lunged at its nearest target, launching itself into the air. It gripped Karl in its claws and clamped its teeth on his neck. Petra stared in momentary disbelief before rallying her senses. She smashed the mallet against the upír's head, throwing it off. It roared in confusion and stumbled back. Bako didn't hesitate. He drove the saber through the fiend's torso until its legs buckled and it collapsed on its side. Petra knelt on the rancid body and plunged the stake into its chest. Holding firm to make sure the hawthorn slipped between the ribs, she struck the mallet twice and the upír went still.

Petra collapsed next to Karl, shaking his arm to rouse him, but he didn't respond. "Help! He needs a doctor! Medic!" She lifted Karl's head and patted his cheek, whispering to him to wake. He groaned slightly, but he was losing blood too quickly. His color paled before her eyes.

Bako knelt across from her and checked their comrade's eyes. "Have a look," he said.

Petra pushed back the lids and saw a brief flash of shadow dart behind the white part of his eyes. "No, he can't be."

"It was a direct bite. His blood is already tainted."

The major stood and raised his saber at the sound of boots running through the snow. His body relaxed when Josef, Viktor, and Dragoş cut through the darkness with the scent of char still fresh on their coats.

"What happened?"

"We lured one away and killed it, but this one leaped." Bako gestured toward Karl's body. "Got him by the throat," he said to Josef. The tenor of his voice implied a hidden message in his words.

Josef dragged a hand over his weary face. "I'll do it."

"You're sure?" Bako removed a carved stake from his belt and offered it to Josef.

"Do what?" Disbelief bloomed in Petra's mind. "No, you can't. He's one of us." But even as she protested, the impossible situation became clear. Karl had been bitten. Shadow already lurked behind the eyes.

Bako forced her to her feet and pulled her away from Karl as he continued to bleed out on the ground.

Josef pressed the back of his hand to his mouth, steeling his emotions as he knelt beside his fallen comrade. "I'm sorry," he whispered, then slammed the stake past the man's ribs with two powerful blows. The body arched, then went still. The hawthorn shaft, with a chain of five-petaled flowers carved into it, protruded from Karl's chest. The black bile that Petra had witnessed in other revenants oozed up through the punctured skin where the spell's poison strangled the budding growth of a second heart. He'd never had a chance once the taint was in his blood.

Josef exhaled and tossed the mallet aside. "Someone collect his body. He and the other upíri will need to be burned together."

Petra blinked through her tears. "That's it? That's all you have to say? The poor man was terrified. He shouldn't have been here. He shouldn't have died. Not like this."

Taken aback by her outburst, Josef appeared as if he might break down in sobs, but then his face hardened into a scowl. "No one should, but this is war," he said before calling to Viktor for help carrying Karl away. "Bodies are an unfortunate part of the equation."

Behind them, Dragoș maintained the spell wall of illusion that had been holding the soldiers back from seeing their work. He used his right arm to channel his energy, but his left hung limp at his side. Blood dripped from his sleeve. Petra waited until Viktor dragged Karl's body away, then ran to Dragoș.

"You're hurt," she said, inspecting his arm. There was a bloody hole in his coat at the shoulder.

His right arm shook and he grimaced. "I can't hold the spell much longer. I'm only good at hiding myself from the police. Nothing this big. Get Viktor. We need to keep the illusion going." He groaned in pain as his arm dropped from exhaustion. Petra picked up the spell energy with both hands before it fell apart and spread the illusion in a full circle around them, using a golden hoop from her inner vision to guide the magic. Dragoş gawped at the force of energy she'd created, momentarily distracted from his pain.

"What happened to your arm?" she asked when she had full control.

Dragoş swayed on his feet. "Bullet, I expect." He hunched over, grabbing his left shoulder before he sank to the ground. He was also bleeding from his head somewhere.

"Help!" she shouted. "He's been shot."

"One of the soldiers fired at us in the dark. He assured me he was fine." Josef pushed Dragoş's coat off and opened his shirt. "It's through the arm," he said and then lifted Dragoş off the ground with little more effort than cradling a small child. "I'll take him to the hospital," he said to Bako. "You stay here and burn the bodies."

Josef looked intent on barking out an order to Petra, too, but stopped, caught off guard by the spectacle of her spell wall. Bands of gold radiated in waves that glowed like the northern lights. His eyes traced the energy with a sort of awe before looking her dead in the eye with . . . what? Fear? Anger? He swallowed whatever words he wanted to say to her and walked away with Dragoş growing pale in his arms. She extended the illusion spell so it wrapped around him until he was safely through the trees, all the while spinning her golden energy as the ring whirled round and round in her mind's eye, encircling them all.

CHAPTER THIRTEEN

Petra had long kept her magic constrained. Pushed under, ignored, rejected. And for good reason. Magic could be reckless, unpredictable, and dangerous in the wrong hands. Her hands. And yet, after so many years of denial, she'd been able to pick up the illusion spell without a second's hesitation. She'd barely had to concentrate. The enchantment had gushed out of her like water sprung from a well.

"Before coming here, I hadn't called up the full force of my magic in such a long time," Petra whispered to Dragoş, who lay unconscious on a cot in the hospital. His arm was wrapped in white bandaging, and a piece of gauze clung to his forehead, held there by a spot of dried blood. His color was sickly pale, and he'd just been given a shot of morphine to help him get through the night. She held no affection for the man. He'd been nothing but rude to her since they met, yet in his unconscious state, he made a good audience for her confession as she sat at his bedside. "Well, except for this." She pointed to where the scar remained hidden on her cheek. "Do you think a small daily spell like that could have kept the magic alive inside me all this time?"

Dragoş continued sleeping with his mouth slightly open, but his silence was all the conversation Petra craved. She might have sat with him all night, until a nurse interrupted.

"Time to go," she said, shooing Petra away. "Let the young man get his rest. No need to worry about your friend. If we can keep the bleeding under control, he should come through just fine."

Petra thanked the nurse but wasn't ready to leave just yet. She couldn't face the others in the barn after the disaster of Karl's death. Not when his body lay just a meter away on a stretcher, his head turned toward the wall as though lost in sleep. Had she trusted her magic sooner, would he still be alive? When the nurse ducked behind a curtain to check on another patient, Petra took the ladder to the attic.

Light from a weak but flickering candle seeped under the door. She'd been asked to stay away by Josef because Yanis was treating a patient there, but she wouldn't be in their way. She just needed a warm place to sit by herself where no one could find her for a few minutes.

The door opened quietly enough. The attic space wasn't large, but it had a warren-like feel from the support beams and maze of crates piled inside. The candlelight was coming from the other end near the darkroom, where the shackles had been bolted to the wooden beam. Petra paused, hearing a low groaning sound. She'd meant to slip behind the crates on her right and hunker down in the corner just long enough to clear her mind and have a good cry, but curiosity overrode her initial intentions. Had it been a groan? Or a growl?

Petra crept closer, trying not to make a sound. She got halfway across the floor when she spotted a man hunched over on a crate with his head between his hands. In front of him lay another man on the floor wearing the straitjacket, which had been chained to the wall through a loop in the back. A rag had been tied over the man's mouth, presumably to keep him from screaming and upsetting the other patients below. What kind of pain did a man have to be in to be gagged and restrained in a hospital attic?

"You were told not to come up here," Josef said, lifting his head. His face was pale and his eyes rimmed red.

"I'm sorry," she said, feeling like she'd intruded on something private she was never meant to see. She hoped leaving right away might render it forgotten. "I'll go."

"No," he called out. "Stay." He motioned to a chair that had been brought upstairs since she'd last been in the attic to develop the film. That seemed like days ago, though it had been only a few hours at most.

The man on the floor groaned and writhed in his restraints, baring his teeth behind the gag as though riding out a painful attack. She stayed on her feet out of an abundance of caution, while Josef casually took a swig of beer from a brown bottle.

"Why is he restrained?"

"It's for his own protection," Josef said. "And yours."

"Is there nothing to be done for his pain?" she asked. "No morphine?"

"You mean you don't have some magical spell tucked away in your pocket to make his distress go away?" Josef took a deep and sullen gulp from the bottle. "That's how he got in this wretched state in the first place. Witches and foul magic." He ran his hand through his hair, with an increasingly inebriated look in his eyes, as he stared at the poor man.

Josef had been unusually flippant with his comment about witches. "He's been cursed?" Petra asked, though given his mood, she half expected him to answer that they all were cursed in the end.

"A curse. A hex. A desecration of the soul." He gave a small shake of his head. "Call it what you want. He'll never be the same man again, I can tell you that."

The man on the floor spasmed, yanking on his restraints. If this was someone in the midst of a cure, she'd hate to see what the full-blown curse looked like. He trembled again and turned his nose to where she stood, following her scent. He growled deep in his throat.

Petra took a step back. "I don't understand. There must be something that can be done for his suffering."

"Could you have saved him tonight?" Josef asked. He pointed his empty beer bottle at her. "With your magic?"

Petra realized he was talking about Karl. Poor Karl. The man had been out of his depth. They all were, but none so much as Karl. The choice Josef had had to make tonight to put a stake through one of their own wrenched her heart and stomach into knots. Could she have intervened and changed the course of events?

She sat on the chair and lowered her head. "I don't know."

Josef exhaled in anger before drinking deeply from a newly opened bottle. "Is that what you do? You witches? You play games with your power to decide who lives, who dies, and who gets tossed into the in-between, depending on your mood?"

With his ire up, there was little she could say to relieve him of the anguish he must be in. "It's possible I could have saved him, yes, but I'm not a practicing witch anymore, aside from a few inconsequential spells I use for convenience's sake. I told you that when you recruited me." She was tempted to tell him the truth to exonerate herself. Remove the illusion spell and show him her scar as proof, but that would require a long explanation she wasn't prepared to give.

Josef paused mid sip. He dragged his eye over her but held his tongue. He seemed to sense she was being honest, despite still hiding the worst of the truth from him.

The man on the floor tugged on his restraints before curling up into a ball by tucking his knees into his stomach. His boots and trousers were those of the tsar's army.

"He just wants to be free," Josef said. His voice was calmer. More introspective. "They've begun bleeding the killing instinct out of him, but the part that wants to run stays in the blood, constantly straining to be let loose." His eyes reddened again, bleary with drink. "He'll be better in a few days."

Killing instinct?

"The treaty talks Yanis mentioned will put an end to this sort of cruelty, surely," she said.

Josef scoffed. "Too late for some." He seemed to recognize he'd slipped into the shadow of malicious melancholy and set his beer down, wiping his hands dry on his trousers. "But, yes, the talks will help. As long as the representatives from each kingdom are able to convince their cohorts to adhere to the tenets."

Petra fell into her own thoughts, letting the conversation rest in a natural silence. This wasn't the first treaty to be negotiated between the interests of mortals and witches. She knew from history the harm a witch could do if unburdened by conscience. Protective covenants had been hammered out to protect witches and mortals from the extremists on both sides. Hexes and curses like the one afflicting the young man on the floor had been deemed unlawful in the century prior, as had witch hunting, but war naturally blurred the lines of right and wrong.

It was rumored the emperor held court with a handful of sorcerers. The tsar too. Or at least his wife. The tsarina was said to employ an entire coven for scrying and fortune-telling for matters of state. Once hostilities began, magic became a potent weapon in their arsenal, covenants be damned, with mortal soldiers paying the price. Men like Marek. And Karl.

"Do you know why I recruited you for this mission?" Josef asked, breaking the silence.

"You thought my photography might be useful. And it was. We found three upír tonight because of it." But even as she said it, she knew there was more to his question. Bumping into a woman in a public square with a camera at midnight was no reason to recruit her for a war with the undead.

"Four months ago I was the wretch lying on the floor, struggling against the restraints." Petra looked up sharply as Josef went on. "I'd been injured in the first skirmish with the tsar's troops. Their army had overwhelmed our flank, and I was taken prisoner."

"You said they let you fight with them."

"They do not like to see a man wasted. Loyalty doesn't matter to them, only the bodies. Wishing to live, I changed uniform."

The man on the floor had gone quiet, listening so that the only noise he made was his ragged breathing through the gag.

"We were patrolling the outskirts of the great fort at the base of the pass. The one the men here are hoping to retake. It was nighttime, and the snowflakes were falling like the sifted sugar my *maminka* dusts the spice cakes with at the bakery." He closed his eyes and tilted his head up as if reliving the moment. "The scent of bread fresh out of the oven wafted in with the snow from a distant village like a dream of home. It was the most pleasant moment." He opened his eyes and took another drink. "Until something charged at me. Knocked me to the ground. The thing tried to maul my neck but only managed to bite my shoulder. My comrades on patrol chased it off before it could sink its teeth a second time."

"Upír?" Without thinking, Petra recoiled slightly before correcting her posture.

Without his ushanka on, his hair hung in his eyes. "No," he said. "You shouldn't think that."

Josef rolled his neck from side to side until Petra heard something pop. He sighed from the relief. "The creature carried the curse in its teeth. The effect of his bite showed up the next day." He gestured to the man on the floor. "Like him, they say I got lucky. A healer woman in a nearby village said she could cure me, if they had the body of the beast that had attacked."

Hana?

Josef stood and gathered his bottles, setting them in a bucket with some used bandages. "They'd hunted down the monster and trapped it after the attack, so I had a chance." He called her over to the other side of the room with a nod of his head. "When I'd come through the worst of it, the woman would sit and talk to me about home and family. Really, I think she was checking my humanity to be sure her cure had worked."

Petra was tempted to ask what the woman's conclusion was, but held her tongue. Suddenly the tonic she'd sniffed at his bedside made more sense. And yet Josef clearly continued to suffer the effects of the curse, judging by Valentina's earlier ministrations.

"One day," he said, "when I was stewing in self-pity and all I could see was a path to revenge, she told me an extraordinary tale about a girl from the village where she'd lived before the war." Petra's heart fluttered from the first pains of panic. "By then I'd already come around to the idea of magic being more than a fantasy story we tell children. After one suffers from a curse, the threshold for belief drops to gut-level instinct, if you know what I mean. But to hear a tale about a witch who could transform one element into another. Smoke into dust, falling leaves into rain, rocks into flame. Magic that didn't come from any curse or spell but from the inborn mystical talent that ran under her skin. *That* gave me hope."

"Hope?" Petra's panic gave way to curiosity. "Why?"

He hesitated a moment, collecting his thoughts. "Because that was something real, something tangible. The way her magic was described wasn't mere love potions or palm readings or twigs and herbs mixed up in a mortar to make a cure. If she could truly manipulate solid objects to change their form, what might she be able to do against curses and the ungodly creatures who attack the mortal soldier on his night patrol? How might she protect the man who might otherwise never return home to his wife and warm bed, all because there are witches on both sides of this conflict who are more than happy to use the war as their personal cauldron for power and glory."

"Oh, we rarely use cauldrons anymore."

Josef blinked twice, interpreting the lighthearted tone of her remark before lowering his head in mild contrition and smiling. "My apologies. Apparently I still have some learning to do."

The color had come back into his cheeks, and his eyes had cleared. She believed the part about the magic inspiring hope in him. The truth was plain to see in the way he brightened just thinking about it. But had he heard the entire tale—or only the shiny parts that lured in a willing audience? Some magic, after all, was only palatable when told as a children's story.

"I heard the girl in that story died," Petra said, fishing around for how much he knew.

"Someone certainly wanted her to be dead." An elderly woman on the attic ladder, who'd overheard at least part of their conversation, climbed the final step into the room. "Have you been telling stories, Josef?"

The old woman clutched her black wool shawl around her shoulders with one hand and held a steaming tin cup in the other. Her gray hair was braided and coiled against her head, and her pale eyes sparkled above rosy cheeks just as Petra remembered. Aside from a few more wrinkles, time had been kind to her face.

Josef helped Hana up the last step. "You said you'd be gone an hour, *babička*."

"Valentina's soup was too salty for me to finish tonight." She waved her hand, dismissing his concern. "I saved my extra portion for the new young man," she said, raising the tin cup as proof. "How is he?"

"Miserable to be alive," Josef said. He held the old woman's arm as he steered her toward Petra.

"Well, that's progress," the old woman said lightheartedly before her eyes met Petra's. Her cordial demeanor transformed into guarded curiosity. "Oh, and who is this young woman?"

"Hana, this is Petra," he said.

"Petra?" The old woman peered at her face, as if probing beneath the physical appearance to recognize something of the metaphysical, until she appeared at least half-convinced the woman standing before her was who Josef claimed she was. "You found her?" she asked, with a tone of disbelief.

"Hello, Hana." Petra's heart thumped in her chest until her ears filled with the rush of blood, a fist pounding against the door of her past.

She hadn't seen anyone from her village since the day she died.

CHAPTER FOURTEEN

Ten years. That's how long it took for the past to find her.

The last time a man had made plans for how to use Petra's magic, she'd ended up staked in a bonfire by Pavel Radek, as ordinary a mortal man as ever there was. Middle-aged, a slight paunch under his belt, a graying mustache he neglected to trim, and eyes that glazed over with greed at the mention of gold. Of course, the word almost always originated in his mouth first, so his was a self-inflicted disease of the mind, eye, and heart.

Petra had been only twelve at the time. Much too young to keep blaming herself for what had gone wrong. She saw that now. In hindsight. Though it did nothing to lessen the pain or absolve the guilt still lurking in the dark corners of her memories.

Yes, she could turn leaves into rain or rocks into fire. Manipulating the structure of physical objects was as easy as changing the shapes and colors she visualized in her mind. That she had the ability to turn bronze into gold was where the problem started. No, that wasn't right. That Pavel was able to root out her unique talent by manipulating her mother's emotions was where the problem started.

But then she couldn't blame her mother either. After living without her own husband for these past six months, Petra understood the loneliness her mother must have felt after her father's death. Uncertainty and isolation as a widow had driven her mother to entertain Pavel's attentions in the beginning. He'd courted her with red roses cut from a neighbor's yard, brought her half-empty boxes of chocolates left over from his trips to the city, and boasted about her bread dumplings, which were never really very good. But once he'd weaseled his way into her heart and her bed as her husband, his true intentions emerged. Her mortal mother had traded her daughter's secret for love. Demands for proof followed.

"A girl who can turn reed grass into rope or stale bread into bricks for the garden wall can surely turn a few koruna into gold," Pavel had argued and argued until one day her mother's resistance had been worn as thin as her threadbare nightgown and she agreed to let him have his way.

"It's a small thing, *myška*. Only this one time," her mother had said to her. She gave Petra a light thump on the head with her finger as if to say it would only go badly if she didn't agree. But even at that age, Petra knew witches weren't allowed to alter money for profit for themselves or anyone else. Not without consequence.

Pavel had worked for the railroad, maintaining the track and signals. Before he met Petra's mother, he'd made a respectable living for a single man with little ambition. Afterward, his dreams of wealth expanded to owning a grand house in the city with a courtyard and fountain, and a two-seater automobile with brass headlights parked in front.

Pavel came to Petra the next evening with a handful of coins he'd been saving to buy himself a new winter coat and spread them on the table. "Your mother says you are ready to be an obedient child." He held up an old cigarette advertisement from a magazine of a cartoon man holding a giant coin. Pavel tapped his pile of money and then the advertisement. "Now, do as you're told and make these into a stack of gold ducats like the one in the picture."

Petra would never forget the hard gleam in his eyes. The expectation of a life-changing miracle. Wolves didn't hunt with as much hunger in their eyes as this man. She spread her hand over his meager coins. The metal was warm from his tight fist and carried a whiff of tobacco. The shape of a golden sun formed in her mind. She watched the orb rise and set in her third eye as she tapped on the smallest coin in the pile and dragged it toward her, obscuring it with her finger.

Part of her wanted to know if she could truly turn bronze and nickel into gold. The ultimate ambition of the old alchemists, her father had once told her. Pavel wasn't the only one to dream of riches when the stomach clenched from hunger. If something as simple as a pile of pine cones could be changed to money, why shouldn't she make her and her mortal mother's life more comfortable, and without need of this *debil* in their home? But that wasn't what her father—the source of her witch blood—had taught her before he died. The craft was a grand gift to be explored, yes, but one must adhere to the rules or the magic would rain down misfortune.

The golden sun she envisioned burned a bright halo behind her eyes. When Petra lifted her finger on the table, a single gold ducat had replaced the koruna. Pavel's hand snatched it up. The coin went straight to his teeth, where he bit down on the gold. "It's real," he said, showing the coin off to her mother. The gleam in his eye had grown into a streak of avarice as he shoved the rest of the coins at her. "More! Do them all."

Petra knew she'd done wrong and thought at first to refuse, but that would only anger him. Yet what could he say if she failed? He had no understanding of the ways of magic to know what was defiance and what was a futile attempt, so she spread her fingers and let her hand settle on the coins. They'd gone cold again while sitting on the table awaiting their turn. This time, instead of a sun, she conjured the image of a cow chewing on grass. When she removed her hand, a hard patty of dry dung had replaced the coins.

"What is this?" Pavel reached over the table and grabbed Petra by her hair. "Where's my money? Put it back, you filthy witch!"

Petra held her tongue, feigning ignorance. He pulled harder and she threw him off by visualizing a wedge between them. His hand let go and he flew backward into his chair. The table tipped over and the ducat and dung fell into his lap. The look on her mother's face told her to run until he calmed down, and so she did.

Thinking back on it over the years, she should have recognized the warning signs in Pavel's calm demeanor after she'd humiliated him. She might have seen he was a man who bided his time like a simmering pot with the lid on. A week passed, and as spring warmed the ground, the people prepared to celebrate the land's fertility as they always had. In the village, the first woodpile for the Walpurgisnacht bonfire was constructed at dawn. Pavel helped load the wood on the pyre, nodding at Petra as she passed. Later in the day, he offered her a sweet cake, letting her believe all had been forgiven. And why not? The ducat she'd produced was worth all the rest of the money put together. She'd done him no lasting harm.

When dusk came she collected her coat and scarf to go to Hana's house on the edge of the village, as she'd been taught by her father from the time she was a small girl. Even in modern times, Walpurgisnacht was not a night for witches to stand too near the fire, so a handful of them from nearby houses would gather together to ride out the mortal frenzy of the holiday. There was no real threat of being burned anymore, but the witches had their own way of celebrating the rebirth of the season—by baking and singing and laying an offering on the hearth before they cast the bones to see into the shadows.

But Petra never arrived at Hana's. Pavel had held the need for revenge in his heart like a sponge holds water. With a smile on his face, he'd offered her and her mother a glass of pear-yellow wine for a toast. He'd served it in the small cordial glasses with the etched pattern around the rim that Petra had never been allowed to use before. She felt very grown up and swallowed the wine in three sips, not knowing Pavel had laced the drink with opium. Or at least that's what she later learned was the knockout drug of choice for mortals with no skill for sleeping spells.

Petra had awakened with her mouth gagged and her head covered by an old flour sack. Her hands were bound behind her, wrapped around some kind of pole or fence post. Her feet, too, were strapped to the pole at the ankles. Heat grazed her face, and an orange blaze filled her field of vision through the sack's fabric. They'd already built up the main bonfire in the square. A tune played on tambourine, fiddle, and the hurdy-gurdy filled the air with folk music until a roar from the crowd rose up to drown out the song. Walpurgisnacht. The burning of the effigy.

Petra's heart ran like a wild animal chased by a hunter's pack. Suddenly the sack was ripped off her head. When her eyes focused, she saw she was at the south end of the main street, near the grocer's, while the big bonfire burned at the northern end, near the post office. Pavel stood in front of her, leering as he brandished a hot poker mere centimeters from her face. The radiating heat singed the soft hairs near her ear. She tried to turn her face away, but he grabbed her chin in his right hand. "You weren't supposed to wake yet, but since you have, all the better. You'll know now you should've never crossed me," he said, pointing her face toward a stack of wood at her feet.

While she struggled against her restraints, Pavel reached in a bucket for a lit torch, the kind the revelers would carry to chase away the darkness after the sun set. "You're a wicked, wicked thing," he said. "And now you'll burn for your unnatural ways." With his left hand, he plunged the hot poker against Petra's cheek. The skin sizzled and her nerves lit on fire until they shrieked with unbearable pain. Amid the shock of the burn, as she gasped for breath, she watched him use the torch to light the dry grass tucked between the woodpile at her feet. The sack came back over her head. She tried to scream, but her sobbing breath caught in her throat. Smoke rose to meet her nostrils. Heat spread at her feet. A man shouted from the square, "Burn the witch! No more winter!"

Walpurgisnacht. The burning of the witches. Pavel had taken advantage of the people's giddy springtime celebration to commit murder right under their noses. What they would believe was an effigy tossed into a second fire was a living witch who'd made the mistake of making a fool out of a dull-hearted mortal.

Petra struggled against the ropes, terrified her clothes would catch fire at any moment. She was trying to still her breathing long enough to concentrate on a spell to free herself, when a woman screamed in agony from up the road. The cry was filled with terror, yet utterly familiar. The main bonfire. Her mother! The crowd erupted in a terrified panic. "It's a woman," they shouted. People screamed for buckets of water. *Yes, put the fire out!* Petra ignored her pain long enough to focus on the shape of dampness. The colors blue and green filled her inner eye. She envisioned the brittle kindling of both fires transforming into mounds of soft, green moss wet from rain. The orange flames at her feet morphed into smoke and steam that smelled like the heart of the forest. At the sound of people rushing to help her mother, she turned her bindings into thread, snapping them at her wrists and ankles. She ripped the sack off her head. The flame had scorched the soles of her shoes and the hem of the black cloak he'd draped her in, but aside from her scalded cheek, she was otherwise unhurt.

The villagers swarmed the bonfire in the square with buckets of water, rushing to release her mother from the stake, but the fire still burned. Petra had only doused the flames of her own fire, the one she had contact with. Her mother's burned body slumped over the steaming pile of smoldering wood as the people looked on in horror and confusion. "How did this happen?" they shouted, but already they called out it must be Pavel's devilry since it was he who'd taken charge of the fire. He who'd propped the effigy on the woodpile. His wife on the bonfire.

In a panic, Petra made a decision, one she would suffer the consequences of for the next ten years. Concentrating on the shape and width of the pole she'd been staked to, she morphed the wood into an effigy of herself burned in the smaller fire, one made of bones and teeth and hair. Pavel gaped at her, still holding the fire poker in his hand. She grabbed the iron and transformed the poker into an ice pick. When he released it in his shock, she stabbed the weapon into his neck with a rage built on a pyre of panic and hatred. His body collapsed into a heap on the ground as blood spurted from the hole she'd made in him. When he didn't move, she ran far away from mortal men with greed in their eyes and magic that punished so thoroughly.

CHAPTER FIFTEEN

In the space between that night and this moment, Petra had grown from the girl thrown into the fire, to a refugee living hand to mouth, to a young woman newly arrived in a city looking for work, to an eager new wife, and now to a war widow fighting under the banner of the Order of the Seven Stars against the undead. All of it converged in her third-eye vision like a halo of light that blinded her momentarily.

Petra opened her eyes and found herself lying on a pile of pine boughs in the barn. Her clothes and hair were damp with melted snow, and her mouth tasted of copper. She shivered and pulled up the blanket someone had carefully tucked in around her.

"You're back." Josef knelt to feel her forehead with his palm.

"What happened?" she asked.

"Your knees buckled and you fainted," he said. "Here, drink this." Josef handed her a warm cup of tea that smelled of mint and chamomile. He propped her head up with his arm to let her sip. She winced as the tea hit her lip. She touched the spot with her finger and came away with a tiny speck of blood on her skin.

"Careful," he said. "You bit it when you fell."

She stared into his smoky brown eyes so close to her own. He knew. He knew everything. He'd sought her out. He'd tracked her down.

Brought her to this place. All because he knew what she could do with the touch of her hand.

Petra swallowed the tea and plotted her escape.

"How did you know I was alive?" she asked. "Even the mayor reported I'd died in the fire. I saw the headline in the newspaper."

He laid her head down again in the pine bed, and she immediately regretted the absence of his arm around her. Yanis peeked around the corner of the stall and nodded in relief to see her awake. Behind him, Bako and Viktor played cards, pausing long enough to acknowledge she'd awakened, while Valentina crushed the woody husks of poppies to get to the valuable seeds inside.

"Hana told me different parts of the story while I was recovering," he said, waving Yanis off as if to say everything was under control. "But we can talk about that later."

She gripped his jacket and sat up. "No, I need to know now." Josef wore his fur hat again, reminding her of the man thrashing against the restraints in torment in the attic. He'd called the man lucky.

Petra leaned back against the wooden slats of the stall, hugging the warm mug of tea. Her head still swam in the clouds, but her focus improved. She looked Josef in the eye, encouraging him to tell what he knew.

"Hana, as you may recall, is not without her own powerful gifts," he said. "She casts the bones and sees into the shadows. At least that's how she explains it." He made himself more comfortable by leaning against the wall beside her and propping one knee up. "After the fire, many in your village were convinced you'd died, even though the bones in the ashes appeared uncharred." Petra silently wondered if her twelve-year-old self had left out that important detail in the transformation. "Pavel Radek was blamed for your mother's murder, but Hana didn't see your death. She saw an image of you in the forest on a path leading far away."

"I went north for a while," Petra said. "A dairy farmer saw the state of me and let me stay in the cowshed and work for his family for food."

He nodded, putting the pieces together. "After I recovered, Hana agreed to cast the bones one more time. For me. To find any last witches in the city to recruit." Again Petra looked for a streak of greed in his eye but found only sincerity. "That's when she saw you walking in the Old Town Square, hovering in the shadows between life and death. I worried that meant you were dying and I might lose my chance—" He cut himself off, not wanting to say more.

"Lose your chance for what?"

Josef wiped his hand over his eyes, buying time to overcome whatever resistance he had to saying the words out loud. "After they reassigned me to Yanis and the Order, I used the recruiting trip to go back to the city and find you. And there you were, just as she said, only you weren't dying. It was your camera that had tied you to the other side. I let myself hope . . . I thought . . ."

"You thought I could transform you. Use my magic to rid you of the curse." A hollow space inside her contracted with regret. "If I could," she pleaded, putting her hand on his arm, "I would. But my magic only works on things. Objects. Not the living."

He looked down at her hand touching his sleeve. Did he still wait for a miracle? Something to rid him of his torment. This man who felt fortunate to suffer only from fever and convulsions in comparison to what might have been. Had he grown disappointed that he'd found her? She'd twice before refused to use the magic he coveted. One member of the team was dead, one shot in the arm and laid up in the hospital, and the rest no closer to figuring out how to rid the mountains of the upíri. And now his own hope of a permanent cure had been extinguished.

She handed Josef the mug of tea. "We need to get back to work."

"It's late," he said quietly. "You should rest."

"Do the upíri rest?" Petra pointed beyond the door, where the ping of rifle fire never ceased. "Do the men fighting out there get to rest? I can't relieve you of your curse, but we can still try to save those men." She threw off the blanket and walked to the center of the barn, where

Viktor and Major Bako used the overturned horse trough as a card table. She threw the two photos of the clouds down on their cards and stabbed them with her finger. "This means something, and the sooner we figure it out, the sooner we can save the next man's life."

Yanis met her at the table and studied the photos for the first time. He pointed to the eyes. "Is that from a smudge on the negative?"

"They're eyes," Viktor said, throwing his cards down after losing to Bako. "Like my mistress moon, only this one hides in the clouds."

"Eyes?" Yanis turned the photo toward the lantern just as the door opened and Hana came in, shaking snow loose from her shawl and saying she needed more elixir for the young patient in the attic. "What do you make of a pair of eyes hovering in the clouds?" he asked with a nod to interest Hana.

The old woman kissed Valentina on the cheek and asked for hot tea before briefly meeting Petra's gaze again in passing. "Whose eyes are we looking at?" she replied to Yanis.

"They're in the photos I told you about," Yanis said. "Petra is able to capture images with her lens that most ordinary vision can't see."

Hana slipped a pair of reading glasses on and took the photo of the clouds from Yanis. After tipping the picture in the light, she clucked her tongue and looked at Petra with concern. "But how did you take a photo of such a thing? It's some sort of manipulation. A spell."

"That's what Dragoş said." Viktor took a short iron punty from his coat and blew through it onto the fire. The flames swelled, creating a dome of heat in the barn.

"It's no trick," Josef said, coming to Hana's side to study the photo again. "That's one of Petra's gifts. She can sense those on the other side with her camera. Their likeness only shows up when she develops the negatives. It's how we found the upíri among the soldiers tonight."

"I never knew such a thing was possible." Hana tossed the photo down on the table and took her glasses off. "This is a zduhać," she said, as if there were no doubt.

"Zduhać?" Bako collected the cigarettes he'd won off Viktor. "What's that? Don't tell me there are undead flying around in the clouds too."

Hana frowned as she glanced from Josef to Petra, weighing the truth for herself. "No, not the same at all," she said. "A zduhać is a spirit but he is also a man." As she spoke she stirred one hand in the air to convey his ethereal nature. "A zduhać is a protector. A man whose soul can leave his body while he sleeps to travel on the wind. He can build the clouds to make rain or turn back a hailstorm to save his crops by sheer fearlessness in the sky. But then he must return to his body exactly as he left it. It's very old and revered magic. One like this is born with the caul over the face. Rare these days to encounter such a being," she said as though still troubled by the idea of photographic evidence.

Bako struck a match and lit a cigar. "Could this kind of man travel out of his body to another place while in this state?"

"Yes, most certainly," Hana answered. "His spirit travels while his body stays put in his bed."

Bako blew out an angry stream of smoke. "Christ, and we thought we had good spies. But a man who flies out of his body? Sounds impossible."

"It isn't," Valentina said. "There is a history of these types of happenings where I live. We don't discount something just because we can't see it with our eyes."

Josef nodded toward the photograph. "Valentina is right. There's a lot we don't understand, but if these eyes are something that can only be explained as supernatural, we have to explore it further. It could be connected to our other problem."

Yanis agreed, leaning against the overturned trough to view the other photos again. He traced a finger over the haunting images of the upíri with their shining eyes. "Does a man like this, a zduhać, have other powers? Can he perform spells?" Yanis straightened. "Could he do spells while in spirit form?"

Valentina and Hana both nodded. "It's not impossible," the older witch said. "You should all take great care."

Petra wasn't so sure. "But he would have to be a master sorcerer to maintain that kind of concentration in spirit form."

"But it could be done?" Josef paced and grew more animated as he talked.

"Theoretically, yes." Hana quickly gathered the ingredients she needed to make the elixir, as though eager to be on her way. "Though I agree it would require the craft of a very accomplished and dangerous witch."

"A man who can manipulate the weather would make sense," Petra said. "What the soldiers said about the wind hitting before the attacks. And the attacks seemingly all happening at night. Or just before dawn."

Josef pointed his finger at her and finished the thought. "When a man is most likely to be sleeping."

Viktor shook his head, unconvinced. "But how could a zduhać control an upír attack by traveling here on storms while asleep?"

"The body is asleep," Hana corrected. "But the man's essence, good or ill as that may be, can travel anywhere the mind can in spirit form."

"Not unlike our jinn," Yanis said. "They prefer to stay hidden in the realm of the unseen but are more than capable of doing mischief in that form."

"So we know it's possible," Josef said, throwing off his melancholy mood. "Which is our first real lead in finding the source of the coordinated upír attacks." He held up the photo of the eyes watching from the clouds as evidence. "Now all we have to do is figure out who these belong to so we can stop his spirit from causing any more damage."

CHAPTER SIXTEEN

The storm continued to batter the barn with wind and snow as though searching for a way to gain entry and eavesdrop on their latest discovery. For a moment, Petra thought she might have to work a spell to keep the roof on, but after a few loud rattles, the wind gave up and died down again. Long enough, at least, for Hana to return to caring for the suffering man in the attic. Petra had hoped to speak with her father's old friend privately to learn more about what had happened after she'd run away, but then Dragoş walked through the door with his arm in a sling and all attention turned to him.

"You're back already?" Viktor asked.

Dragoş shut the door behind him, still wobbly on his feet. "They needed the operating space, so it was either go to the church to recover and get infested with lice from the other wounded or walk the extra hundred steps here and collapse on my own blanket."

Josef stood and patted him on the back. "Welcome back. Not too much blood loss, then?"

Dragoş cradled his bad arm. "Bad enough I might fall over if I don't sit down soon."

"Of course." Josef led him to his stall in the barn. "Valentina, can we get him something stronger than tea?"

Dragoş settled on his blanket with an audible sigh of relief. He accepted a tin cup from Valentina filled with beer from Bako's hidden supply. "*Na zdraví*," he said, looking each in the eye before drinking.

"I stirred some calendula and garlic in it," Valentina said. "It will help with the pain and keep the blood fighting against the wound."

Dragoş frowned at his cup as he inspected the contents more closely.

Bako came around and poured everyone a small drink of pálinka, drawing a few raised eyebrows. "It won't last anyway," he said with a shrug about his private stash of apricot brandy. The major emptied the last of the bottle into Petra's cup and then raised his own. "To Karl and Dragoş," he said. "Men who each, in their way, sacrificed the ultimate today." Before he drank he gave a slight nod to Petra, catching her eye as if to say he included Marek in his sentiments.

"To Karl and Dragoş." The group toasted in unison before swallowing their drink in somber silence. Josef kept his head down a moment longer before taking a sip and setting his cup aside.

Dragoş brushed off their tribute, saying he was only glad to be back in the barn. "I don't know how the doctor faces the horror of that hospital every day," he said. "It's a gruesome place. Every man that dies has to go through that wretched ritual. Must be a dozen a day at least."

"Ritual?" Josef asked. "You mean he performs some religious ceremony?"

Dragoş leaned back to rest his head, wincing at the pain it caused his arm. "The hearts," he said. "Cutting them out and collecting them in a bucket before burning the slop in the fire."

Yanis set his cup down. "The doctor is doing this with *all* the dead?"

"Macabre bastard," Dragoş said. "Three in the few hours I was there, at least while I was conscious. Sometimes the doctor would get interrupted by more wounded coming in, and the dead would sit on the table like that for an hour with their chest cut open." He shook off some image in his head and set aside the last of his draft.

"I'd say he's being overly cautious," Yanis said, looking to Valentina for validation. "The heart serves as a vessel for carrying the tainted blood of the upír curse, yes, but there's hardly a need to do this to all the bodies. I'll have a word with the doctor about it."

"You may try," she replied. "But many here believe the hearts need to be rendered to ash to rid the upír curse from rising again."

Petra got an uncomfortable pain in her stomach, wondering if Marek had met the same fate on the doctor's table. She set her palinka aside and tried to put the thought out of her head.

"The medical staff has been told to screen the patients for signs of unusual illness or infection," Bako said, confirming there might be a reason for the doctor to scrutinize the dead soldiers in his care. "For the ones we don't catch."

The report infused Josef with that caged-animal energy again, the way he got whenever they started to talk about the upíri. "Either way, the doctor seems to appreciate the dead don't always stay dead."

And the past doesn't always stay buried, Petra thought, watching Josef pace.

It was nearing midnight, but Josef only grew more spirited. He'd caught scent of something earlier regarding the photo of the eyes in the clouds and needed to chase it down. "Let's go over this zduhać theory one more time," he said to a handful of tired groans. He was right, of course. Any time wasted could be the difference in how many men ended up on the doctor's operating table, so Petra spread the photos out for everyone to look at again. "For Dragoș's sake, let's get caught up," Josef said, imploring their patience while he filled their wounded comrade in on what they'd come to believe about the wind's connection to the attacks.

"Yes, please continue," Dragoș said. "But don't take it personally if I pass out before you finish."

Josef acknowledged the young man's need to rest before testing his theory out on the group. "I think there's a good chance whoever is doing this is one of the tsar's men," he said. "When I slipped into their camp last night, it was fairly obvious their troops have not been targeted by the upíri as they have been on this side of the ridge. I saw no evidence of men hanging amulets around the camp or carving protective symbols into tree trunks to ward off evil like they do here. That cannot simply be because their men are less superstitious."

Perhaps they fear something other than upíri on the other side, Petra thought, still watching Josef closely after their earlier conversation.

"Who's their commander?" Viktor asked.

Josef reached for the collection of photos on the table before answering. "A man named Andrei Demichev."

"Any chance he could be a zduhać?" Valentina asked.

"Not on your life," Bako answered. "He's a shrewd strategist, but he's no magician. He'd have wiped out the Empire's entire army by now, if he were."

"That's a good point," Josef said. "The attacks have been horrific, but there have only been a dozen or more in this camp. The tsar's army could easily take out ten times that many men with their howitzers pointed in the right direction."

"But we already suspect the upíri attacks aren't about how many are killed," Petra said. "It's the superstition and fear that becomes demoralizing. What if that's the main point? Look at the photos. Aside from those we know are upíri, you see fear on the men's faces. Troops are deserting every day. And the ones that stay *do* hang amulets and crosses, and whatever else they can find, to give them peace so they can find sleep."

"It isn't often mentioned, but the number of suicides among the men has risen too." Josef exhaled and rubbed the back of his neck. "Many because of the unbearable winter conditions they're forced to endure. But, as you say, many also live with debilitating fear on a daily basis. They're desperate to be gone from this cursed place. If you're trying to win a war of attrition, having the enemy's army living in a constant state of distress would only aid your cause."

Valentina stood next to Josef, leaning against the table so that their shoulders met. "So how do we find out who is doing this? How do you find a zduhać on the wind?"

Petra had to shoo away the hum of bewildering jealousy buzzing near her ear again at the sight of Valentina sidling up to Josef with her curly hair and cinched waist.

"You said the attacks have been building in frequency." Viktor lifted his colored glasses so they rested on top of his head. "What if it's because whoever this zduhać is, he'd been wounded before, but now he's getting stronger?"

"What, you think this zduhać got himself shot like me and now he's sleepwalking in the clouds wearing a sling?" Dragoș laughed out loud and stared at the ceiling from his bed.

"I didn't say that. You always twist my words."

"Because you're an idiot."

"Enough," Josef said. "Viktor makes a valid point. There could be a correlation we're missing."

"What if this zduhać isn't getting stronger, but instead he's getting nearer?" Petra said. "Proximity could account for the increase in activity. The closer he gets, the stronger the magic."

"Is that how the magic works?" Bako asked.

Valentina weighed the likelihood with a tilt of her head. "Proximity matters in a spell," she said with an eye on the barn door as it rattled in the wind. "The storms have been getting stronger too."

Josef's head snapped up. "When I was in the Imperial army's camp, they were preparing for a visitor," he recalled. "Someone important. Not likely to be the tsar himself, though he has been known to show up to inspire his troops."

"We'd know, if that were the case," Bako said. "Even our spies couldn't miss a tsar on the move."

"Somebody else important, then," Josef said. "Men were busy polishing anything made of metal. Clearing the ground. Saluting right and left."

Bako pulled a half-smoked cigar out of his breast pocket and lit it. "Could just be a general coming in for an inspection to see why they haven't obliterated the Empire yet," he said, squinting through smoke.

Josef chewed his lower lip and stared at the floor as he thought. "Who's representing the tsar's Imperial army in the witches' treaty negotiations?"

"I've not seen the final list." Yanis folded the front of his robes around him as he crossed his arms. "King Wahaj is arriving on behalf of the sultan. He is king of the western jinn, near where the fighting has begun on the peninsula. The jinn normally do not interfere in the wars of men. It is beneath them, but it is said the sultan did not wish to be excluded from the talks, should there be a way to exploit magic to his advantage. He would need to generously bribe the jinn to action in such a case, however," he said with a tilt of his head.

"Wouldn't the Empire send Ava König?" Viktor asked. "I've read she has the emperor's ear. The newspapers suggest she's merely one of his mistresses, but she's a well-known sorceress. There was a rumor she was the one who put the notion of dreams and their interpretations in a certain doctor's head after serving him tea laced with a divining spell. The fallout has reverberated for years throughout the capital's back rooms, with everyone lying on a couch talking about their fantasies and what they mean. Some said she was just flexing her mystic powers for the emperor's amusement."

"The tsar has his mystic too," Yanis said. "He claims to cure people of disease and cast out demons. Would he be considered a high-profile-enough dignitary for an army to pause shooting at us long enough to polish their boots?"

Josef got that determined look in his eye that said he was on the verge of doing something dangerous. "I need to go back over the ridge," he said, holding up the photo of the clouds. "Whoever is coming, whether it's this mystic fellow or someone else, we have to know if he could be the zduhać. If he's been working his magic from the tsar's palace, imagine the horror he could unleash from a mere kilometer away from the front."

The blood drained from Valentina's face. "You can't go back so soon. You're not strong enough yet."

"And yet we don't have any choice," he said. "The treaty negotiations are scheduled to start in two days. Less than fifty kilometers from here. If we're right about this, he could do his worst damage yet."

Valentina implored him with a meaningful look of unspoken warning. "The elixir still needs time to work through the moon cycle."

"You see these pictures?" Josef grabbed the photographs of the men with shining eyes and held them up for Valentina. "Three of these men proved to be upíri tonight. Sitting among the soldiers like normal men. Grinning and smiling and waiting to rip their comrades' throats out with their teeth. If they were waiting for orders from this zduhać, then we have to find out who that is and stop him before he signals more chaos in the camp. Or your brother could be next," he said. "Or Petra's husband."

His final words hit like a stab to the heart. *Marek.* Petra had somehow let him slip free from her thoughts again. She caught Bako's eye and exhaled in disappointment.

The major cleared his throat and looked away uncomfortably.

"What is it?" Josef had noticed the emotional thread that had been pulled taut between Petra and Bako. "What's happened?"

Bako nudged his chin toward the photos and suggested Josef take another look. He went through the motion of thumbing through the photos, tossing them on the table one at a time before shaking his head in ignorance at the final one.

Bako clamped his cigar in his teeth and tapped on the top photo. "The faded soldier standing in the background."

"Who is he? Is he an upír? Did anyone try to find him tonight?"

"There was no need," Petra said. "He was not an upír. He was my husband."

"Was?" Josef studied the photos again. Understanding hit, and he dropped the last photo. The edginess left his body until all that coiled energy he'd been building up unspooled. "Is this how you learned of it? You didn't say anything."

"I couldn't," she said. "There was too much happening."

Josef pulled his ushanka off and gripped it humbly in his hands. "If there's anything you need. Anything we . . . I . . . can do, let me know. We will arrange transport for you to return home as soon as possible. Right, Bako?"

"No." Petra cut off the major before he could reply. This time it was her turn to insist. "I'm heartbroken over Marek's death, but we always knew it was a possibility he might not come home."

"Oh, my dear," Valentina said, giving Petra a squeeze around the shoulders. "You poor thing."

Petra gently shrugged her off by feigning an almost forensic-level interest in the photos again. "I'm not leaving," she said, studying the images of the men with shining eyes. "Not yet. Not until we figure out who this zduhać witch is. Besides, where would I go? I have nowhere to return to. This is my only home at the moment."

Bako and Josef exchanged a look and nodded. "If you're sure, we'd be grateful to have you stay and work here with us," Josef said.

"I'm sure." Petra scooped up the photos of Marek and put them away in her coat.

CHAPTER SEVENTEEN

Valentina continued to argue with Josef over his plan to cross the ridge to spy on the tsar's army again. It was too soon. It was too dangerous. He'd never get out alive a second time. In the end, though, with the threat of an escalation in upír attacks—if the photos were an accurate reflection of how deeply they'd infiltrated the army—all agreed the risk was worth the intelligence that might be gained concerning the zduhać. How else would they ever stop an army of undead unless they could cut off the head?

Unable to convince Josef there was any other way, everyone called it a night and planned to see him off in the morning. Yanis opted to return to the farmhouse attic to help Hana with the difficult patient overnight. Before he left, Josef asked the sorcerer to verify the doctor's practice of tending to the dead by removing their hearts.

Petra cringed at the thought and curled up in her corner of the barn, where she removed another photo from her pocket. One she hadn't shared with the others. She hadn't been wasteful with her supplies. She hadn't printed the entire set of negatives from her personal roll. Just the last one. The group photo she'd taken before the recruits had jumped into the truck to head to their final destination. Only two days ago, yet it felt like the distant past already, so innocent had she been then of what awaited them in this frozen place.

Leaning toward a stub of candle to see better, Petra studied the men's faces in the photo—Viktor clutching his satchel, Dragoș with that constant smirk on his face as he watched a pigeon fly away, Karl seemingly unaware of fate's eye upon him, Bako chewing his cigar, Yanis carrying the weight of the supernatural world on his shoulders, and Josef brooding beneath his fur hat. All of them clear-eyed but one.

She'd hoped she'd been wrong. She'd hoped she hadn't seen what she had, but it was undeniable. Josef's eyes shone silver in the photo. Josef, who'd once needed to be chained to a wall in a straitjacket like the man fighting for his life in the attic now.

"What's that you've got there?" Valentina asked. She'd brought a bedroll with her and laid it out next to Petra. "We women have to stick together, yes?"

"It's a photo of my husband," Petra said, not ready to confide anything to this woman. She took advantage of Valentina's distraction while straightening her blanket to switch the group photo for the one of Marek she kept in her pocket. "He was a private," she said, showing her the photo he'd had taken before he left for war.

"I'm very sorry. He was a handsome one," she said, handing the photo back. "Are you sure you don't need to go home and be with family at a time like this?"

Petra nearly laughed. She had no family anymore, and the one she'd tried to make her own had rejected her out of hand. "I couldn't bear to face my in-laws. He was their only son. A mortal prince in their eyes who'd married a much too common girl."

"Ah, they didn't know what you are."

Petra shook her head. "Neither did Marek."

Valentina gave her a curious look before settling under her blanket. After a pause, she rolled on her side, propping herself up on her elbow. "It's an unusual talent, isn't it? Your ability with the camera?"

"You mean capturing images of the dead?" Petra put the photo away and stretched out on her back. "I'm still figuring it out, to be honest. I only took up the camera after the war started."

Petra caught a whiff of herself while they talked. She wished she could have washed up before sleep. She was beginning to feel grubby after wearing the same clothes so many days in a row. *Marek's clothes.* The disguise was necessary enough to be able to walk among the men, but her feminine side was suffering a bout of inferiority next to the curly-haired, bright-eyed Valentina, who smelled of crisp green herbs.

"You must have some connection to the underworld," Valentina said. "Maybe even to Veles himself. Imagine that, the king of the dead." She smiled in a mildly teasing way, but it was nothing Petra hadn't considered herself. Yet she knew the magic with the camera was connected to her ability to change objects. In a way, everything connected to her magic was a manipulation of physical energy: some seen, some unseen. The camera was merely the device that brought the other realm into the visible spectrum.

"And you?" Petra asked. "Have you always been an apothecary's herbalist?"

"How did you know that's my craft?"

Petra enjoyed stealing the sweet smile off Valentina's face, if only for a moment. "You have the scents of mint, cinnamon, basil, and maybe some bay on you. The oils are embedded under your nails and skin from crushing them with the pestle."

Valentina checked her fingernails for grime before claiming she would have to do a better job of scrubbing her hands next time. "War is no place for me. I usually help women find love with my spells. And later I sometimes assist them when love finds them ripe with child."

"Out of curiosity, what was the interesting concoction you made for Josef?" Petra asked. She'd hoped the woman might share the potion's full ingredients, because it would tell her a lot about what the spell's purpose had been, but Valentina grew cagey.

"Oh, it's just a simple mixture I use to settle the stomach and clear the head when he gets overexerted," she said.

After the short exchange, Valentina claimed she was too tired for any more talk, so Petra blew out the candle.

Before sleep overtook her, Petra again thought about the men in the photos with their shining eyes. All of them hiding in plain sight. Pretending to be just another soldier among the others, waiting with their rotting breath and knotted hearts for the chance to steal the life-blood out of those nearest. She wrapped her scarf snugly around her neck and tried and failed to sleep with one eye open.

In the morning, a half meter of new snow blanketed the ground. And yet there was still the morning call of artillery fire in the distance. Rifle shots too. The fighting had shifted from day to day since Petra had arrived. Sometimes near, sometimes farther away. Major Bako had told her the gunfire was the result of skirmishes meant to keep the line between enemies taut. One had to remain aware of where the line was between one empire and another so they knew which side of the ridge to stay on. The instruction carried new meaning as she stared at the boot tracks in the snow outside the barn that led toward the forest.

Valentina joined her at the door, handing off a steaming cup of mint tea. "He'll be fine, if he's careful," she said. "He's a canny survivor. And I made him take both bottles of elixir with him, just in case."

Petra nodded and accepted the tea. "How long have you known him?" she asked.

"He was injured last fall. Back then there were very few surgeons this close to the fighting." Valentina offered her a hard roll for breakfast to go with her tea. "My aunt and I tended to him for weeks. Why?"

Petra turned from the doorway. "So, his injury was a bloody one?"

"Most are, but he's recovered now, except for the occasional setback."

Setback? Was that what she called his sudden illness and rapid recovery all within a few hours? This curse he suffered from?

Petra followed Josef's tracks in the snow with her eye as far as she could see before they disappeared into the trees. Half of her wanted to follow just to see how he managed to walk into an enemy camp without being shot. There were too many unanswered questions swirling in the new snow. Yet despite her craving to know more, the other half of her was mildly relieved he was gone and had taken his intensity with him.

Valentina packed hard rolls, the last of the cheese, and a fresh vial of elixir in a basket and set off to relieve her aunt. Petra reluctantly closed the door behind her. With her and Josef gone, Bako off dealing with command to find out the details of Marek's death, and Yanis and Hana still tending the special case in the attic, she felt the loss of Karl more keenly. He'd been the quiet type, happy to sit in the corner and carve his delicate flowers in wood. Now she was left with Viktor, whom she liked but suspected was slightly touched with moon madness, and Dragoş, whom she didn't like and who seemed to do nothing since he returned from the hospital but sit on his blanket and glare at her while she drank her tea. She also thought he could do with some soap, as the stench coming from his side of the barn had overpowered her own need for a bath.

"He won't make it back," Dragoş said.

Petra reluctantly looked up from her tea. "He made it back before. I suspect he'll do it again."

"Not in that snow," he said in his leering way. "The wolves will eat him for lunch."

"Not if he eats them first," she said simply to shut him up.

It didn't work.

"Do you ever wonder how he found you? Or any of us?" Dragoş sat up and rolled a cigarette with the last of his tobacco. His nails were long and rimmed with black filth, his lips cracked from the dry air, and his hair hung in greasy strands that formed parentheses around his forehead. "Think about it. None of us were eager to join up. We were all hiding our magic to stay out of the war, and yet he knew where to find each of us." He licked the rolling paper to seal it and struck a match. "And I know for a fact my name wasn't in any roll call of witches. They expunged my name years ago."

Petra wanted to ignore him. Josef had already told her that Hana had found them all by tossing the bones. "Why did you agree to come, then?"

Dragoș laughed briefly. "I've been asking myself that same question ever since I got shot. Only I didn't have any choice. I was set to spend the rest of my life in Old Saint's Prison near the river when he found me."

"You were in prison?" Why was she not surprised?

"He said I had certain skills he needed, skills that could earn me my freedom."

"Skills?" Petra made eye contact with Viktor across the barn, pleading for him to pay attention.

"I think he meant the stealing, lying, and murdering part." He laughed again, knowing it made her nervous. "I had illusion spells I used for years that went undetected by the authorities before I got caught."

"What's all this?" Viktor asked. Petra breathed a small sigh of relief when he came and sat at the table with her.

"And you, sir!" Dragoș grew livelier, as if he were a stage performer baiting an audience. "What were you hiding your magic for? Let me guess: there's a law against venal thoughts about celestial bodies," he said, giggling at his jab.

"Actually, I wasn't hiding," Viktor said. "I volunteered the first day they posted notices asking witches to aid the war effort."

"So why didn't you serve earlier?" Petra asked.

"They turned me down," he said.

"What, too mental, even for an army of witches?" Dragoș suddenly got to his feet.

So did Viktor. "That's right. They didn't know what I might do if confronted."

"A loose cannon, are you?" Whatever aggression Dragoş had let build inside him, it shrank by half when Viktor didn't back down.

"Should you be up?" Petra asked. "You're still recovering."

"This?" Dragoş held his cigarette in his lips while he tore off the sling. "Good as new," he said, winding his arm around, then punching the air with each fist like a boxer.

Something was very wrong. Even for Dragoş, the behavior was hostile. Then, as he danced around the room, punching the air, she saw past his loosely buttoned shirt to his chest. An abbreviated incision, angry and red as if recently cut with a scalpel, ran down from his collar to his breastbone. Right where a man's heart was. Two, if he'd been compromised.

Her gaze lifted from the wound to his face. There was no shine to the whites of the eyes. No spark of life behind the irises. If she were to take his photo, she was certain the ghost light in his eyes would leave a glow on the film.

Petra suspected now the Dragoş she'd been recruited with had died from his wound in the hospital. This reborn revenant who'd returned to the barn was some sort of undead doppelgänger. The voice, the demeanor, and even its memories were intact, but this thing was not alive, merely animated. There was a stake near her blanket, but could she get to it quicker than Dragoş could attack? Was Viktor ready? Had he seen what she had?

Petra listened for the rattle of wind against the roof, some sign Dragoş was being told what to do by the zduhać, but the weather remained calm.

"Oh, he's coming, don't you worry." Dragoş stopped his frenetic movements and stomped his cigarette out on the floor.

"Who's coming?" Viktor asked.

Dragoş ignored the question. "He's very interested in you, Petra. And in the magic you've been hiding deep under that painful memory of your mother's death."

Petra shook her head. She stood up from the table. He couldn't know anything about that.

The door opened and Yanis walked in. He'd been out all night, watching over the young man in the straitjacket. His eyes were barely open as he tossed his satchel down and arched his back to stretch it from the long hours he'd stayed awake. He opened his mouth to say something, but his instincts, honed from years of walking into dangerous encounters with the supernatural, picked up on the unusual energy holding everyone in their place. His eyes narrowed as he spotted Dragoş without his sling and Petra reaching for her weapons.

Yanis went for the hawthorn stake he kept fastened to his belt. Dragoş unhinged his jaw, exposing a double row of razor-sharp teeth. His feet never left the floor as he flew with enormous speed toward the sorcerer. The pair crashed into a horse stall, barely avoiding being impaled by a muck rake when they fell. Viktor readied a flame in his hand but resisted hurling it aimlessly for fear of burning Yanis. Without thinking, Petra lunged at Dragoş, slipping her arm around his neck to pull him off. His rotting smell hit her, making her wince as she yanked him backward.

His strength was shocking for a creature decaying from the inside out. Once she'd lost the element of surprise, he twisted his wiry body around, breathing his putrid breath in her face. His eyes, flat like a dead fish's, stared into Petra's. His lip quivered in anticipation of his first bite. Her hands pressed against his throat to keep him off her. He spread his mouth open wide. His teeth were vicious, pointed things made for tearing flesh. She had to stop him. Blunt his bite. But would it work against a creature half-dead, half-animated?

An image of a polished stone came into her mind, but just when she was ready to risk punching him in the mouth to transform his teeth, he held back. Wind rattled the barn walls and he relented, releasing her ever so slightly as he shuddered from the agony of unfulfilled bloodlust. Something had changed. Instead of lunging for the kill, he panted as though trying to control his rage. Petra used the moment of distraction to smash the flat of her hand against his protruding fangs. Dragoş's head snapped back. His teeth transformed from rows of deformed enamel to rounded pebbles that wedged in his mouth. In his fiendish state, he tore at his teeth with his claws. He screamed and thrashed until he suddenly arched his back in torment and fell forward. Yanis stood over him, still holding the mallet he'd used to drive the stake into his back.

But it wasn't a killing blow to the heart. Dragoş lifted himself up with immense force, throwing Yanis back. Petra scrambled to her feet as Dragoş screamed and clawed at his mouth. "Now," she called to Viktor.

Viktor called a brilliant orange flame into his hand. He drew his arm back to cast the fire at Dragoş when his target leaped into the air, clinging to the wall of the stable. Viktor released the flame, but the upír jumped down before the fire struck. Dragoş grabbed Petra by the waist with one arm and stole her away as if she were no more consequential than a corn-husk doll. Viktor's misspent flame had overshot its mark, only to find the dry rot hiding in the beams. Smoke billowed into the barn. Yanis and Viktor covered their faces and called out for Petra, but their voices quickly faded in the distance as Dragoş dragged her off her feet and into the nearby forest at a sickening speed.

CHAPTER EIGHTEEN

Dragoș ran too quickly for Petra to make sense of where she was or where they were going. All she saw were trees and snow and rocks as he carried her over his shoulder. His claws dug into her side as they leaped over a fallen log, yet she did not think he meant to kill her. Not yet. They had run far enough from the farmhouse and barn that he could have stopped and devoured her at any opportunity, yet he kept going deeper into the forest, past the ridge and past the alarmingly frequent gunfire dividing one army from the other. He ran with purpose, motivated by something beyond his own base desires.

Twice Petra had tried to concentrate long enough to turn whatever blood he had running in his veins to mud, but she was constantly jostled—biting her tongue twice—plus the smell coming off his body kept her on the verge of losing her meager breakfast. At one point he stopped to sniff the air, turning his head left to right before stomping through knee-deep snow. His strength was superhuman, as if aided by some demonic power. Was that what happened to the undead when they came back to life as these despicable creatures? Did the weight of their humanity get replaced with the speed and agility of winged devils?

Dragoș finally came to stop in a clearing surrounded by towering spruce trees. Their tops swayed in the breeze as he dumped her off his shoulder into a thick pile of pine boughs that had been arranged in a bed on the ground. A fire burned in a stone circle, and a raven squawked from a branch above as snow flurries swirled in the air.

"What is this place?" Petra demanded. "Why have you brought me here?"

Dragoş snarled at her, but without his sharp teeth, a degree of ferocity got lost in the translation. Still, it was strange how his aggression toward her had changed. He avoided her, constantly sniffing the air as though trying to catch the scent of something. Or someone. He stayed well away from the fire as well, letting her warm herself while he stretched his neck to see past the trees. Petra let a spell swirl in her mind's eye, waiting for the moment she could connect with his rotting skin. Before she could lure him closer, Dragoş lifted his head as if he'd fixed on something moving toward them.

"You'll regret casting your magic in this clearing," he warned, though with his mouth full of pebbles, the words came out all mumbled together, making it difficult to take his threat seriously.

"And who will stop me?" she dared to ask.

Dragoş grinned as half a dozen of the tsar's soldiers—each wearing a thick wool greatcoat, a fleece *papakha* on their heads, and a bayonet attached to their rifles—stomped through the snow into the clearing, dragging a body with them. "Them, for starters," he said before retreating to stand at the edge of the clearing, where he gnawed on the bark of a tree, determined to rid his mouth of the stones.

The first two soldiers to arrive pointed their rifles at Petra while the others dropped the man at her feet. She knew without seeing his face it was Josef. They'd beaten him and stripped him of his hat and coat, but he was alive as he moaned and collapsed onto his side. When he turned his feverish face toward her, it was clear that, aside from the beating, he was also suffering from the same ailment Valentina had treated him for earlier, as he sweated profusely in the cold air.

Petra dropped to her knees. "What have you done to him?" She cupped Josef's face in her hands, feeling the fire smoldering under his skin. His left eye was bruised, and his lower lip had a split in it that had left a trail of blood down his chin.

Josef, barely conscious, whispered "zduhać" so only Petra could hear. She patted his face to show she understood.

"We haven't killed him yet," said a man who'd entered the clearing behind the soldiers. "That is the main point I wish you to take from this." Tall and gaunt, with long hair and a beard that flowed over his chest like the tail of a Friesian stallion, he wore a black greatcoat with a fleece collar that was belted around the middle. On his feet were a pair of tall, black *sapogi* still gleaming from a fresh coat of polish. His eyes were somewhat occluded by the round glasses he wore, as they fogged over when he spoke. He was no soldier, no officer, yet an air of authority crackled in the aura around him.

"Who are you?"

"A friend," the man said. "I'm called Grigori Zimin."

The tsar's mystic? The words he spoke, like Yanis's, were mismatched with the movement of his lips as her ear interpreted the new language. She could only assume he understood her through the same manner of spell.

Petra held Josef a little closer to her so that his head rested against her leg. She slid one arm over his chest as though she could protect him from these armed men. Josef reached up and held her arm in place with his bloody hand. A plea to not let go? Or a warning? A round of artillery exploded nearby, answered by a blast of gunfire.

"Your comrade attempted to infiltrate our ranks," Zimin said, holding his hands behind his back. "As you can hear by the fighting, he caught up to us just as the army was preparing to execute a long-planned advance to sweep the emperor's troops from the pass. I myself am likewise on my way to plead the tsar's case in the treaty negotiations concerning magic in warfare. You'll forgive us if we don't have time to entertain either of you properly. I hope you'll also appreciate that it is entirely within our rights to shoot you both." In response to his threat, the other soldiers raised their guns.

Dragoş snickered from his place behind the trees. The noise caught Zimin's attention, and he walked over to better observe the young man gnawing at the bark. Dragoş cowered at first, but the mystic put his hand on the upír's head as if blessing him. "You did well finding her and bringing her to me as I asked," Zimin told him. "I know we did not plan on this next phase for you." He took in the state of the young man with a pitying look. "But you have my blessing. Sin and you will be forgiven. Go and feast now. I release you." He directed Dragoş to the forest where the armies clashed. When the upír stayed where he was to sulk instead, Zimin inspected his mouth. "She did this to you?" he asked, squinting at Petra. When Dragoş nodded, the mystic rested his hand on the upír's shoulder, drawing him close, as though to embrace him in a fatherly hug.

Suddenly Dragoş dropped to the ground. A needlelike stake protruded from his chest and he fell face-first into the snow, where his remains sizzled from the burn of enchanted wood.

"That was unnecessarily cruel of you," Zimin said. He flipped Dragoş on his back and pulled the stake out. "You could have at least left him his front teeth to eat." He knelt to wipe the stake clean in the snow before shoving it back up his sleeve.

"Stopping him from eating me was rather the idea," Petra said, turning away from the desiccated, shriveled thing Dragoş's body had become.

Concentrating on Josef again, she pressed a handful of snow to his bruised eye as his body began to shake in her arms. She needed the vials of elixir to make him better, but they must have been in his coat, which they'd removed. "What do you want with us?" Petra looked at the two soldiers nearest, who still aimed their weapons at her. "Why did Dragoş bring me here? Who are you really?" Petra wasn't sure how this man controlled the undead to do his bidding, but his presence had an unsettling effect on her own thoughts, as if his mind were pressing up against hers, trying to gain access.

"I haven't always been the man with the tsar's ear you see before you." The mystic stood again and held his hands behind his back, his glasses still fogging slightly and his long hair hanging neatly past his shoulders. "I come from very humble beginnings, but cream always rises to the top, as they say. Though sometimes it has to swim through a watery stream of tepid milk first." He looked up at the treetops, tilting his head. "Pavel Radek died a violent death, but not the one you think he did."

Petra's body shivered at the mention of the name. How did this man know about Pavel?

"The insufferable man remained alive for three more years after he last saw you." He lowered his gaze to measure Petra's reaction.

"Impossible." She knew it was, because she'd killed him.

Zimin stretched his hands out over the fire to warm them, displaying a star-shaped scar on his right palm, the mark of a witch condemned for murder. "Years ago he and I and"—he glanced quickly over his shoulder toward the nearly disintegrated body on the ground—"our young friend Dragoș were inmates together at Old Saint's Prison. It's not a period of my life I'm proud of, traveling your country like a vagabond until being arrested, but it did help shape the man I've become."

You mean the killer I see before me? Petra did not yet know his power, nor the temperament of the men he'd brought with him, so she held Josef and listened.

"And while I was there," he went on, "Pavel told me the most extraordinary tale before eventually meeting his end. A story about a young girl who could turn ordinary objects into the extraordinary."

"And does a grown man always believe in fairy tales?"

Zimin swept his coat back and reached into his tunic pocket. From it he produced a gold ducat, which he manipulated through his fingers like a common magician showing off his latest trick. "Imagine having a talent so concentrated in one discipline that one is able to transform matter from one element into another. Not just in appearance but in substance. That's a witch who could change the world." He flipped the coin in the air, then caught it in his fist. "Or, at the very least, one man's fortunes."

Josef gripped her arm with renewed purpose. She looked into his fevered eyes as he shook his head. "That's not why I wanted to find you," he whispered through gritted teeth. Behind his pain, his eyes had changed hue from a deep brown to a golden color, and his front teeth had elongated slightly. Something was transforming within him, something she'd begun to suspect, and yet not in the way she'd thought. His eyes had light and life in them, unlike the upíri, who wore the eyes of the dead. Still, he suffered as he fought against the change coursing through his body.

Zimin held the coin up between his thumb and finger like a tiny golden moon against the sky. "It is the very same coin," he said. "Pavel smuggled it into prison with him, swallowing it every few days to keep it safe. Though . . . how safe, really, is a man's belly against a blade in a place like that?"

Petra's stomach turned over hearing the callous admission. "You murdered him?"

Zimin laughed out loud. "For the last ten years, you believed you were the one who killed him, a young girl stabbing an animal like him, and now you find it offensive that he died by another's hand? Too rich."

"The girl you're looking for died in the fire," Petra said. In so many ways she truly had.

"I should have finished my earlier thought," Zimin said, squatting beside Josef and Petra. "With the right motivation, I believe such a witch could be persuaded to exercise her unique and profitable talent for another's ambition."

Before she could object, he held up the first of two small brown vials. The elixir Valentina had concocted to help Josef. "This is what he needs, is it not? One dose now. The other before moonrise?" He waved the bottle in front of Josef, whose chest rose and fell in quick bursts at the sight of the drug. He swung his hand out weakly to snatch the vial. Zimin easily lifted the bottle out of reach, adding a chiding "tsk" sound as he pulled it away and straightened his glasses. "Not so easily, my friend. We are still haggling over our price."

Petra wondered how he could watch another man's suffering, knowing he held the cure in his hands. Then again, she was facing an admitted murderer. One willing to gut a man for a gold ducat. Or stab a friend in the heart with a wooden stake because his usefulness had run out.

"What do you want?" she asked. If there was going to be a conciliation, then they needed to get their true intentions on the table.

Zimin stood to his full height, towering over her like some wooden carving of a pagan god wearing spectacles. "You will escort me to the site of the treaty negotiations."

"And?"

"There you will use your particular form of magic how I see fit. I will instruct you on the specifics when we arrive."

Petra took the measure of the man, knowing he'd grown accustomed to manipulating both the living and the undead like pawns. A man who thought nothing of using his talent to do harm to others and with little other concern but for what it enabled him to gain.

"Do this for me," Zimin said, "and I will give the first vial back to your comrade. By the state of him, I assume he will either die without it or fall through to the other side of transformation, never to return to his present form again. And if you do not care for him as I think you do, then you may assume you'll both die in this clearing."

The soldiers gripped their weapons tighter—their knuckles white, their breath rising in the cold, their fleece caps slipping down their foreheads as mortars exploded less than a kilometer away. The first soldier pressed the muzzle of his gun to her head, grazing the skin at her temple. The contact was all she needed. Did Zimin truly know what he'd bargained for when he stole that ducat from a coward's stomach? Borrowing the vision of all the springy components of Bako's gun while it had been taken apart, she fused the guts of the soldier's weapon so that the bullets, bolt, and trigger all merged into one piece of solid metal. To the eye the weapon looked the same, but the gun would be of no more use to the soldier than a medieval cudgel.

The mystic dangled the vial. "What is your answer?"

Petra stood and faced Zimin. He was not as good at hiding his ambition as he hoped. Desperation flared in his eyes while he waited for her to agree to his terms. The tsar's mystic didn't care about Josef or Dragoş or any of the men he'd brought with him, only her and what she could do for him. But there was still too much at stake to let this man slip away and no other way to save Josef from certain agony, or the countless others who'd be mauled by his growing army of undead, unless she conceded to his request.

"If you will give my friend the elixir he needs," she said, feeling a bruise form over her heart, uncertain if she'd sealed his fate or not, "I'll go with you to the treaty site."

"Petra, no," Josef rasped.

Zimin set the first vial down in the snow and straightened again with his hands held in the air to show there were no tricks. "You'll find I'm a man of my word. I'll send someone back for him to administer the second vial once we are on our way to the treaty site and I know your magic is true."

Petra knew it was a lie, but she picked up the first vial, took a sniff to make sure it was viable, and then slipped it in Josef's hand, hoping it would be enough. "He will need his coat and hat returned," she added when he shivered uncontrollably. "Nonnegotiable."

The mystic snapped his fingers, and one of his men obediently slipped off the greatcoat he'd taken from Josef. A crushed ushanka fell out of the pocket onto the snow. A hat made of fur the color of wolves in winter.

Snow began to fall in big flakes as both coat and hat were left with Josef. The fire was banked and stoked, the soldier with the fused rifle was left to stand guard, and the contents of the first vial drained past Josef's lips. With their deal negotiated, Petra followed Zimin out of the clearing, leaving one member of their group lying dead in the snow and another fighting for his humanity. Holding her hand out, she counted seven snowflakes in her palm before they melted and made a wish for the one who yet lived.

CHAPTER NINETEEN

Despite wanting to remain defiant in Zimin's company, Petra accepted the black tea he offered with lemon and sugar. A servant had brought it to her in a tall glass nestled within an ornate metal sleeve with a handle. She turned the *podstakannik* in her hand to admire the embossed coat of arms, then resumed her stony demeanor as Zimin dismissed the boy harshly from his tent.

"Tent" was an understatement. The mystic traveled in comfort at odds with their harsh environment. Outside, the snow fell in heavy clumps, intermingled with the rain of distant gunfire, delaying their departure momentarily. Yet under the canopy of Zimin's private quarters, they enjoyed heat from a coal-burning brazier, cozy cushions spread on a bench that doubled as a cot for sleeping, and small hors d'oeuvres of pastry paired with black caviar and smoked goose liver. The food left her wishing for some of Valentina's salty cabbage soup, but she ate what she was offered, as one never knew when they'd see another meal when held in captivity.

Petra wasn't exactly a prisoner. She could leave at any time. Escape was simple enough, should she choose to use her craft, but if this man sitting before her, slurping his tea with as much grace as a dog lapping up water, was to be stopped, she must first learn his weakness. And that meant traveling with him to study his habits, his routines, and the reach of his arrogance so she might find the chink in his armor.

The last point, of course, was already on full display within his lush surroundings. Zimin refused to give up the warmth of his tent for the uncertainty of icy roads. If he were a zduhać, couldn't he vanquish the storm so they could be on their way? Yet instead of dissipating into his spirit form, he seemed to think their time together was better spent understanding the parameters of her magic, judging by the questions he peppered her with.

"How is it a witch learns to change wood to bone without uttering a single incantation?" he asked, stirring more sugar into his tea. "Only witches with years of experience show any true skill with silent spell-casting." He was deliberate in his movement—slow, methodical, calm, tapping the spoon exactly three times against the rim of the glass—yet she sensed his impatience to know everything about her skittering just beneath the surface of his carefully calculated demeanor. Hunger for power, gray like a storm cloud that builds and gathers into a tornado— that was what she sensed from him. She suspected he was searching for a way to hoard her magic for himself. After all, why should such a valuable talent be wasted on a young peasant woman too illiterate to string a few rhyming words together.

"My father once said the magic comes from a wellspring rooted in the earth." Petra took a sip of tea. "It flows up through me in shapes and colors that form in my mind." She wiped the corner of her mouth with a cloth napkin. "No words needed."

"You are the source?" He questioned her answer, scrutinizing her rough appearance to see what he'd missed.

"No, you misunderstand me." She enjoyed correcting him, as he seemed to her a man who'd climbed very high in his station in life by scrambling over the tower of bodies he'd piled up on the way. "I'm not the source," she said. "I'm the conduit it flows through."

"So anyone could tap this energy?" He grew intrigued. Calculations and manipulations spun in his eyes, and Petra found herself grateful she hadn't swallowed whole his lies about being a man of his word. "Show me." Zimin shoved a plate of caviar in front of her and asked her to transform it. "Something simple. No need to impress. Just show me what you can do."

Petra hesitated. She wanted to gain his trust long enough to sort out how best to stop him but hated being used for parlor tricks. Still, she had to do something to keep him invested in their bargain. She turned the plate around until the fish eggs transformed to chocolates.

Zimin picked up one of the confections. He narrowed his eyes at her behind his glasses, then put the sweet in his mouth almost as a dare. His grimace faded as the chocolate melted on his tongue. He swallowed and called to the young man outside the tent. The servant entered, and Zimin whispered something in his ear. The boy's eyebrows tightened in confusion, but he bowed his head obediently and left. He returned a minute later with a live chicken tucked under his arm.

"What can you do with this?" Zimin asked.

"That's a living creature," Petra said.

"Yes, of course. I'd like you to demonstrate how it works on animals now. For instance, does your magic work on people? Could you turn my servant into a newt?"

Petra hoped the question was a joke, but the young man's eyes widened in concern as he set the chicken down and backed up toward the exit.

"It doesn't work that way."

"Why? Because you are squeamish? Because you hold some reservation about experimenting on lesser creatures?" The man steepled his fingers, waiting for her to admit she was afraid to try so he could convince her why she was wrong, while the chicken clucked and flapped its hapless wings. "It worked on the caviar. Was that not once a living thing?"

"If the magic worked on the living, do you think you and I would be sitting here having this conversation?" she asked. Zimin's body flinched at her implied threat, but he refrained from lashing out. "I can't replace your arm with a tree limb," she said. "I can't slip vinegar into your veins instead of blood. Not while you're still connected to the life force." She used her fingers like scissors to snip the air. "My father reasoned that once that connection has been severed, what's left behind is mere matter. In that state it can be altered, because it's no longer growing or becoming."

"It's in a state of decay," he said, understanding.

"It's why I can change an acorn into a thimble, a plucked apple into a teacup, or even an upír's teeth into stones."

"Because they're undead."

Petra nodded. She hadn't been sure about that part until she'd tried it on Dragoș, but there was nothing left of life in the body she'd altered. "So whatever it is you want me to do for you at the treaty negotiations, I won't be turning someone into a pillar of salt when they say something you don't agree with." Petra drained her tea, with one eye on her host.

Zimin smiled beneath his mustache. "I am the tsar's representative in this matter," he said, affecting an air of regal legitimacy he didn't naturally exude. "My mission is to secure favorable terms with the witches of the other regions so that we might bring a quick end to this war."

And by "end" she thought he meant to push the Empire into oblivion. At least on a magical scale. But if he was counting on her for that, he would find himself gasping from want.

Zimin snapped his fingers and pointed to the chicken. "Take it away." The young man scooped the animal up in his arms and bowed at the waist as downy white feathers sifted to the floor. "And tell them to prepare my car," the mystic said, inhaling the cold air wafting in from outside. "The snow will be stopping in a few minutes, and we have a meeting to attend."

Outside, the handful of soldiers assigned to remain behind with the tsar's mystic moved out of the way as a large black automobile rolled to a stop before Zimin's tent. The hard-topped car was a great, gangly goose of a thing that had been fitted with a caterpillar belt made out of metal links for traction over a double set of rear tires. A pair of skis had been fitted inside the front wheels to help it glide through deep snow.

"After you," Zimin said. He held the door open and gestured to the back seat draped with a bearskin cover.

Petra had never been in such a luxurious vehicle before. She was given a small brazier with warm coals for her feet and a renewed glass of hot tea for her hands. Two men, a driver and an armed guard, climbed in the front seat with guns and shovels awkwardly propped beside them. They nodded curtly over their shoulders without uttering a single word. Zimin secured a black *papakha* on his head, pointed ahead, and whispered, "*Skol'zit'.*" Or at least that's the word his lips formed. Her ears heard the command *glide*. The fog and ice lifted from the windshield, the last remnants from the snow squall swirled away from the road in fanciful eddies, and the car took off at a lurch before skating over the icy ground.

Zimin told Petra their destination was an hour away, but he lost his taste for talk once they were moving and soon crossed his arms and leaned against the door, closing his eyes. Petra regretted telling him her magic didn't work on living things. She might have preferred to have him behave a little more warily around her, sleeping with one eye open, rather than nodding off. And yet this zduhać had fallen asleep right beside her. Would he leave his body? Was his spirit out in the clouds even now? Or was he simply exhausted from constantly directing upíri to kill in his sleep at night?

Petra glanced at the two soldiers. The one on the right had been fighting sleep himself. He hugged his arms and slapped them several times to warm up and stay awake, but inevitably his lids would get heavy again. While she wondered how quickly hypothermia would set in should she choose to kill the car engine and make a run for it in the middle of nowhere, she thought it best to see the ride through to their destination. No doubt, her seatmate had already deduced she'd do nothing of the sort as he snored on, fogging up the window. Or was it fog? Petra looked again, and the hazy cast she'd seen on the glass had moved to the roof of the cab.

Petra waited until the guard's head bobbed forward. She pushed the front of her coat open and removed her camera, quietly unfolding the lens. She angled her body sideways until she captured Zimin in the viewfinder, then took the photo. The click made the guard's head bounce up, and he slapped his sleeves again in a sort of self-flagellation. The driver looked over his shoulder to see what had made the noise, but all he saw was Petra bundling her coat up against the cold and slurping her hot tea.

Petra didn't know what she expected to find on the film. Maybe the tsar's mystic was merely sleepy after a busy day of murder and kidnapping, but curiosity had her wanting to see if the camera could record the zduhać traveling out of his body the same way it had captured the eyes in the clouds and the ghosts in the town square.

As the day wore on and the air turned bitter cold, she worried about Josef. Had he fully recovered after swallowing the elixir? Was he still shivering in a forest? Had he lost the battle and transformed into the cursed creature he'd fought so hard against? She never would have left him had she not seen his body recover in record time the day before. Or if she hadn't rendered the soldier's gun inoperable. She held on to the hope he had the strength to survive and vowed, as she looked at the man sleeping beside her, she'd do the same.

The car slipped over the snowy hillside as they drove in the narrow space between trees that the driver insisted was a road. Petra could see tire tracks from other vehicles, so she tended to believe him, but every rut they slid in and out of had her doubting they were destined for anything but getting stuck in a ditch.

And then they suddenly dropped into a valley where the smoke from a dozen chimneys rose into the sky. A steepled church with a bell tower emerged above the red-tiled roofs of the small settlement, where a meandering river ran black against the snowy ground. A cow mooed from a field as they neared the outskirts. She nearly wept at how normal the village sounded after her whirlwind introduction to war and the undead.

Zimin's eyes opened and he leaned forward as they bypassed the village. "There," he said, pointing to the remains of a medieval stone castle on the hill overlooking the river. The driver steered the car up the narrow road, sliding as he rounded the final corner, where Zimin ordered them to stop just short of the summit. Tire tracks from other vehicles already making the climb were evident in the snow.

"Why this place?" Petra asked, looking up at the thick stone fortress.

"Despite its looming presence over the village, the castle is isolated and abandoned, and therefore easy to shroud in spells to discourage the curious," Zimin said. "To the majority of the world, our kind does not exist; therefore this meeting does not exist." He stared at the castle through the window, as if looking for proof of what he'd just said.

"And what do I do now that we're here?" she asked, awaiting his demands.

Zimin ordered the two men in the front seat to step out of the car. Once they shut the doors and walked three meters away to smoke their cigarettes, he removed a small leather book from his coat. The sun was setting, but even in the half-light, she could see letters glowing on the paper when he thumbed through the pages. A spell book of some kind. "This was my father's, and his father's before him," he said. "Our family heritage, my birthright to the craft, is bound between the worn covers."

Petra felt a twinge of envy. She had no such book from her father. No written spells to study and practice. Her father had marked his incantations down. She remembered seeing him write by the fire while her mortal mother embroidered, but if he'd had a spell book, it had been lost to the ages after his death.

Zimin offered the grimoire to Petra so she might examine it. "I want you to re-create it," he said. "An absolute replica. Make it out of whatever you wish. Whatever will help the magic produce the perfect copy. Sense the history. Absorb the energy. Get an impression of the generational knowledge embedded in the pages. I want that feeling to translate into the new book you create. It must exude authenticity."

Petra was almost disappointed. She'd expected a request for gold, or cash, or diamonds. She'd only ever transformed the one gold ducat, but the coin had confirmed she could do it. Though at a huge cost to herself in the end.

Doing as he said, she concentrated on the spell book in her hands, turning the pages, smelling the ink and leather, and observing the peculiar way the handwritten letters, spidery thin, shimmered in the sunlight. But why make a copy that felt authentic when the real thing already existed?

"I need an object to transform to create the book." Petra searched the car's interior for something suitable. "It's best to use something similar in size."

"Like that camera of yours?" He arched his brow at her as if to say he knew what she had hidden under her coat, though she didn't think he knew she'd snapped his photo while he slept.

Just how much can he see?

"Too many moving parts," she lied, desperate to keep her camera.

Zimin removed his hat and tossed it at her. "Perhaps this is simple enough."

Petra turned the *papakha* over and nodded. She placed the hat on her lap and blew warm breath on her hands while rubbing them together. Outside the vehicle, the two men hunched their shoulders against the cold while waiting for the signal to return. They would have to wait a few more minutes. The book, with its glowing letters and numerous pages, made for a complex image. Petra closed her eyes and inhaled its scent until a shade of reddish brown, like polished rosewood, flooded her mind's eye. Something about the aged quality of the hue translated what she'd sensed from the book, so she concentrated on replicating that with just a tinge of gold around the edges to account for the gilded undertone of the lettering.

The fleece hat transformed under her fingers. She opened her eyes and flipped through the pages. It appeared correct, but she worried about the mystic's scrutiny as he snatched it out of her grip.

"Yes," he said at last, after turning the pages to read various spells and compare strange splatters and blotches that stained the original paper. "This will do nicely."

Petra knew better than to ask what he intended to do with it. Honestly, she didn't care, so long as she was free of their bargain.

"We have more in common than you know," Zimin said. "I, too, come from humble country beginnings." He closed the book and tucked it away in his breast pocket. "It was only after I learned to wield my magic as the powerful weapon it is that I began to rise from my unfortunate circumstances. Once I understood the righteousness of sin and the exquisite potency of redemption. They are the pair that work in harmony to propel one upward."

Petra knew it was practically unheard of for a man of such humble birth to climb to a place at a table of nobles. So close to the seat of power that his words traveled directly from his mouth to the tsar's ear. And yet his talk bordered on fanaticism.

"Is that all you needed me to do?" she asked, ignoring the way his eyes glittered at the sound of his own preaching.

"Almost." Zimin shifted his body to confront her, adjusting his glasses on his nose. "Before I go in I want to see your true face. The one beneath the spell."

Petra reflexively touched the scar on her right cheek, where Pavel had burned her as a child and where she'd kept an illusion spell in place for most of those ten years to hide it. "How did you know?"

"I might not be able to manipulate physical objects, but what I can do is see beyond the obvious." He checked the grounds around them again, as if looking for someone. "Quickly—we haven't much time."

"It's merely an illusion. Not a true physical alteration," Petra said, somewhat uncertain. She hadn't shown her face to anyone since she was a child. He scowled at her to get on with it, and she let the veil drop.

The mystic examined her cheek as one might verify an address before dropping a letter in the post. He nodded, approving. "He said he'd left his mark on you, and there it is."

Zimin waved the two frozen men back to the car, and they drove up the last part of the hill to the castle door, stopping beside a dilapidated horse-drawn cart that had been ditched in the weeds. A precursor to the state of the abandoned castle they found themselves staring up at. Petra resumed her illusion spell, expecting to wait in the car with the soldiers, but then Zimin opened her door. "Follow me," he said.

"But I did everything you asked."

"And now you will also do what I tell you," he said. "Get out."

He led her inside the vestibule. There was no one there to greet them, no host to tell them where to go. The place appeared as deserted as Zimin had claimed it was. Oughtn't a castle protected by spells at least have furnishings, a coat of arms hung on the wall, a chandelier brimming with fat white candles? Zimin shoved her into an alcove and put a finger over his lips in warning. For an instant she thought the worst after his sin-and-redemption speech. "Quickly," he said. "Can you change your clothing to something worthy of a palace secretary?"

Petra looked down at her trousers caked in mud and blood. "Yes, but why—"

"Just do it. And quickly, before anyone sees you," he said, turning his back to her.

Petra changed her dirty clothes into a burgundy suit with delicate embroidery along its edges. She'd seen the two-piece ensemble in a shop window in the city before she'd been swept off to the frozen mountains full of bloodshed and misery. It wasn't that she thought she deserved it. She never did this sort of thing for herself. She never wanted to attract the scrutiny of the authorities after what she'd done to Pavel. Or rather, what she had thought she'd done. Had he really survived that night? Only to be done in by this murdering mystic? If so, she was done with hiding her true self. This man needed *her* powers, not the other way around.

Taking full liberty—and because her body was frozen through to the bone—she turned Marek's cap and scarf into a floor-length cape with a fur-lined hood to keep her warm. One with a pocket deep enough to hold her camera. When she was finished, she stepped out of the alcove, braiding her hair and twisting it into a knot so as not to appear a total shambles.

"Tonight you are part of my entourage. My secretary. Keep your mouth shut and do as I say until we're finished and I'll see that the second dose of the coagulating elixir is administered to your comrade."

Petra questioned whether there'd be enough time. They were more than an hour away by car, and Zimin seemed to think Josef needed the second dose of elixir before moonrise. She wondered, too, what made him think the elixir was meant to thicken Josef's blood. Before she got the chance to pursue her thoughts further, a door on the other side of the entry hall opened. A tall gentleman in a black suit, with gray hair that hung to his shoulders and a long staff with a sickle on the end, bowed at the waist. He introduced himself as Stefan, temporary caretaker of the castle sent by the Ministerial Council for Magical Affairs.

"Grigori Zimin?" Stefan brushed a cobweb off his sleeve. "The others have arrived. If you'll follow me," he said, not bothering to acknowledge Petra. The caretaker escorted them to a stone-lined stairwell, where they descended in corkscrew fashion to a depth two levels belowground. No torches burned in the stairwell, yet the way was lit by a soft light that seemed to travel just ahead of them. Almost as though a will-o'-the-wisp guided their steps. The thought of being led astray in the underground tunnels of an abandoned castle put the chill back in Petra's blood, and she clutched her cloak high at the throat.

When they reached the bottom, the soft blue light hovered at the end of the corridor. Stefan pressed on, ignoring the pools of water on the flagstones, the cobwebs clinging to the old iron brackets where torches once burned, and the odd clicking sounds emanating from the shadows over their heads.

"Just a little further," the caretaker said, as though encouraging them to ignore their instincts and the voices in their heads telling them to turn back.

"The Ministerial Council chose the location," Zimin said to Petra from behind her shoulder. "They love to remind everyone what they're capable of."

When they reached the source of the light, Petra was surprised to find a room lit by four large candelabras whose candle flames glowed warm and bright. An enormous round oak table stood in the center; around it were six high-backed chairs covered in royal-blue velvet and gilded trim. In the middle of the table, inlaid in dark wood, was the likeness of a sacred linden tree with three pentagrams centered beneath it. A silver tray containing a decanter of red wine and four crystal glasses had been placed aside the inlay.

A middle-aged man stood and straightened his waistcoat as Petra and Zimin walked in, while a woman adorned with a wide-brimmed hat trimmed in fur remained seated with her hands resting atop a walking stick with a cut crystal handle. Neither of the others had brought an underling with them. Apparently Zimin was the only one who needed the aid of a secretary in these matters.

Before anyone spoke, Stefan poured each of them a glass of wine, ignoring Petra until Zimin insisted she be included. "Please drink the Lingua Franca in full," the caretaker instructed after scrounging up an extra glass for Petra, one smeared with fingerprints and the ghostly outline of lips that had once pressed against the rim. The man and woman both drank their wine in two sips, while Zimin swirled his in his glass first, as if he didn't trust completely what he'd been given. Once the others had finished theirs without incident, he swallowed his glassful of the enchanted wine, urging Petra to do the same.

Once the effect of the wine had made its way from their stomachs to their ears, the witches made their introductions.

"Hello, Grigori." The woman tilted her head formally in greeting, yet the informality of using only his first name suggested a shared history.

"Ava." Zimin bowed his head in kind. The interaction was familiar yet chilled with the tension of reciprocated distrust. Or professional rivalry perhaps. Ava König, a middle-aged woman with blonde hair and wrinkles near her eyes that creased heavily every time she forced a smile on her face, was the famed witch of the dual monarchy. Apart from her interference in the field of psychology as Viktor had recounted, it was said her spells held the Central Powers together with a centripetal force, though one had to wonder if all that inwardly pointed energy wouldn't lead the empires to eventually swallow their own tails one day.

Zimin kept his manner aloof as he introduced himself to the gentleman, reaching out to shake hands. "Grigori Zimin. Pleased to make your acquaintance," he said before bowing stiffly, as though unaccustomed to the practice in a diplomatic environment.

The gentleman, dressed in pinstripes and smelling of tobacco smoke, held his beefy hand out. "Otto Schultz." He puffed his chest out slightly, like a toad hoping to make itself appear larger in the eyes of a predator. "Dirty tricks, this calling up of revenants," he said, not waiting for the air of pleasantries to clear the room before jumping into the middle of the muddle.

"And yet a little dirty business has its place in one's repertoire of deeds, too, does it not?" Zimin spread his arms out, ignoring Schultz's confused smile. "And where is our jinni king?" the mystic asked when Schultz backed away to pour himself a second glass of wine.

"Oh, I imagine he's already here," König said, baring a hint of a smile as she tucked a stray blonde hair under her hat.

On cue, a burst of flame shot out from one of the candelabras, jumped to the floor, and rose up as a man appeared in brilliant blue-and-silver silk robes, unlike anything Petra had ever seen before. "Peace be upon you," he said with a slight bow of his head. The silk flowed with his every move like flame itself.

"Ah, the infamous King Wahaj." Zimin squinted slightly, sizing up the fiery jinni, before offering his hand. The men completed their greetings and took their seats.

Zimin offhandedly introduced Petra as his secretary, forgoing the mention of her name, which was barely met with any acknowledgment except for a worrisome glance from König. Presumably, Petra was meant to take notes, though she carried no pen or paper. She also presumed when you're a member of the invisible underclass, no one takes notice of such details, so she refrained from conjuring any props to assist with the ruse. Zimin had her take the seat beside him at the end of the table nearest the exit. Once everyone was seated, Stefan, sickle in hand, stepped out of the room and shut the door behind him.

"I believe we're all here, so let us begin." König waited for everyone to place their hands flat on the table, reminiscent of a séance gathering. When they were in position, she called out through the door to Stefan that they were ready.

A moment later the candles in the corners of the room flickered and a thin blue stream of electrical light spread out to form a circle of spinning energy over their heads. Something slumped inside Petra, as though a space beneath her heart had been hollowed out and collapsed. The others displayed mild recognition of the same sensation, frowning slightly. Whatever effect the light had on the room, afterward all of them, one by one, glanced in her direction with a distinct look of recognition for a face they couldn't quite place. She couldn't say the same for any of them. Other than Ava König, she was certain she didn't know either of the men by face or reputation.

"Now that's done," König said, removing her hands from the table, "we may continue."

"If I may speak first?" Schultz cleared his throat. "The kaiser wishes for us to recognize there must be a denouncement concerning the level and cruelty employed by all sides in the conflict, and yet he must firmly condemn the recent hexing of our mortal men crouching in trenches on the western front." Schultz pounded his fist on the table. "Yes, yes, I know. We're not here to talk about that part of the continent, but to send in the rats and lice to eat soldiers alive in these numbers is simply inhumane. The kaiser wants it duly noted we formally protest this and the harvesting of our fallen soldiers' blood to awaken the undead in the mountain forests."

He'd directed his remarks squarely at Zimin, who simmered with a sort of sadistic delight behind his crystalline eyes. "Which is no more egregious than a curse that renders a soldier half-man, half-animal if bitten by one of König's pack." The mystic's cool demeanor had thawed. He let a new level of hostility bleed through as the accusations of cruelty went around the table.

Petra sat up straighter. Had he just accused König of initiating the vicious curse she suspected Josef suffered from? The very affliction that had brought her here to save his life? Was it possible there was a permanent cure? Something stronger than a few herbs brewed together over a fire? Zimin had held her hostage and forced her to come to the castle using emotional blackmail, but if there was another way to help Josef besides his elixir, it might just be fate that had brought her to this moment. If only she could find a way to appeal to Ava König alone before the negotiations ended.

King Wahaj and König exchanged a conspiring look after Zimin's accusation, one that suggested that, yes, she was responsible for the curse. Meanwhile, across the table, Schultz stared at Petra, biting his cheek and tapping his finger against the edge of the table with an insistence suggesting he believed he knew her from somewhere but couldn't figure it out.

"No doubt we all have summoned dubious magic we later regret onto the battlefield in the heat of the moment," Wahaj said. He waved away any shame in it with a flick of his hand. "Pride tricks us into believing our fiercest efforts always have merit. Later, cool heads see the inflicted cruelty and decry it as unfair. Unethical even. We can and must do better. While some of my kind find pleasure in interfering with mortal wars in this way, the majority do not. And I vow they will not meddle going forward, if that is the desire of this council."

Petra was agreeing with the jinni when she caught Schultz staring at her face again. The continued attention made her uncomfortable, so she pivoted in her seat to face the other direction.

"Thank you, King Wahaj," König said. "I wish all of us had your humility and commitment to peace." The witch purposefully glared at Zimin, giving Petra hope that she might be able to persuade König to help her. "And while I agree we all should take a step back to prevent further unnecessary death, there is one among us who has not only put the lives of our soldiers at risk but those of every citizen along the great spine of mountains dividing our countries." She faced Zimin directly, making her accusation obvious. "To recklessly unleash upíri on hapless mortals is a dereliction of decency, not to mention outright murder."

Schultz pounded the table again in support of König, finally taking his eyes off Petra.

"And yet without drawing universal condemnation," Zimin said, "how does one attract the most prestigious witches of the belligerent kingdoms we each represent to one room?"

His comment was met with confusion and distrust. König and the others shook their heads as if he'd misspoken. Petra, too, wondered what his purpose was in antagonizing the others in the room. Had he really insinuated he'd broken every covenant concerning the use of magic during war *and* peace with the sole intent of drawing them to the negotiating table? What reward could be worth risking one's reputation and international prestige for?

Schultz nearly spit out his wine. "What are you playing at, Zimin?" he asked, mopping his lip with a napkin.

König paled with almost prophetic dread as her eyes traveled from Zimin to Petra. "What have you done, Grigori?"

Zimin took obvious pleasure in their discomfort, yet it was also clear that he craved attention and admiration, no matter the price. A grandstander in a black tunic. A sideshow magician who relished the collective awe of the crowd. "What have I done?" He laughed and leaned back in his chair. "I have brought you opportunity," he said. He sobered and stroked his horse-tail beard. "For the right price."

Money seemed to be a language they all understood with or without the aid of wine. Their postures relaxed, as if it were expected that negotiations would come down to bribes in the end. King Wahaj, however, was the first to understand the mystic's true position as he scrutinized Petra just as Schultz had earlier. His body relaxed as he crossed his arms over his robes, keen to observe how the opportunity would unfold.

"You wish to accuse me of war crimes," Zimin said, challenging them. "Of forbidden magic. Breaking covenants. But when has greatness ever come from meekness? When has timidity ever brought glory and riches?"

"Or maybe delusions of grandeur, my friend," Schultz said.

Zimin leaned forward on his elbows. "Grander than you can imagine."

König banged her walking stick against the flagstones. "Grigori, what is this about?"

"It's about the young woman," the jinni said. "I believe her name is Petra, is it not?"

At the mention of her name, Petra's intuition flared. How did this man from halfway around the world know her name?

Schultz and König glanced at Petra again, only this time they had the advantage of having a name to put to the face they vaguely recognized.

"It can't be," König said. "Petra Stamitz?"

Petra's palms sweated even though her skin had gone ice cold. "How do you know that name?"

The witch let her eye drop to Petra's cheek long enough to suggest she could see the scar plainly on her face. "The same way you know who I am," König said, studying her more closely. "Your reputation, at least, is well known within the witching community."

Zimin cleared his throat when Petra shot him a look of confusion. "I may have misled you as to the precise reason I invited you here," he said with smug satisfaction.

"Invited?"

"Very well," he said, indulging her protest. *"Persuaded."*

King Wahaj raised a finger in the air to pause the conversation. "Please remind me. Why do we care about this girl with the burned face?"

Petra touched her right cheek. Had her illusion failed? She'd grown so accustomed to the constant vibration of the spell against her skin she hadn't noticed the contact had been broken.

"I think what Zimin is proposing is a finder's fee for being the first to apprehend the girl," Schultz said shrewdly, suggesting he was calculating a fair price for her in his head.

Wahaj remained nonplussed, so König explained. "The young woman is rumored to possess a valuable and unique skill for a witch. If true, this one can change the physical form of an object into anything she'd like." Wahaj shrugged, unimpressed, so she added, "I imagine it's much more common among the jinn, but with witches such magic is cast with an illusion spell. Sometimes permanent, sometimes temporary. This one, however," she said with a nod toward Petra, "can actually manipulate the structure of matter, which is why our friend Grigori Zimin thinks he can fetch a good price for her."

"It's why he summoned the undead to the battlefield," Schultz said, his face contorting as the reality of what Zimin had done became clear. "To execute a spell so audacious that even his fellow witches would balk at the brutal outcome and demand a meeting to discuss the dissolution of the spell. Or make him face a tribunal before the Ministerial Council for Magical Affairs. He wanted us all in the same room together to show off his stolen treasure."

But if that had been Zimin's intention all along, he would have had to know about her whereabouts long before she came to the eastern front. Long before Josef recruited her. How else could he have been so certain he could deliver her?

Petra's body flooded with adrenaline, and she jumped to her feet. "This is madness." She tried to leave, only to find they'd been locked in. She pounded on the door to get Stefan's attention on the other side, but he ignored her pleas. Petra stiffened with anger. *As if they can keep me contained in a room I don't wish to be in.* She concentrated on the door, visualizing an oak plank after the saw blade has bitten through the wood. She closed her eyes and pressed her hand against the door to let her magic do its work.

But instead of finding a pile of sawdust and a gaping hole to escape through, Petra faced a door that remained as solid as before. She pushed against the wood to test its resistance. "I don't understand," she said, gasping at her failure to alter the door. "Why didn't my magic work?"

König made eye contact with Schultz but said nothing. Zimin, acting as if his pet monkey had just embarrassed him, patted Petra's chair. "There's no need for hysterics," he said. "The room is surrounded by a spell that intercepts our connection to the All Knowing. It's primarily used in prison settings to disarm witches, but it also has its applications in situations where there's a lack of mutual trust."

König rolled her eyes and clicked her tongue. "A standard security protocol while we carry out our negotiations."

Petra rattled the handle again, trying to force the door open. "What's happening? Why did you bring me here? How do they know who I am?"

"Your illusion spell was disrupted the moment we put our hands on the table and lost the connection," Zimin said, tapping on his cheek to clue her in.

Schultz cleared his throat. "I suspected it was you the moment I saw the scar. It's very unique."

"I admit I wasn't sure if your particular skill set would be affected by the room's energy." The tsar's mystic helped himself to more wine as though he were at a cocktail party. "But now that it's been demonstrated you're as toothless as the rest of us for the moment, you really should sit before you exhaust yourself trying to get through that door."

The stern faces staring back at Petra convinced her to do as he said, though she made sure to sit at the very edge of her seat, ready to run at the first opportunity. "All right," she said. "So which one of you is going to tell me what happens next?"

The emperor's witch, who'd been watching and studying Petra from the moment she'd learned the truth, curled her lip at her directness. "Quite simply," she said, "we'd come to debate Zimin's punishment, but now I think it's your future we're interested in and what your skill is worth to us." König produced a leather valise from beneath the table. She slid her wineglass aside to make room for the bag, which appeared to have some weight to it.

Before Petra could protest, Zimin interjected on his own behalf. "I've already tested her skill. She's far more adept than first thought. In truth, I wouldn't mind keeping her for myself. We could have great fun together. Unfortunately, at the Imperial palace I have position and power, and yet so little money of my own."

"And thus you've brought her to market," Schultz said. He, too, produced a suitcase and slid it on the table. He opened it to show stacks of colorful banknotes wrapped in paper bands. Presumably, they'd all shown up with money enough to bribe their way to a solution to peace, but it wasn't enough for Zimin.

"I've seen what she's capable of." Zimin gulped his wine down in one go. "She could make me twice that amount of cash out of a pile of old telegrams," he said and pushed his empty glass aside.

"Do that and you'll see the entire might of the Ministerial Council for Magical Affairs come down on your head," König said.

"No need for that. Here is a small example of what she can do." He slid his private spell book on the table, followed by the exact replica Petra had made. "I'm sure one of you will pay for her unique talent so that I might avoid prison."

"So what do you want?" Schultz asked. "Do we bid against each other, or do you name your price and we see who can pay?"

"Hmm, I like the sound of naming my own price." Zimin stroked his beard, toying with them. "Though I'm certain none of you brought enough, considering these bags are full of token bribe money to get me to stop calling up the undead."

Schultz slid his suitcase forward. "It's a fair price for a young woman whose talent is known to me strictly through rumor and gossip. Unlike you, I don't have the advantage of actually seeing what she can do before striking a deal, other than this book you suggest she supposedly copied." He looked at the two spell books side by side but remained unconvinced. "Take it and we'll double the amount when I get her safely out of the country."

Petra's hands trembled uncontrollably. She had avoided this moment for ten years. From the moment she had run from home, she'd hidden in cowsheds and caves, monasteries and refugee shelters, sometimes not eating for days. She'd covered her face in illusion and kept her true magic stowed away, all so she would never be forced to perform for greedy men ever again.

"Stop it!" Petra rose to her feet, unable to listen to another minute of their haggling over her as if she were a pig at market. "I'm not some

Lipizzaner dancing horse. I don't do magic tricks to entertain bored nobles or whatever you call yourselves. I'm not for sale. Not to you or anybody else."

"No," König said. "You are the daughter of an accomplished alchemist with an unnatural ability to change the shape and function of matter." The emperor's witch stood to speak eye to eye with Petra. "We've known about you since you went into hiding, of course. The rumors circulated through the salons for years, so we're very curious to see for ourselves what you are capable of. The Empire would be willing to pay double any offer these men put on the table." The witch returned to negotiating with Zimin. "We'd also be willing to oblige the tsar's earlier request for a three-month cessation of hostilities. No curses, hexes, or deadly incantations inflicted on his troops. *If* you give her to me now."

Petra glared at Zimin. "And you get a bag full of cash for turning me over."

"As stated, the money is simply a finder's fee," Zimin said, peeking inside the valise the witch had offered before leaning back, unimpressed. "A reward for being in the right place at the right time to snatch you up."

"And just how did you do that?" she asked. "How did you know I would be recruited to come to the front? Right here, right now to offer me up?"

The smirk on his face told her he'd played the long game. "I always knew you were alive, but I didn't know *where* you were until your friend was captured by the tsar's army."

Josef?

"He came to us with an unusual wound. An obvious curse. Per protocol, I was alerted right away about all incidents involving the supernatural. He should have been put down like any other rabid animal, but then a healer woman claimed she could save him with her elixir. I was curious to know if it was possible, of course, but I grew even more curious about what this healer woman, who hailed from the same village as Pavel Radek, could tell me about you."

Hana. Josef wasn't the only one she tossed the bones for.

"In the end, she proved quite adept at divination. Once I got Dragoş released from prison through diplomatic channels and he confirmed where you lived, we escalated the attacks so the Ministerial Council for Magical Affairs would have no choice but to call a truce. Our plan was to grab you off the street, but then your friend's mission brought you to us instead. All Dragoş had to do was volunteer and ride along with you. After that, he kept me updated on your whereabouts using pigeons. An old but effective means of communication for witches in these turbulent times."

"And you rewarded him with murder," Petra said.

"His was an unfortunate end. I tried twice to have an upír bring you to me first, but they always gave in to the bloodlust. With Dragoş, I had the advantage of his previous commitment to the plan to help override those same impulses after he'd been bitten, but there was nothing to be done after what you took from him. He was already doomed once he couldn't feed."

"Because of your wicked magic."

"Which, I must insist, I be allowed to continue experimenting with after our quaint intervention here is over," he said to the others. "I've grown rather fond of having heartless, soulless beings under my control. Like a taste of my own small kingship. In that vein, I must also insist I keep hold of the young woman until the money can be delivered in full."

König balked. "You're getting greedy, Grigori. We haven't even seen for ourselves what she can do. The book could be a forgery. A simple printing press copy. Rumor may set the opening bid, but proof will dictate the final price. For all we know, you've taken some underling of yours, burned her face, and now you're here trying to pass her off as the Stamitz girl." She held her hand up when he attempted to protest. "Don't bother asserting you're incapable of such a thing. You and I both know you are."

The tension between them plumbed to a depth only those with a long history together could traverse. A chasm created from pleasure on one side of the divide followed by pain on the other.

"Frau König makes a good point," Schultz said. "We demand to see proof of the young woman's skill. And if she is who you say, I could persuade my government to allow the continued barbaric practice of raising the undead, though we'll disavow any knowledge of it."

All of them nodded, agreeing they could promise the same from their governments if she proved authentic. All but King Wahaj. The jinni grew uncomfortable, shifting in his seat and folding his arms over his chest as their talk escalated alongside their obvious greed. What little Petra knew of the jinn involved being trapped in lamps and bottles until called on to fulfill another's desires. Was that what he was witnessing now from the other side? Could he see her being stuffed into a bottle and set on a shelf to await their wishes? Did it taste like bitter truth in his mouth to see himself aligned with those who found nothing wrong with their greed and ambition?

This couldn't be happening again. Pavel had bribed her with sweets to first perform her magic, after her mother had confided in him what she could do. How wide his eyes had grown when he watched his spoon transform into a harmonica, his shoe into a coal scuttle, and his prized pocket watch into an ashtray. After that he'd promised her the moon, if only he could see her turn bronze into gold. And now these people, these dignitaries, were doing the same thing for the promise of instant wealth. Only they were so dazzled by the prospect of being granted anything they desired, they were willing to tolerate cruelty and death to get it.

Zimin held his hands up and consented to their demands. "If it will ease your concerns, we shall have a demonstration of what she can do."

"But how?" Schultz asked. The kaiser's man searched for confirmation of his concern in his colleagues' faces. "If we restore the magical connection in the room, her powers could allow her to escape. Or worse. I'm very quick with a disarming spell, but I'm not so sure this is a good idea. Can we not bind her somehow first?"

Petra had to find a way out. If they were willing to sacrifice their own soldiers huddled on the mountain ridge to those fiends in the name of advancing their governments' agenda, then they were willing to cage her and keep her for as long as her magic proved useful.

"Her compliance is already assured," Zimin said, glowing with self-satisfaction.

"How can you assure our protection, should we allow this demonstration?" Schultz fidgeted with his tie, his watch, his waistcoat.

Petra would turn all their chairs into horse dung and let him sink in it, should they be so stupid as to unleash her!

"She will do nothing outside the parameters of the test," Zimin said. Petra was about to promise she'd do anything but cooperate until he reached in his pocket for the second bottle of elixir he'd stolen off Josef. "That is, if she wants to see her friend recover from his painful curse." He set the bottle on the table for her to see, knowing it was the one thing standing between Josef and the misery the young man would suffer should he not receive it.

"Which curse?" König asked. "And who is this friend?"

"A young man hired by a quaint organization called the Order of the Seven Stars," said the mystic. "He's the one leading the team whose sole purpose is to undo all of my hard work." Zimin leaned in toward Petra. His round glasses reflected the blue light overhead as he stared into her eyes, as though trying to read her thoughts. "But he's grown into more than a mere team leader for her, I think." He snatched the bottle off the table and sat back. "She'll do what we want as long as I have what the young man needs to make it through the night. A result of one of your special curses, Ava."

Petra's eyes watered at the cruelty. Josef had been right. There were witches on both sides of the conflict eager to use the war to advance their personal ambitions. Not caring who they hurt or who got killed, as long as they profited at the end of the day.

"And what about our agreement?" Petra asked before König could respond. "Why should I believe you'll give the elixir to him? Why should I believe any of you about anything?"

The dignitaries went momentarily silent. They'd nearly forgotten Petra was there in the room with them, they were so wrapped up in their strategies to outscheme each other.

"This young man . . . is it the wolf curse?" König asked.

"I don't know," Petra answered honestly. "I believe so. There's some fight going on inside his body. The elixir lets him stay in control of the change, but at a terrible cost." She recalled the eyeshine in the photo and the physical change she'd noted in his irises. He had writhed in pain, as though every fiber in his body were being bent to accommodate a different shape from that of a man. All Petra had was her intuition to go by, but Josef was no creature of the undead. His eyes were tainted in the photos, yes, but he had life in him still. A spark of the wild mountains in his gaze. The eyes of a wolf.

König's attention focused on the bottle in Zimin's grip. "May I?" she asked, holding her hand out for the vial. Zimin hesitated at first but then slid the elixir to her. König uncorked the top and inhaled. Her eyes closed as her nose took in the scents of common self-heal and calendula. "Hana," she whispered, opening her eyes in what Petra thought might be pleasant surprise. König capped the bottle, pausing before sliding it back across the table. "A temporary cure indeed. But I can do better. *If you become my prize.*"

"What say you?" Zimin addressed the group, tapping on the vial. "Do we proceed?"

König pivoted in her seat with her hands braced on her walking stick. "I say we see this demonstration."

After some throat clearing and jacket straightening, Wahaj and Schultz agreed to let Petra access her magic. Zimin knocked on the door to give Stefan the signal to terminate the blue cast blocking their access to the All Knowing. The light dimmed, and the slump in Petra's chest filled with static energy.

There was a tingle in the air for just a moment. Not from the restoration of magic but from the energy of distrust and fear. It radiated among them, riding on a current of uncertainty. For that one second Petra was the most powerful creature in the room as König's words flashed in her mind: *I can do better, if you become my prize.* She needed the elixir, yes, but Zimin hadn't proven himself a man of his word. She had no reason to believe he would hand it over even if she did cooperate.

Petra held her hands against the table, envisioning a jack-in-the-box with the latch released. The table expanded to twice its size, spilling the wine and knocking Schultz, Zimin, and König to the floor. All but King Wahaj, who'd disappeared in a thin wisp of smoke the moment his magic was freed. Petra didn't wait to find out where he'd gone. She used the force of the expanding table to thrust herself toward the door, where she turned the oak to pulp and bolted for the corridor, leaving the witch council to scramble to their feet.

CHAPTER TWENTY

The lower level of the castle reeked of mold and damp as Petra huddled in the dark at the far end of the corridor, past where the blue light hovered. Her chest rose and fell as she forced herself to take long, calming breaths. She had to think. The stairwell was no good; Zimin and the rest had all run straight for the exit in search of her. And even if she had beaten them to the courtyard, where would she go? She'd made a rash decision to escape, and now she wasn't so sure it was the right one. Despite her earlier logic about Zimin's lack of integrity, she really did need that bottle of elixir.

Petra listened for voices, footsteps, or anything that suggested Zimin had returned to the bottom of the stairs to search for her. Poor Stefan still moaned on the floor from where he'd fallen after she rammed into him. She'd had no choice but to turn his sickle into a ship's anchor and trap him beneath it. She thought someone would come to his aid, but they seemed to have left the man behind for the moment. A thing she had to do too.

The corridor led deeper inside the castle's bowels. The space exhaled air from some unknown passageway, drawing her in with the hope of discovering another way out. The risk was finding later that the path terminated in a storage room, but onward she must go, if she had any hope of escaping with her freedom and magic intact.

With her hand pressed against the wall, Petra crept cautiously forward in the dark. Old crates and empty sconces smudged with soot and candle wax lined the curved corridor, while moisture seeped through the cracks between stones. The water had to be coming from somewhere above. An outer wall perhaps? If she could find another way up to the main level, she could get through the wall, but the earth was too full of living things for her magic to work from where she stood. She had to keep going or risk having the side of the castle cave in on her.

Petra had already passed two empty rooms that proved dead ends when she found the true purpose to the underground corridor. A large room, arched in stone, opened up. Inside were seven stone sarcophagi with plaques written in Latin affixed to each one. Long abandoned to the indifference of time, the crypt had lost the luster of reverence. It was now a place for dust and cobwebs and the faint flicker of ghosts.

An angry shout echoed in the hall behind her. *Zimin.* Petra searched the crypt for a place to hide, but aside from the stone coffins, there was nowhere she wouldn't be seen. And she was *not* using her magic to do that. Instead she quickly altered her cape into a dusty, moth-eaten drapery that might have once hung on the wall. She hunkered down below it in the corner when Zimin shouted her name. The threat was followed by a blast of spellfire that spiraled down the corridor in a brilliant shade of orange as it grazed the crypt entrance. The fire fizzled just before it reached her, sizzling in a puff of sulfuric smoke.

If that was Zimin's best attempt at eliciting a scream out of her, he'd already failed. She wondered briefly if she should turn the crates and barrels in the corridor into a wall to hide the crypt but decided against it. The wrenching of stone and wood changing shape in the confined space would crunch as loud as an old man cracking his knuckles, and she wanted Zimin to fret in his uncertainty about where she'd gone. She briefly heard his panicked breathing as he ducked into the crypt and searched behind the three main sarcophagi. She feared he'd pick up the dusty old cloth and throw it out of frustration. Instead, he swiped a decorative cup off the first casket, then turned on his heels and left. When she was certain he'd given up and returned the way he came, Petra tossed off the drapery, trading it back for her warm cloak, and continued searching for another way out.

By Petra's reckoning, she must have completed a semicircle deep below the castle. There'd been no choice of which direction to go when she'd first been led down the stairs, so logically, if there was another stairwell going up, it ought to be on the other side, simply out of a matter of convenience to the castle occupants wishing to visit their ancestors. Of course, any one of the council witches still roaming the main level may have already figured out she hadn't left the castle yet and could be waiting for her at the top of a second staircase. That is, if one actually existed.

There were two niches, one on either side of the sarcophagi. She'd just ducked her head in the alcove on her right when a soft, tingling sensation brushed against her neck. Not a cobweb. Not a cold draft seeping in from a crack in the foundation. No, this was something else. Something *there*. In the room with her. Someone watching her.

Her fingers itched to get her camera out, but this wasn't quite the same shiver she experienced when she followed ghosts. This impression in the air was palpable and—she sniffed—smelled of cinnamon, nutmeg, and coriander. An odd brew for a castle crypt.

"Hello?" she whispered.

The air beside her fogged with fragrant smoke as the figure of King Wahaj materialized. He held a finger to his lips as he drew her deeper into the niche. "They are searching," he said, looking up to the ceiling. His silken robes rustled softly, like an owl gently fluffing its feathers.

Petra feared he'd come to steal her for his own. His powers were unlike the others'. He could whisk her away or strike her down and no one would ever know the truth of it.

"They are yet befuddled, but they'll find a way to trap you soon, and when they do, they will not make the same mistake with you twice. You will be imprisoned. It is a story I have seen many times."

"Why?" She shook her head. "Why can't they let me be?"

The jinni gave a small shake of his head. "Your talent is too valuable to be overlooked. No different than the rubies and sapphires their nations have stolen from faraway places to encircle a conquering king's crown. Men's eyes have always shone with the light of greed and will take what they covet."

"But not you?" she asked, hopeful.

"Your magic is not rare where I come from," he replied with a modest tilt of the head.

"Will you help me?" She didn't want to beg, but she knew she'd be trapped otherwise.

The jinn king seemed to be contemplating the balance between assisting her and protecting his own interests in matters of negotiation. After a heart-stopping pause, he relented. "It is a thing I can do."

The jinni waved his hand, and an illusion of a stone wall fell away from the alcove where Petra stood. The elusive stairs she'd been searching for. King Wahaj held up a finger. "Do not rush headlong to freedom," he warned. "There are already spells floating through the cobwebs."

Petra nodded. She understood. There could be fog laden with knockout gas, flagstones embedded with fine dust that would track her steps, or even enchanted spiders that could bite her ankle so delicately she wouldn't notice, yet the venom might render her all but paralyzed until whoever had cursed her came and carted her off. But all she needed was to get outside unseen and run to the village at the bottom of the hill. With luck, Zimin and the others had already given up on her, but that kind of optimism, she knew, was for fools.

Wahaj bowed slightly and bade her safe travels, but he was done with Westerners and their games of deception. He dissipated, shimmering into thin air. Petra almost wished he could have taken her with him until she thought of what that sort of transformation might do to the body of one not made of smoke. She whispered a quick thank-you, then entered the hidden stairwell.

The steps were wooden, unlike those at the front of the castle. Yet they wound around in the same fashion, climbing through a dark and damp tower. The wood creaked and moaned under Petra's weight, forcing her to step slowly and test each riser before moving forward. To be safe, she kept the image of a steel bridge in her mind as she went, hoping to gird the structure beneath her should it give way.

When Petra reached the top, she pressed her back against the wall. Had she climbed high enough? Was she aboveground? The spiral had disoriented her sense of direction. Was her back to the outside wall, or was freedom in front of her? She paused and listened for the smallest sounds—an exhale of exasperated breath, or suit fabric shifting in the dark, or perhaps a high-heeled boot pivoting on stone—before plunging ahead. But other than the odd complaints of an old building in winter, the room on the other side of the door felt absent of anyone's presence, so she emerged from the stairwell into what appeared to be the kitchen.

Broken bottles were strewn on the floor, an old broom stood propped in the corner, and remnants of dried herbs still hung from the wooden rafters above the hearth. Cobwebs clung to the walls and ceiling, and dirt smudged the thick glass window embedded in the wall beside the oak door. Daylight's last rays shone through, giving her hope.

Petra nearly lunged for the latch on the back door. If she could get to the trees, get to the village, and find a car and willing driver, she'd have a chance. She reached for the knob, when the jinni's voice echoed inside her head, warning her to be cautious. Petra stepped back from the door. Mastering the urge to rush forward, she inspected the doorknob and frame for signs of jinxes or hexes that might trip her up. If any one of the other witches had already been there to cast their spells, she'd be walking right into their hands.

Her eye caught sight of a single spiderweb in the upper right-hand corner. Heavy with dust, the swag swayed clumsily in the air as the castle inhaled and exhaled through the doorframe. But had it been tampered with? She took the broom from the corner and lifted the spiderweb with the handle. There was no shimmer in the low light, and the dust easily fell away. She lowered the thread back where it was.

Time was running out. If Josef didn't get the second dose from her, he'd have to get it from Valentina. If she hesitated any longer, she'd never make it in time to drive him back to the field hospital. *If* she could even find anyone in the village who owned a car. Petra's hand gripped the latch and turned the lock. The door opened easily enough, and she thought she'd made it out—until a sensation of stinging ice zapped her skin. The intense cold climbed up her arm, through her elbow, and over her shoulder to reach her jaw. She couldn't open her mouth; she couldn't speak. Only her eyes and breathing still worked. And the voice inside her head damning her for being such an idiot. Wahaj had warned her and she'd still walked right into a spell. She closed her eyes and tried not to give up.

Just as she feared, a minute later a woman's high heels clicked against the flagstones.

König.

Petra sucked in her breath and opened her eyes.

"Thank the heavens I got to you first." The emperor's witch came very close and whispered in her ear. "I meant what I said. There is a cure. I can help your friend, but you have to promise to come with me. Will you do that? Blink if you agree."

Petra had no option but to agree. She blinked several times until König tapped her walking stick on her shoulder and whispered, "Frost and snow, a chill in the bone, let go of this one, leave her alone."

Petra's jaw loosened, her hand released the latch, and her voice thawed. "Can you really do it?" she asked. "Can you reverse his curse?"

König motioned for her to keep her voice down. "Yes, of course. But first we have to get out of here. You're in grave danger. We both will be, once they realize what I've done." She ducked her head into the hallway she'd entered from. "Zimin is searching upstairs. Schultz is checking the courtyard and grounds, but they'll be back soon." The witch's eyes were alight with fear and determination. "That door is covered in hexes. One step outside and you'd have fallen straight into a trance."

Petra shook off the last of the ice-cold prickles in her arm. "I couldn't see them."

"I made sure to apply my jinx to the handle so you'd get stuck on this side of the door. Thank goodness you didn't turn the wooden door to dust and walk through like before." König put a hand on Petra's shoulder. "I knew your father at university," she said with a wan smile. "Honza was a brilliant alchemist. He was doing things then that others could only imagine. If you have even half his talent, I believe you'll do wonders to advance the field of magic." She lowered her chin and steadied her gaze at Petra as if looking for something briefly. "Has Zimin touched you in any way? Has he made promises in exchange for teaching you his magic?" When Petra mentioned the only promise was to help her friend, König nodded as if she hoped it were true. "I know you have no reason to, but I need you to trust me right now and do as I say. Can you do that?"

Being asked to trust someone who had earlier been willing to pay any price to control you was like seeing a rope thrown over an icy ravine and being asked to grab on and jump. Taking hold could save Petra's life or be her demise. But there was a change in the witch's demeanor that Petra couldn't deny. Had she really known her father? The woman's sincerity landed on Petra's instincts like freshly fallen snow.

Was this the answer to the wish she'd made in the clearing? Could a single snowflake be the magic that would save Josef?

Petra grabbed on to the rope and jumped.

CHAPTER
TWENTY-ONE

König held her walking stick against Petra's neck like a knife as they walked through the castle's great hall. Their footsteps echoed against the emptiness without reply. Petra tried not to fret about the feel of the stick's crystal handle against her skin, but once König had explained that the cane worked both as an aid to walking and as a conduit for her magic, the nearness of so much vibrating energy to her vital arteries set her nerves afire.

The women got halfway across the floor of the great hall before Schultz came in from the cold, stomping his feet. "What is this?" he asked.

"I'm claiming my prize," König said. She pressed the oversize wand firmly against the side of Petra's neck to defend herself, with the business end pointed at the man. "I found her. She's mine. That's what we all agreed when we split up to search the place."

Petra waffled between believing what König told him and what she'd said five minutes earlier about getting out of the castle alive. Petra held firm to the rope of trust. For a moment longer, at least.

Schultz bristled. "Here, now, we can still have a discussion about it, can't we? Nothing is settled yet."

"Don't take me for a fool, Otto." König ordered Schultz away from the door. He responded by stepping to his left to better position himself between her and the exit. Silver pools of light danced in his eyes as he called up his magic.

The witch's heart thudded against Petra's back as she spun them around to keep the kaiser's witch where she could see him. "Stand away from the door. We're leaving."

"Do not be in such a rush, my dear." The witches looked up to where Zimin leaned over the second-floor balustrade above the great hall. "We still have the matter of money to discuss."

König released Petra from her grasp and poised her walking stick in both hands like the weapon it was. "The young woman belongs with me. She is a daughter of the Empire. You had no right to bring her here to sell to the highest bidder."

Zimin smirked beneath his beard. "And yet here we are, doing exactly that." The mystic suddenly leaped over the railing, defying the laws of gravity. He swooped down until the soles of his black *sapogi* lightly touched the floor. König took a reflexive step backward, placing herself precariously between Zimin and Schultz, who seethed with pent-up magical energy.

Petra had to wonder just what the woman's walking stick was capable of, considering no one rushed in to try and overpower them, not even Zimin.

"There's still the matter of my recompense." The mystic's eyes had gone flat, as though he stared in an unfocused trance. He hadn't blinked, not once, since he jumped. It was almost like they were staring at a sloughed-off husk of the man, a shed snake skin that still revealed the slits for eyes. Or a projection of his body while his true one slept somewhere. This zduhać's powers seemed to allow his spirit to take other forms besides clouds.

"Whatever the offer, my government will increase the amount by an extra thirty percent," Schultz said, taking a step closer to Petra.

Zimin raised his open palms in a gesture suggesting all offers were still welcome. "You see, Ava, we cannot let you rush off just yet."

"We had an agreement." König's fingers tightened on the cane. "The money will be transferred, once I return."

"Ava, we are allies," Schultz said. "Let us work together. Combined, we can give him the offer he wants."

Even Petra knew his words were a lie built to buy time.

"And I suppose we'll simply share Petra's talents?" König tightened her grip on her wand. "It's been lovely, gentlemen, but I really do think it's best she come with me. We can discuss any arrangements later."

Schultz called König's bluff. He scooped the air with his hand until a great crackling ball of energy formed. "And what will your people pay with?" he asked. "Gilt scraped off the walls of yet one more extravagant music hall? No, I think the witch comes with me."

Zimin laughed, though his face barely moved. "I'm afraid your promissory note is not enough to secure your stolen goods, Ava. The young woman remains in my care until the money is paid in full."

"She will be a gift for the kaiser." Schultz pushed the ball of energy at König to knock her off-balance. But the witch was ready. She pointed the crystal handle atop the walking stick at the man's chest and released a stream of enchanted flame that disintegrated the sizzling energy he'd launched. Brimstone filled the air as sparks turned to ash and sifted to the floor. Beyond, a sickening sight emerged. The flamethrower had ejected the spellfire with such force it had overshot and enveloped the man's suit. His hair caught fire and blistered his head as his body turned into a conflagration of skin-melting misery. He screamed and rolled on the flagstones until König showed mercy and doused him with a slumber spell. One he would never wake from.

Petra, reminded of her mother's gruesome death, gasped at the sight. The effect was horrific. Ghastly. The sickening smoke made her gag, and she covered her face with the back of her hand. Yet there was no time to give in to panic. There would be retribution, and soon, now that the standoff had turned deadly.

König knelt over Schultz's charred body, staring as though shocked by the power of her own magic. Giving up on their ruse, Petra took hold of her by the arm and forced her to stand. "We should go. Now," she said, giving the witch's arm a tug.

König got to her feet somewhat unsteadily as Zimin's spirit body advanced. Petra supported the woman to the door, but Stefan, somehow freed from his anchor, got there first. "Out of my way," Petra said. "Or find out in the most painful way why there's a price on my head."

The calculations the caretaker made were plain on his face. At first he planned to defy Petra and cast a spell of his own, but he thought better of it and scowled, uncertain what she was capable of after seeing her turn his scythe into a near death trap. In the end she decided to give him a lesson anyway, as she was tired of waiting for men to get out of her way. She reached her hand out and took hold of his suit jacket. She let an image of buckles and straps fill her mind. The buttons on his suit popped, the sleeves extended, and the fabric morphed into white canvas as his arms were wrapped up in a straitjacket like the one she'd seen in the farmhouse attic. Out of caution, she secured the whole thing with a leather belt and a gag for his mouth.

The man squealed, unable to move his arms. His face turned bright red before he became unbalanced and toppled over. Petra stepped around him, pulling König with her to leave, when Zimin stopped in the center of the great room and raised his arms. "You don't want to go yet, Ava. Not when the show is about to start." Threads of static, like filaments of lightning, shot out from his fingertips, forming a cyclone of energy above his head. Soon, storm clouds gathered, building up along the ceiling.

König stopped moving, mesmerized by what she saw swirling above. Her mouth hung open at the sight of the roiling gray clouds as they thundered inside the building and drops of rain began to fall. "No," she said, shaking her head. "Not again."

Petra, too, had been captivated by the magic. The underside of the clouds had an unnatural shimmer that seemed to radiate a faint aura. Or was it an image? In the time she'd looked up to make sense of what she was seeing, König had slipped away to stand in the center of the great hall beneath the storm.

"No, this way," Petra called out to König again, but the witch stood stock-still, unable to look away from the spinning clouds. Zimin hadn't just cast a spell on the ceiling when he summoned his storm; he'd somehow managed to set hooks in König so deep she refused to move, even to save her own life.

Zimin taunted the witch with his haunted eyes. He invited König into his orbit of magic, taking liberties when she neared by encircling her and tracing the contours of her body with his hands.

Petra tried one more time to coax König to her side, but the woman wouldn't take her eyes off the clouds, even when the gaunt, bearded mystic pawed her body and smelled her hair in his ghostly form. Petra couldn't understand. The clouds had no effect on her, yet König saw something in them that triggered a heart-wrenching shudder in her body. She began to cry and buried her face in one hand as though trying to hide from the glare of shame. "No, not that," she said.

Petra risked stepping farther into the room. She feared getting too near the mystic and falling under his spell, but she couldn't let the woman be tortured any longer.

"Yes, come join us," Zimin said, though his lips never moved. "It is a dance we do to get closer to the source of all clear thought." He slashed his finger against König's cheek with his lightning energy, drawing blood. She gasped and covered the scratch with her hand, not trying to defend herself. "Do you believe that to be saved, one must first sin?" König shook her head, but he cut her other cheek and she nodded through her tears.

"Stop it. Leave her alone!" Petra rushed Zimin, ready to turn his tunic, boots, and belt to lead the moment she touched his clothes. Instead, he lifted off the ground like a leaf on the wind. He rose, melding into the clouds until his body dissipated and all that was left was a raging storm that began to spit lightning as he embraced his zduhać form. From her new vantage point beneath the clouds, Petra finally saw what had held the emperor's witch entranced and ashamed. Images swirled on the underside of the clouds like a motion picture film. Lurid frames of a dozen men and women engaged in sexual wantonness scrolled by. König. Zimin. Petra also recognized the tsarina from the newspapers, but the rest were unknown to her, though not the lust in their eyes. Her stomach heaved at the mystic's sin-and-redemption logic on display.

While Zimin's spirit retreated into the clouds, they'd been given a reprieve. A second chance to escape. Petra had no intention of wasting it. Not when she knew what fiends he was capable of calling up in that state.

"It doesn't matter," Petra shouted. "None of it." She wasn't leaving without König, not when the woman held the cure to Josef's curse. Not when she'd likely saved Petra's life by defending her against a man who eagerly awaited the opportunity to exploit her. Petra locked her arm around König's. "We're getting out of here."

Zimin's departure into the clouds had severed his spell over König. She came out of her stupor with damp cheeks and her energy drained, and yet eager to flee. Together, she and Petra ran for the door. Outside, the mystic's two men stood shivering beside the car, stomping their feet to keep warm while sipping from small silver flasks. Petra nudged her head toward the castle. "Negotiations went better than he thought," she said, stealthily plucking a pair of brass buttons off König's fur-trimmed jacket. "He asked me to send you both inside to help him carry some heavy boxes." In a flash, she manipulated the buttons into gold ducats, and handed one to each man.

Their eyes lit with curiosity and the hope there might be more gold where that came from. They didn't look twice at the disheveled König as they swept past to help their boss inside and gain his favor.

"Get in." Petra opened the passenger door, then ran to the driver's side. Her feet barely touched the pedals, and the glass was frosted over so her view was limited out the front, but she touched her finger to the ignition and listened as the car rumbled to life.

"Do you know how to drive this thing?" König tipped her walking stick toward the windshield. A prism of colored light emanated from the handle, forcing the frost to recede.

Petra shook her head. "No, but I watched an ape in a wool coat drive it here. How hard could it be?" After sorting out which pedal did what, she put the car in gear and whispered "*Skol'zit*" as she'd watched Zimin do. The car pulled out of the courtyard with a lurch just as the two stooges came running out the door after her.

The car fishtailed around the bend in the road as they headed toward the setting sun. Moonrise wasn't far off. Petra didn't have the vial of elixir, but she had the witch who could reverse Josef's curse. All she had to do was figure out how to get back over the roads the way she'd come. The landscape whipped by as they took the turnoff for the village, sped past the outlying farms, and drove the car west through the hilly forest. They were so close to freedom they nearly began to sing.

"Watch out!" König yelled. She braced her hands against the dashboard as Petra slammed on the brakes. The car skidded sideways, bumping into a tree before coming to a stop.

Five meters in front of them stood a large gray wolf staring directly at them from the center of the road.

CHAPTER
TWENTY-TWO

"He's still watching us." König cleared the frost from the windshield again with the tip of her walking stick. "Why doesn't he move?"

The heavy rumble of a vehicle drew nearer on the road. It was coming from the opposite direction. A truck. But not just any truck. One with hard bench seats and a canvas top stretched over the back.

"Because he's here to help." Petra kept her gaze on the wolf as she opened the car door. The wolf lifted his ears before turning to watch the vehicle approach. Instead of running away, it trotted over to the side of the road as if waiting to greet the driver.

"Be careful." König gripped her walking stick and opened her door. "He could be one of mine."

"I truly hope so," Petra said, stepping out of the car. The wolf sat on his haunches as the truck rolled to a stop several meters in front of them. She nearly cried when Viktor, Bako, and Yanis jumped out of the cab.

"Petra, thank the stars." Yanis limped over to her on his false leg. "We thought we'd lost you."

"We escaped, but he's still here," she said. "The zduhać. It's Grigori Zimin." She scanned the trees and road, looking for the wolf, but he'd disappeared. "How did you find this place?"

"Josef," he said. "Josef led us to you."

Petra greeted Bako and Viktor with a quick handshake before searching the back of the truck, where she found Josef's ushanka resting on top of his folded greatcoat. His boots leaned against one of the benches. She was confused about the discarded clothing, until an image formed in her mind that wasn't altogether unpleasant. "Where is he?" she asked. "Where'd he go?"

Viktor pointed to the trees, where the sleek silhouette of a man stomped through the snow in his bare feet, still buttoning his shirt. Petra had to restrain herself from running to him. Her chest rose and fell as he crossed the road to greet her. "You found me," she said. "Again."

He drew nearer and inhaled. "You're wearing a different coat, but you still have the linden leaves you carried in the city." He touched his nose. "The scent is strong."

Petra looked down at her cloak and reached in the pocket. The amulet she'd carried from the first night they'd met had stayed with her even after she'd transformed her clothes. "But how are you still standing on your feet?" She looked him over for damage or weakness. "You were shivering and ill when I left you back in the clearing. I tried to get the second dose, but he snatched it away. I had to run. I couldn't get it before we escaped."

"One vial is enough to recover," Josef said, putting his hands on her shoulders to calm her. "You negotiated well with Zimin. He believed I needed the other to survive."

Because she'd believed it too. "What about the guard?"

"Funnily enough, his rifle locked up on him. I may have introduced the back of his skull to the thick end of a stick after that." Josef sat on the tailgate of the truck and slipped his boots on over a pair of dry socks. "Anyway, I'm only sorry I wasn't able to protect you. Did he hurt you? Are you all right?"

"We're fine," Petra said, though a halo of doubt clung to her, recalling the distressing images she'd seen of König and the others dancing in Zimin's illusion. "But he's still there. At the castle."

Josef nodded, but something wasn't right. His breath caught in his throat, and his face went pale before he toppled forward onto the ground.

"What is it? What's wrong?" she asked, holding his head up while she called out. "Help! I need help. He's fallen."

"I seem to have exerted myself again too quickly," he said as Viktor and Bako knelt beside them and got their arms under his shoulders. "But at least I found you first."

"Oh, no, Josef. No, no, no, not now." Petra eyed the sky with worry.

"It's all right," Bako said. "We'll get him in the truck. He just needs his medicine after changing again."

Josef's skin grew warm to the touch as they lifted him into the truck bed. His neck glistened with perspiration, and he began to shake from a chill in the blood.

"I don't have the second dose," she told Viktor. "Zimin still has it."

"He's hiding in a castle up the road," Josef moaned, before collapsing in the back of the truck.

"He was still there when we left." Petra watched the sky, where heavy clouds roiled above the village. "He's already changed into the zduhać."

Bako secured two wooden stakes to his belt and checked his pistol. "Can we get up there? Is it protected? If not, I say we head up to the castle and finally put a stop to this upír army of his by cutting off the head." The major tossed two more stakes to Viktor before jumping out of the back of the truck. "What do you say, Kurková?"

They had no choice. Petra agreed but begged for another minute. She laid Josef's coat over him and whispered, "I have good news. The emperor's own witch is here with me. She says she can cure you. No more elixirs. No more shivering under blankets. It's her curse you suffer from. She can reverse it."

"She can reverse it," he repeated, squeezing Petra's hand before convulsing and passing out.

"He wouldn't stop until we found you," Viktor said after Petra jumped out of the truck. "He'd barely broken his fever when he . . ." He looked over his shoulder at Yanis, who gave him a nod to explain. "You see, it's the energy it takes to *not* fully change that does him in."

"Into the wolf?"

"Into the *vlkodlak*," Yanis said. "A man who wears wolf skin to hunt his victims."

Major Bako secured his saber and pistol to his belt, shaking his head. "He tried to keep it from all of you at first, but a curse like his doesn't stay hidden for long."

"One of my best." König gathered with the others to gape at the sky. "And worst," she admitted. "Remarkable that Hana was able to halt the most vicious aspects of the transformation with her elixir, but then Honza always said she was a very talented healer."

"He was lucky," Yanis said. "They apparently found Josef right away after he'd been attacked. His comrades caught the wolf an hour later."

"They captured the host that bit him?" König pursed her lips, thinking. "So, Hana has inoculated him with the wolf's blood. Or perhaps a few hairs mixed with the right ingredients. Very creative, but not quite a permanent solution, not if he continues to fall ill with each transformation. I can help him with that part, but he'll have to recover first. He'll need his strength." She checked with Yanis and the others. "I assume he changes at will and not with the moon, since he's able to conform to normal social situations otherwise?"

"Correct," Yanis said. "To my knowledge, he's never attacked anyone or shown any aggression. Well, where it wasn't warranted."

"Now that we've got the man's animal temperament all sorted," Major Bako said, "we've still got a zduhać to track down, or have you all forgotten?"

Viktor removed his dark glasses and pointed to the sky. "Looks more like he tracked us down," he said. What had been a calm winter sky grew dark with nimbostratus clouds that threatened on the horizon.

The trees rocked and swayed, knocking the freshly fallen snow off their branches as thunder echoed in the distance.

"It's Zimin," König said.

"What do we do?" Petra accepted a pair of wooden stakes from Bako.

"There's nowhere to hide, and we can't outrun that." Viktor watched his emerging moon get swallowed up by the clouds. "Can we?"

"We'd never make it back the way we came." Bako searched the area for a form of defense, but aside from the trees and rocks, they had only their magic. "If this zduhać can build a storm that fast, he can flip a truck and then call his undead devils to tear us apart."

Petra glanced at Josef, still passed out in the back, his body vulnerable and unaware of the impending threat. How would they protect him in his fevered state?

"Are there enough of us to band together for a single spell?" König asked. "Something to thwart Zimin's energy or spirit?"

"With four witches?" Yanis was skeptical.

"Wait, that's it." Petra looked from the sleeping Josef to the clouds, where she knew a pair of eyes hovered above, watching.

"I've seen what you can do with a spell wall," Yanis said, referring to the illusion she'd suspended in the air to prevent the soldiers from seeing while they'd fought the upír the night before. "But would it hold against that kind of power?"

"Never mind that. We have to go back to the castle. It's our only hope." She scrambled to see if she'd avoided getting the car stuck in the snow when she'd swerved to avoid the wolf . . . er, Josef. She shook her head again at the revelation.

"Go back and do what?" Viktor asked, trying to follow her line of thought.

"We know from the photos I took that Zimin's mind and spirit are there in the clouds," she said. "But he's a zduhać, which means his body is back at the castle."

"Asleep and vulnerable." Once he understood, Yanis checked the speed of the approaching storm against the distance they'd have to travel over the road to reach the castle. "If we can get to the body, we can sever the tie between his physical self and his spirit. His spirit would be stranded in the clouds."

"He can't sustain his spirit form for longer than a few hours without returning to his body to recover," König said. "Like your friend, there's a cost built into the equation of changing form so often."

"But how do we get there in one piece?" Viktor asked. "That storm cloud of his is bearing down fast."

"We don't," Bako said. "At least not all of us."

"He's right, we'll have to split up." Yanis shut the tailgate on the truck and pulled down the canvas flap. "We need a diversion. It's the only way. Otherwise Zimin will see what we're doing and cut us off."

Petra stood up from inspecting the car. Fear and adrenaline had spiked in her bloodstream, making her nervous and unsure, but knowing Josef must get on his feet again flushed a new emotion through her veins. She could no longer deny the way he made her feel. It was confusing in the midst of so much death and grief and urgency to be attracted to someone again. The seesaw of emotions left her shaking her head. But if she wanted to pursue whatever attraction was there, she'd have to get through this moment first. She'd come on this impossible journey because she thought she could save lives with her magic. Right now that came down to saving her comrades. Saving Josef. But first she had to get him well long enough so König could cure him permanently, and that meant saying goodbye.

"Someone has to drive Josef back to camp. Back to Valentina," Petra said. "He needs his medicine, and if we can't get it from Zimin, at least he'll be on his way toward help. The rest of us will drive to the village and then split up so our zduhać has to track us in multiple directions."

"I'll drive Josef," Yanis said.

"Frau König, would you ride with Josef?" Petra asked. "As soon as you get the elixir and get him stable, you can reverse his curse. And then we'll talk about the other half of our arrangement."

The emperor's witch nodded. "I'll be happy if I never go anywhere near that castle again," she said. "He'll kill me if I do." König wished them all luck and jumped in the back of the truck beside Josef.

"Once we split up, we can leave the vehicle in the village and approach the castle on foot," Petra said. "We'll have a better chance of getting inside unseen."

Bako considered her plan and agreed as he climbed behind the car's steering wheel. "Right. Let's go."

With the fragments of a plan in place, Yanis started the engine while Viktor and Petra climbed inside Zimin's car with the bearskin seats. The truck rumbled to life beside them, and the two vehicles diverged. Petra watched the truck disappear behind them with her hand held over her lips. She knew Yanis would use protection spells, but she still worried as the treetops shook violently in the wind, and rain and snow pelted their windshield. Cold seeped in through the vents and windows, freezing her fingers and stinging her nostrils, as the truck disappeared behind them in a vortex of swirling snow.

CHAPTER
TWENTY-THREE

Petra, Viktor, and Bako had traveled nearly a kilometer and were in sight of the village when two massive Douglas fir trees toppled in front of them, blocking the road. The crash of the wood reverberated through the earth to shake them in their seats.

Bako slammed on the brakes. "What do we do now?"

The engine idled as two more trees fell behind them, trapping their vehicle between roadblocks. Petra opened her door and ran to where the trees crossed each other.

"Petra, what are you doing?" Viktor jumped out, watching the sky churn above them.

"This has to end," she said. "Tonight."

She put her hands on the trunks and willed the bark and pulp to change to paper. She wasn't certain it would work so soon after the trees had been uprooted, but enough of the living tissue had been severed from its life force. The trunks shrank to half their size, withering away to cardboard. She dragged them off the road, sending the vehicle through. As Petra climbed back in the car, Viktor and Bako blinked at her as if she were a carnival contortionist who'd just escaped drowning after being wrapped in chains and submerged in a tank of water.

The group drove to the village at top speed. The stormy weather followed, buffeting them in their seats, but there were no more obstacles thrown in their way. Had Zimin grown curious about why they'd driven back to the village? Did he think the others had slunk off to escape his wrath? Who did he want more, her or König?

After winding down lanes where gas lamps flooded cobblestones slick with ice, Bako parked the car beneath an enclosed bridge that arced between buildings. It wasn't perfect, but the semi-occluded spot might provide a small opportunity for them to escape the car unseen. Petra and Viktor jumped out of the vehicle and put their backs to the wall deep in shadow. They waited for Bako to join them, but he stubbornly stayed in the driver's seat.

"Listen," Bako said. "You two go. I'll keep moving. Make him think we're still together."

Petra shrank against the wall. "What? No."

"It's the only way. Otherwise he'll know what we're up to."

Bako didn't wait for them to argue. He drove on as though he'd only paused to get his bearings under the bridge. It was difficult to tell from the ground where the storm's energy had concentrated. Had the zduhać followed the car with his stormy eye? The truck? Or was he waiting to pounce like a cat after a mouse and strike them with lightning the moment Petra and Viktor showed their faces from under the bridge?

Viktor nodded he was ready, and then he and Petra made a run for it. They dodged down alleyways and up stairways hidden in secret gardens carved into the hillside until they reached the grounds leading to the castle. The cloak Petra had conjured for herself fended off the worst of the wind compared to Marek's jacket, but the frigid air still took small bites out of her exposed skin. Viktor, on the other hand, seemed impervious to the cold. He pushed forward, not even turning his face from the wind. She wondered if he'd become so adept at fire spells the residual heat had settled permanently under his skin.

Above, the clouds swirled, flashing with lightning and rumbling like an angry, impudent god shaking his fist. Is that what Zimin felt while soaring in the clouds? A godlike creature, watching the earthlings below? Traveling on the wind to raise an army of undead while he slumbered tens of kilometers away? What man or magician could resist such a temptation? And yet for all the power he'd been endowed with at birth, he still didn't have the touch of gold at his fingertips. No, that was something he'd tried to take, just like Pavel Radek.

Above, the roiling anger in the clouds had subsided, replaced by a still sullenness that sank over the village, except for where silver moonbeams peeked out between the cracks in the clouds. Desperate to get to Zimin's body before he returned, Petra suggested they run the rest of the way while the lightning had ceased, but Viktor stopped her when they found themselves constantly stumbling over rocks and logs.

"Wait," he said, unloading his satchel at his feet. He took out the vase he used to draw down the moon and set it on the ground. Petra had tolerated his odd deity worship before, but she nearly throttled him for his lunatic thinking at a time like this. "She's nearly full, so her energy is strong," he explained. "I'm going to ask her for help."

"Now isn't the time," Petra tried, but he wouldn't budge until he whispered to his *bella luna*.

Viktor held his palms up, closed his eyes, and said his invocation. Petra eyed the full, ripe moon rising in the east above the clouds like a graceful floating orb, and for a moment even she believed in the beneficent goddess as Viktor stood mesmerized as usual, drinking in the beauty before him. But his behavior was the definition of lunacy.

She was ready to make a break for it alone when a trickle of moonlight seeped into the vase, swirling like glowing water behind the cut glass. The luminosity mesmerized the eye, making it nearly impossible to look away. Had he been telling the truth? Did the moon speak to him? *Through* him? *Impossible.*

Viktor smiled. "She's here."

"The moon?"

The glassmaker picked up the vase, still glowing with a soft white light inside the colored glass. "She sent us a moonbeam."

Yes, a wonderful trick, the way he captured the light inside the vase, but what use was it to them in that moment? "What can a little moonlight do to help?" she asked, begging her comrade to see sense and give up his illusions, at least until they finished what they came to do.

She'd barely finished her plea to him when the sky went unnaturally dark, inkier than night ought to be. The kind of primordial darkness that made a person jump at every movement that skittered in the shadows. The moon had disappeared. The stars too. Eclipsed by cloud or shadow. All that remained was the faint glow inside the vessel, where some of the silvery beams seeped out. The light spread over Petra, making her skin radiate with a shimmer that permeated her bloodstream until her sight took on the sheen of luminescence.

"What is this magic?" she asked, watching her hands glimmer briefly before the light retreated again.

"She says hello," Viktor said. "Come on. She'll lead us there."

Petra hadn't believed Viktor, not in the deepest part of her heart where truth resided. Even when she saw the light respond to his command, she still doubted. But she could no longer argue after Viktor held the vase up and a soft violet light illuminated a pathway before them, leading to the castle grounds, one she just knew would be invisible to the unaffected eye watching above.

"Oh, Viktor, you mad genius!"

As they walked unseen in the pitch black, Petra could almost feel the weight of the clouds lower above them, as if Zimin had been plunged into a sea of ignorance concerning anything and everything that scurried on the ground. He could sink as low as he dared to hunt for his clues, but he would not see them without the touch of the moon in his eye.

"This way," Petra said, following the final stretch of the violet pathway as it led them up a jagged wall of rocks. "Quickly, we're nearly there."

When they reached the top, they held back, hugging the ground as they peered over the top of the rock outcropping. The two cars that had been parked out front were gone. She could only assume Zimin's men had departed after she and König had escaped. Stefan, too, if he wasn't still bound in a straitjacket. And yet, despite giving off the impression of being abandoned, a torch continued to burn in a basket outside the imposing front entrance. She hoped it was a sign Zimin's body was still inside, sleeping somewhere in the maze of rooms.

"König said there are spells guarding the side doors," Petra said. "It's possible the front has been hexed by now too."

Viktor lifted his vase, letting the moonbeams cast their glow against the castle walls. The light revealed an intricate web of spell energy encasing the doors and windows.

"Now what?" Viktor asked. "I'm not practiced enough in counter-spells to reverse someone else's jinx on the spot."

"Maybe we don't have to," Petra said. "Follow me."

Recalling the layout of the main floor, she crept around the castle's side, making certain to keep out of the glow of the torchlight. Viktor trailed behind with the bottled moonlight. The wall where they stood appeared free of spellwork for several meters. "What are you going to do?"

Petra tipped her head to take the measure of the wall, then closed her eyes and envisioned the whorled shape of a seashell. She made a silent plea the entire fortress hadn't been jinxed, then placed both hands against the stonework. Gray masonry transformed to marble, metamorphosing with little more noise than a gristmill grinding grain into flour, as a spiral staircase embedded itself in the side of the castle.

"Come on," Petra said, ignoring the swelling in her fingers after manipulating so much matter at once. "König said she last saw Zimin in his physical form on the second level."

It took Viktor a moment to close his gaping mouth and find his footing on the staircase, but moments later he and Petra emerged in a darkened hallway on the second floor. Rooms ran left and right around the center atrium where she'd seen Zimin's spectral body jump.

"This way," Petra whispered. With no clue where to start, she began opening random doors to hunt for the mystic's physical body. The rooms varied from empty and dust-ridden to filled with old furniture stacked away in storage. She'd assumed at first she was looking for a bedroom, but she supposed a man could sleep anywhere.

And so he did. The fifth door she tried led to a room draped in red velvet. There was no bed, and no chair, but there was a stand-alone porcelain bathtub. An elegant thing with clawed feet trimmed in gold, a leftover perhaps from the castle's last legitimate occupant. An unconscious Zimin lay slumped inside the tub with his hands crossed over his body. Almost as if he were asleep in an open sarcophagus.

Petra didn't hesitate. Viktor whispered for her to wait, but she charged over the threshold to take the elixir off Zimin in case he returned to his body. She had to get that first and know it was safe; then they could deal with the body.

She got within a half meter of the sleeping man when a creature, no bigger than a small dog, leaped out from under the tub to sit on Zimin's chest. With long limbs that bent at knobby joints, almost like a praying mantis with a woman's face, the unusual being seemed to be wearing an old pillowcase draped over its body. The thing turned and hissed at Petra.

"What is it?" Petra asked, waving her hand without luck to shoo the odd being off Zimin.

Viktor lifted his vase to let the light of his goddess graze the creature's skin, casting it in a slightly green tone. "My employer has one of these. He calls it a *hlídač*," he said. "A guardian of dreams and slumber. He really doesn't like to be disturbed during his afternoon nap."

"Friendly?"

"Sworn to defend the sleeper to the death, if need be." Viktor raised the vase higher to see deeper inside the tub, but there was only the one.

Of course Zimin has a guardian to watch over him while he terrorizes the entire eastern front.

The creature squatted on Zimin's chest, never taking its eyes off Petra as she took a step back. "It isn't very big." She scanned the room for something she could transform into a weapon. "Couldn't we just swat it with something? Or stun it maybe?"

The guardian bared its teeth, revealing two incisors made for puncturing skin. Viktor reached in his coat for his iron punty. "What can you do with this?" he asked, handing off the stunted glassmaking tool. The short punty turned into a two-meter spear in Petra's hand, stunning Viktor yet again by the ease in which she manipulated matter. "How do you do that?"

Petra hefted the spear in both hands and jabbed it at the ugly, shrunken guardian with the intent of flinging it off Zimin. Instead, the creature, defying its small size, took hold of the pointy end of the spear and lifted Petra off the ground.

"Whoa, whoa, whoa." Viktor set his vase down to keep it safe. "Let go of the spear," he said to Petra before she got tossed out a window. He grabbed her legs, pulling her down to the floor again. The creature snickered and tossed the spear across the room, where it split a wooden plank in the door.

Viktor decided to give it a try, using his fire to frighten the creature away. He kept his flame thin but hot, staying within the blue spectrum. With saber-like proficiency, he thrust the flame at the creature to get it to back off. The guardian merely straightened on its long limbs and let the fire pass between its legs. Whichever way Viktor sent his flames, the creature evaded it.

Too quick, too smart, and too damn loyal to its sleeper, the *hlídač* held its ground over Zimin. Everything they tried to get near the body failed in a frustrating defeat. Time was running out. They had to get the elixir and dispose of the body before Zimin's spirit returned. But what could break a guardian's duty to its sleeper?

"Is it controlled by a spell?" Petra paced in front of the tub, running out of patience. "How does someone even get a personal *hlídač* to protect them?"

Viktor shrugged. "I think my employer pays the one he uses."

"That's it?" Petra stopped and studied the creature in a new light. "So, you're motivated by money, are you?" The creature bared its teeth in what Petra took for a greedy smile. Shaking her head, she asked Viktor for any spare change in his pocket.

"I don't think it will be enough," he said, handing over a few meager hellers.

Petra gave him a watch-and-see look as she jingled the small coins in her hand. She'd sworn to never use this magic again, yet here she was, about to turn nearly worthless objects into gold for the second time in one night. She cupped a single heller between her palms and envisioned a golden sun. The nickel coin transformed into a golden ducat. The guardian rose on its hind legs to get a better look. "Enough?" she asked the creature.

The creature frowned and squatted. Petra transformed the remaining hellers until she held four golden ducats. "How about now?" she asked, extending the coins in her palm.

The *hlídač* scurried off Zimin's chest, snatched the ducats from Petra's hand with its bony fingers, then hid under the tub, where a tittering sound and the clanking of coins echoed off the porcelain.

"Right. Now what do we do?" Petra asked.

Behind her, Viktor had gone pale. "You're her, aren't you?" He stared at her hands and at what she had done with the coins. "They all talk about you. The alchemists. I never truly believed you were real until just now."

"Never mind that," she said and squeamishly patted down Zimin's tunic to search for the elixir. The mystic exhaled, whistling through his nose and ruffling his mustache as her hand hit on the gold ducat he'd stolen from Pavel Radek after gutting him like a fish. The weight of everything it represented threatened to sink her on the spot, but she palmed the coin and kept searching Zimin's coat until she found the vial tucked away in a breast pocket. "Got it." She held the bottle up in triumph, but they were only half-done with their mission. "Now what do we do with him?"

Viktor had been staring at her with a sort of awe, but he shook it off as she backed away from the body to stand beside him. "Stake through the heart?" he suggested.

Petra looked at Zimin's body in horror. With the upíri it'd been different. They'd attacked first. The fiends weren't even alive anymore when they'd plunged stakes into their chests, just reanimated corpses that needed to be stopped. But to kill a man in his sleep? She'd thought she'd murdered a man once before, and it had nearly ruined her life. "I don't think I can," she said.

"I . . . I don't think I can kill him either," Viktor said. "But we have to do something."

Petra tried to remember everything Hana and König had said about the zduhać's powers. He was a spirit, but one that had to return to the physical form to renew. The safety of his body was so important, the man had hired a guard to protect it in sleep. But if the spirit and body couldn't reconnect, then what? If the spirit had to spend its last energy looking for a body it would never find, would it get snuffed out like a flame that had run out of wick?

"Come on," Petra said, getting an idea. "Get under his arms and help me move him. If he can't find his body, he can't reanimate."

"If he can't return, he can't survive," Viktor said, understanding her meaning. "He'll die in the clouds." The glassmaker tucked his vase safely away in his satchel again. Together they slid Zimin's sleeping body out of the tub and down the hall, dragging him by his arms as his heels scraped against the wood floors.

"Now where?" Viktor asked.

"Another room somewhere." Petra considered their options. "We just have to get his body out of sight."

Taking small, quick steps, they dragged the unconscious man into the room with the stored furniture. A blanket chest with a solid oak top proved a useful size. Together they heaved his body into the chest, closed the lid, and stacked a set of ornate andirons from the fireplace on top. In the end, if it worked, they would still be taking a man's life, but somehow the deed rested easier on Petra's conscience, recalling the war crimes Zimin had committed as the zduhać. He deserved a bloody end for what he'd done, but it wouldn't be from her hand. Better to let the flaw in his magic kill him in answer to the way he'd abused the power for his own ends for so long.

"I'd add the candelabra for a bit of extra weight, if I were you," said a familiar voice.

Petra spun around. "King Wahaj?"

The jinni reanimated in the shadows behind a grandfather clock, making Viktor jump. "The alchemist's daughter and a jinni in one night." Viktor blinked several times before smothering a laugh behind his hand.

"Why are you still here?" Petra asked Wahaj.

The jinni king looked around the cluttered room as if it were obvious. "It is a quiet place to think and watch the snow. It is so seldom I get to witness such a thing." He picked up the candelabra from the dining room table and set it on the chest between the andirons. "There—now he is safely hidden inside."

Petra hadn't counted on anyone else being in the castle. "You saw what we were up to."

"Oh yes." The jinni's bright eyes turned on Viktor. "I was drawn by the most delightful light."

The glassmaker, taking a cue from Petra, opened his satchel and took out the vessel containing the moonlight to show the jinni. "Moonbeams," Viktor said. "A gift from my *bella luna.*"

The jinni king beheld the glow in Viktor's hands. "How does one attain such a gift?"

"Love," Viktor said, as though it were plain.

The jinni acknowledged the truth of it with a nod, unable to take his eyes off the soft light. He held out his hand, a gesture one might mistake for an invitation to dance. A trickle of light escaped the mouth of the vase to accept the offer, illuminating the jinni's arm and face. The old king laughed like a giddy child as they took a turn around the room, moving in rhythm to a song only they could hear. When their dance ended, the moonlight encircled his head once before grazing Viktor's cheek and floating through the window to return to the sky.

"Thank you," the king said. "Thank you for sharing your beautiful gift. I will now share mine with you. What may I give you in exchange?"

Viktor glanced at Petra, unsure what to do or say. "I . . . we—"

"We need to return to our friends on the road," Petra said, holding up the vial. "I have medicine for a man who is ill. He needs it urgently, but we have no way to get there."

"Ah," the jinni said. "You require quick transportation. That is a thing I can do."

"Really?" Viktor tucked the vase away and slung his satchel on his shoulder.

"We had a car," Petra said. "But it's in the village." She thought to explain about the zduhać watching and waiting for them, but she suspected the jinni already knew Zimin's true heart.

"Then we shall have to improvise," King Wahaj said, widening his eyes in mischief.

They descended the marble staircase and met the jinni in the courtyard. There, he waited for Petra and Viktor to take notice of the horse-drawn cart in the weeds.

"You can't be serious," Viktor said.

"She will sail like a ship on the air," Wahaj said with a smidge more optimism than either Petra or Viktor felt. "You shall see."

One wheel was missing, and the floorboard was nearly rotted through, but the jinni made good on his promise and magicked the wagon upright. He encouraged them to climb in with an eager nod of his head. "You shall see, you shall see," he kept saying as board by board the cart grew solid and sturdy. The missing wheel reappeared, a velvet cushion covered the seat, and the all-important reins were reinstalled. The jinni waved his hand, and the wagon lifted a half meter off the ground as if the wooden sides were made of hollow bones and downy feathers. Viktor grabbed the reins, for all the good they did him without a horse attached.

"As with most things in life, it will follow the road you choose," Wahaj said. "I prefer a woven rug myself, crafted by the premier weavers of my homeland, where the air is soft and warm. However, this will take you where you wish to go." The jinni bowed and bade them safe travels before they had a chance to object. "Peace be upon you," he said as he dissipated before their eyes.

"Ready?" With no other option but to try, Viktor gave the reins a slap. Petra nodded and the wagon gently slid forward, lifting them higher off the ground. After a few steady moments in the air, Viktor grinned wide like a crescent moon. "It really is no different than guiding a horse."

"Perhaps a Pegasus would be more apt," Petra said, clinging to the side of her seat as they rose cautiously higher. But the more confident they grew, the faster they went, until they were gliding above the ground on a current of cold night air.

How and where they would eventually land, however, was up in the air as well.

CHAPTER
TWENTY-FOUR

At the speed they were moving, Petra hoped they might catch up to Josef and the others in the truck before they reached camp. Then she remembered the barn had burned and the tsar's army was on the move. If the others had arrived, would Valentina have even been at the field hospital anymore to administer the elixir?

"Oh, do hurry," Petra said, thinking of Josef suffering from fever in the bed of the truck. She squeezed the vial in her hand as though it were an amulet, holding it tight against disaster.

Viktor let out the reins, and the wagon soared higher until it ascended over the tops of the trees. The rush of air was exhilarating, but while Viktor had conjured a ball of fire at their feet to keep them warm, a storm brewed in the distance, filling Petra with cold dread. Lightning flashed from cloud to cloud like angry fireflies trapped in a jar. Or a zduhać rattling the sky to show his power. She feared now that Zimin had chased the truck after his vision had been plunged into darkness outside the village. The moon shadow had given them the time they needed to get to the castle and hide the body, but at what cost?

Beyond the electrical storm, another kind of light punched holes in the darkness. Artillery fire lit the undersides of the clouds with flashes from its deadly fireworks. Viktor and Petra were certain they ought to still be several kilometers east of the ridge, yet they were getting dangerously close to the fighting. Fearing they would sail straight into the teeth of battle, they slowed the cart and descended closer to land.

They had just settled into an easy hover a meter above the road when Viktor pulled hard on the reins. The wagon dropped onto the ground with a thud, skidding sideways off the road and coming to a stop between trees. Ahead of them, they spotted the truck their friends had been driving. The vehicle lay mostly on its back with two of its wheels still spinning on the axle. Smoke rose from a blackened hole in the ground in front of the hood. It looked like a grenade had exploded.

While they surveyed the damage, an arm struck out from the other side of the wheels.

Petra jumped out of the cart. "It's Yanis." The sorcerer moaned in pain as she approached. His face was bloodied and his clothes were covered in dirt and snow as he leaned against the truck's front bumper. "Are you all right? What happened?"

"Zduhać." He pointed to the sky. "He used lightning to crash the truck."

"Are you hurt? Can you stand?"

"My ribs," he said, wincing from the pain it caused to talk.

Petra let Viktor take over checking the sorcerer's injuries, then frantically searched the back of the truck for Josef. She found him on his side tangled up in a blanket, with wooden stakes and extra canteens strewn around him.

"Josef!" Petra tossed the blanket aside. He was feverish, and his cheek bled from a cut below his eye. "I'm here," she said. "I have the elixir." When he didn't respond, she crawled over the canvas siding, cradled his head in her lap, and pressed the bottle to his lips. "Drink. You'll get your strength back." She rubbed his arms and chest to get his blood flowing. Seconds later his eyes flew open, wild and disoriented. His nose caught a scent on the air and he reached out, gripping her hand on his chest. "Are you hurt?" she asked. "Anything broken?"

He shook his head, but she still feared he'd been injured in the crash. The truck was lying on its side, which meant he'd hit the ground hard. As gently as she could, Petra tucked the blanket under his head and checked his arms and collarbone to see if anything was broken. She moved to his legs next, bracing her hand against his thigh as she gently bent one knee and then the other.

"I'm just bruised," he said, sitting up. "But I won't complain if you want to continue your examination. It's important to be thorough."

Petra sat back, too relieved to see him regaining his energy to scold him for his teasing. "I'm just glad you're all right."

He reached out, cupping her cheek in his hand. "Thank you," he said.

Petra softened at his touch, closing her eyes, if only for a second, to absorb the feel of his skin against hers. There was so much more of him she wished to feel. "You're going to get better," she said, opening her eyes. "Ava König can cure you. She knows what to do. As soon as you're stronger. All this will be over."

He brushed her cheek with his thumb, then let go, exhausted. "I hope you're right," he said.

Petra helped Josef crawl out of the truck and wrapped him in the blanket. Viktor had started a fire for Yanis, but it proved a temporary reprieve as the sky exploded with orange flashes and streams of smoke. The fighting was getting close enough they could hear men's screams in the distance. And the wind was picking up under the churning clouds.

"Where's König?" she asked. Viktor shook his head, not knowing, but Yanis pointed toward the trees, suggesting she'd gone there to shelter away from the truck in case Zimin returned. "She can't be far," Petra said. "I'll go find her."

Shoe prints in the snow led to a stand of beech trees. Drops of blood trailed beside. Petra quickened her pace. "Frau König?" Her call was answered with a frightened sob a few meters ahead. Petra stomped through the snow, pushing weedy saplings out of the way until she spotted a lone figure sitting on a log.

"He did this." König lifted her head. A gash on her forehead was bleeding into her eye so that she squinted up at Petra. "He can send thunderbolts from clouds. How does one man get that much power?" She wiped her sleeve against her face to clear the blood, but the wound kept pumping out more.

"Come back to the truck." Petra turned her head at the snap of a twig through the trees. "We have a fire going. You need to warm up and get that head looked at."

"He'll strike the truck again." The witch shivered under her fur-lined coat. "He's been watching us. Waiting. He knew you'd return."

Petra worried the witch's head wound was more serious than a mere cut. She needed to get her back to the fire, back to safety. "Come with me," she said. Petra held König's hand, stepping nearer to her with the same caution one used when approaching a stray dog. But the emperor's witch was right. The energy in the air had subtly changed. The evening sky had been black and orange with the firestorm of war. Smoke had trailed through the trees and over the road, filling the air with the scent of gunpowder. Petra listened, but she could no longer detect the sounds or sights of battle. Yet there was a distinct new stench on the wind. One of decay.

"What is it?" König stood and searched the trees around her.

"Shhh," Petra said. The smell grew stronger until she secretly wondered if König had stumbled onto an unmarked grave site. And then she saw them through the trees. A dozen men in uniform surrounded them. Only they weren't soldiers. And they weren't men. Not anymore.

Petra searched her belt for her hawthorn stake, but of course it was gone, along with her husband's clothes. She had no weapon on her but her magic and her wits. Would they all come at once? Could König defend herself? She must.

"Do you have your walking stick?"

"It's them, isn't it?" König reached for her stick. "He's called his upíri to us."

"That or the wound on your head has lured them here." Though it was hard to see how the trickle of blood spilling from her head could compete with the horror taking place a mere kilometer away. "Get ready to direct your fire at them, if you can."

The first fiend sprang from the trees. Ava König deftly aimed the crystal handle of her powerful wand at the upír, unleashing a stream of fire. The creature burst into flame and was incinerated on the ground, but their respite was short-lived. A pair of ghouls that looked like they'd recently crawled out of the earth eyed Petra. Their hair was matted, the clothes ripped and ripe with blood. Limbs, ears, and fingers were missing. They rushed, and she raised her hands defensively, catching them both by the arm a second before they bit. With her touch, she turned their busted-up bodies to stone that crumbled at her feet.

"Behind you!" Petra watched König swing around just in time to burn another revenant at the end of her walking stick, but they were quickly being outmaneuvered. Three upíri taunted Petra by smiling and creeping closer while they unhinged their jaws. She knew she could transform one of them, maybe two, but the third would likely kill her.

Petra picked up a stick and backed up, buying time. The first one jumped, mouth open. The stick transformed in her hand into a two-meter stake. She raised the sharpened tip just as the upír leaped, skewering it on the landing. The force of the impact nearly snapped her wrists. She managed to hold on, but the weight of the creature trying to wriggle loose knocked her backward, and she tripped on the hem of her cloak. The other two fiends lunged. Petra let go of the stake and braced for the attack, ready to turn them to ash with her hands.

She never got the chance.

Viktor torched the first revenant with his flame, while Josef slammed a stake through the other's back with a mallet until black blood oozed through its shirt. Viktor pivoted and burned another before it could swipe its claws at König's legs. She blanched at how close the thing had come to striking her before she'd noticed it was there.

"Protect the emperor's witch," Josef called out to Viktor as he swung around to defend himself against an attack on his flank. The upír moved with surprising quickness, evading the swing of Josef's mallet. But the creature had backed into Petra, who turned it into shreds of paper that blew away in the wind.

Josef watched the pieces float away. "How did you do that?"

Petra brushed her hands off. "They move like people, but they're as dead as sticks and stones."

He gave her a nod of approval before pulling another stake from his belt. Petra scanned the trees. There were three more upíri biding their time. Was Zimin holding them back? Was he watching? Were there others coming? The trees swayed in the wind as the roar of trucks rumbling on the road grew closer. The bombing had stopped, replaced by a smattering of gunfire exchange and the occasional explosion of a grenade. In the wake of calm, the air grew foul with the taint of smoke and char. The energy shifted again, elevated by the current of fear and adrenaline passing from man to man.

"They're retreating." Josef bit his lip, thinking. "The tsar's men must have finally breached the pass. The army is pulling out. We ought to go now too."

Petra tuned in a second longer to the hum of energy, then spun back around to face the upíri. One of them had disappeared. "Where did he go? There were three of them; now there are only two."

Viktor and König shook their heads. Josef tilted his ear toward their overturned truck. "Yanis. He's in trouble," he said and broke into a run.

How stupid! They'd left Yanis, injured and alone, by the fire. Petra followed. As they ran, the two other upíri chased after them, ignoring Viktor and König, who lagged behind. Josef slowed and let the fiend on his left catch up, then swung his mallet into its jaw just as it lunged. Far from a killing blow, Josef and the upír locked arms as they struggled and fell to the ground. Petra nearly gave up her dash for the truck, until Viktor caught up from behind and yelled at Josef to get out of the way. Josef rolled right and the glassmaker torched the revenant's body.

Petra had no such luck. The second upír outran her, making straight for Yanis. Ahead, she could see the other one had already found him. It hissed and lunged over the fire but refrained from attacking after being distracted by a hawthorn bush in the sorcerer's hand that continued to grow more berries.

"That's right," Yanis said before grunting with pain from his broken ribs. "Count the berries. Too many to ignore." He let his eyes meet Petra's as the second upír arrived with its mouth open.

Petra knew he couldn't defend himself for long as he waved the hawthorn weakly. She took a breath and rushed the second upír from behind. She got her hands on his rotten flesh as rage filled her mind, fiery, red, and full of fury. The revenant twisted in agony as its body morphed into a blackened log, already half-eaten by fire. She took her hands away a second too late. The sizzling charcoal blistered the tips of her fingers, yet she felt nothing as adrenaline pumped through her veins.

Yanis was still in danger. His hawthorn spell seemed to be losing power as he winced in pain from his injured ribs. The upír bared its teeth, ready to tear the sorcerer to pieces as the hawthorn berries shrank. Yanis waved the branch as he taunted the fiend, daring it to leap. Josef grabbed Petra around the waist and pulled her back just as she moved to interfere. The upír charged and Yanis dropped the branch into the fire. The flames leaped a meter high, ignited by a second spell and the brittle dryness of the branch itself. With a swipe of his leg, he knocked the ghoul into the fire, where it was scorched by the flame. It struggled to free itself, raising up onto its knees, until Viktor landed the final blow with a ball of spellfire that incinerated its putrid body.

Yanis screamed in agony at the cost to his broken ribs from defending himself. But there was little time to comfort their friend. Behind them, a single gray cloud appeared directly above Ava König, casting a shadow over her. Unlike the earlier roiling skies that had threatened to topple trees and tear shingles from rooftops, this threat was isolated. Shrunken. Pathetic. Had Zimin's energy finally run out? Could he already sense that he'd lost his tether to this earth?

"Frau König, come. We need to leave this place." Petra waved the emperor's witch over as she watched the cloud swirl overhead. "He is nothing," she said, eyeing the patch of rain cloud. "A wisp of air without physical form. He has nowhere left to go." Unable to resist taunting Zimin one last time, she shouted, "He will soon fizzle out and fade from the sky forever."

König took strength from Petra's bold claim. She wiped the blood away from her eye and nodded, as though she finally believed she was free from him. "Coming," she said just as a spindly bolt of lightning shot out of the cloud, striking her walking stick.

Electricity shot through the crystal, exploding in a shower of sparks that cracked like a whip in the air. Flashes of electricity zapped König, ensnaring her in a halo of white light, before she shuddered and collapsed in a final tremor.

Above, the cloud rotated, darkening at the center, until a small tornado formed with a wicked tail. The wind churned around the witch's body, kicking up leaves and sticks. Petra feared Zimin meant to obliterate the truck and everyone near it with his remaining power. She searched for a shelter they could run to, but then, just as suddenly as it had started, the wind died down. The rotation in the cloud slowed until it was nothing more than a band of mist and fog. The faint scent of rain permeated the air a brief moment as the cloud evaporated into nothingness. True to form, the zduhać had exhausted the last of his energy on one final act of vengeance.

CHAPTER
TWENTY-FIVE

Petra stared open-mouthed at the woman's singed corpse. There was no question König was dead. A thin stream of smoke rose from her charred remains, yet Petra went to her anyway with the hope she might still wake. Josef gripped her by the shoulders to hold her back.

"Leave her," he said. "There's nothing to be done."

"But this is all my fault. She was going to cure you."

Josef folded his arms around Petra. "I know all too well what's been lost, but it's gone now," he said just as a grenade detonated a hundred meters away.

Across the clearing, men ran past—caps flying off their heads, rifles and haversacks slung loose in their hands. They ran for their lives through the trees. They ran to trucks forming a convoy on the road below, ready to race to the nearest train station. They climbed into truck beds, grabbing their wounded comrades by the collar and hauling them up with them. The emperor's army was fleeing from the mountains by the thousands as the ridge they could no longer defend was overrun by the tsar's men.

"We have to go." Josef turned Petra around, not letting her look back at the woman on the ground as he walked her toward their overturned truck. "Can you fix it?" he asked, making her focus on the task before them. When she didn't answer, he looked at Yanis and Viktor. "Can you get the truck upright. Any of you?"

"The radiator is shot," Yanis said.

"We have to get to the trains." Josef tried flagging down a truck as one after another drove past. "We have wounded," he shouted, but the trucks drove on, too overloaded to carry more. "Damn it, where is Bako?"

"We can take the wagon," Viktor said, pointing to the cart wedged between the trees. Josef glared at him like he thought him a madman. An unfortunate look Viktor was forced to suffer often, but he took it in stride, walking over to the horseless cart. "It should be able to hold us all."

"And how do you propose we move it?" Josef inspected the wagon as if wondering how it got there in the first place. "Am I to be the beast who pulls?"

"No, it flies," Petra said. "A gift from King Wahaj."

Yanis ceased grimacing long enough to ask, "You saw him? King Wahaj granted you a gift?" He hobbled over to the wagon, clutching his side to examine it with a new appreciation. "This is a great honor."

"Did you say 'flies'?" Josef knocked the notion away with a swat of his hand. "I'm not going anywhere in that thing."

A pair of grenades exploded nearby. Close enough this time to make their ears ring.

"I don't think you have any choice," Viktor said. "Get in!"

"It doesn't even have wings. Or an engine!"

"No, it has magic." Yanis sat on the edge of the wagon bed and slid inside. "Magic I trust. Human ingenuity, not so much."

With a growl loud enough to let even the emperor know he was displeased, Josef crawled in the back of the wagon and hooked his arm around the struts beneath the front seat. Petra climbed in beside him, acknowledging his bravery with a weak smile, while Viktor grabbed the reins. With a slap, the wagon pulled forward.

"An illusion spell wouldn't be out of order," Yanis said, lying down on his back when he was no longer able to fight the pain of sitting up.

Petra got to her knees and raised her energy. Her fingers were blistered and sore, but she conjured a spell wall filled with the colors of the northern lights. As the wagon lifted higher, she spread the spell out to hide them from those on the ground. Josef's breath came out in huffs, and his skin turned an unhealthy shade of pale with every bump in air current, but even he settled down once he was certain they wouldn't imminently crash to the ground.

Petra watched the last of the Empire's men run for safety below them. Where the trees had once been thick on the mountainside and the winter snow undisturbed by men's footsteps, there were now scenes of splintered timber and blackened craters. Packs and tents and playing cards strewn on the ground. Machine guns abandoned in rocky crevices. Bloodied ground and broken bodies left behind on a snowy mountain slope where only Morana, walking aside the fox and lynx, belonged in the dying days of winter.

From the air, the war changed shape in Petra's eyes. What had seemed like a fleeting moment in the life of a marriage all those months ago, when Marek had confidently declared he was off to join the fight, had transformed into the demise of naivete. There'd been no quick homecoming by Christmas. No medal pinned to his chest. No stories of bravery to be recalled in old age, when their children and grandchildren were gathered around the table. Perhaps they never were destined for such future shadows of a life together, but the war had stolen their choice. The coldness of Marek's death sank inside her. A frozen splinter of ice permanently embedded in her side to sting the skin whenever she might have cause to remember this place.

And still the wound she carried could not compare to the scars she witnessed on the ground. Witches' curses had taken their toll on this place, but for all their cruelty, mortals had proven more than equal to the task of inflicting their own brand of pain and destruction. With their bombs and guns and careless decisions, they'd unleashed more ruin than any spell had wrought.

Petra leaned over the side of the wagon and watched one army rush out of camp only to see another swoop in. From the air she recognized the farmhouse and the burned imprint of where the barn had once stood. Packs of men searched the field hospital with their weapons pointed in front of them. What would they make of the doctor's work on the dead? Or of her darkroom in the attic? Or the straitjacket and scratches on the wall? She snapped a photo of the tsar's troops, curious to see how many of the emperor's unseen soldiers walked among them—those who had no more reason to rush anywhere.

As the wagon trailed away from the scene, Petra followed the road with her eyes to where the trucks fled, one after another, heading for the nearest rail station like a great migration of lumbering elephants. And there, at the back, racing to catch up, she spotted an odd black car with skis aside the front wheels.

"It's Bako," she said, pointing. "He's made it. He's following the trucks."

Josef lifted his head and strained his eyes in an attempt to look, but he couldn't find the courage to let go of the seat strut long enough to see over the side of the wagon. "I'll take your word for it," he said. "He's a good man. He'll find us once we put this thing down."

"Uh, and where should that be?" Viktor called over his shoulder.

Josef's and Petra's eyes met. "Home," they said in unison, though for Petra no such place existed any longer, outside of the back of the wagon.

"We heal up in the city, and then we reform as a group," Josef said.

Petra was surprised yet relieved to hear his plans. "To do what?"

"The war isn't over yet," Yanis said. He took a strip of willow bark from his haversack and tucked it between his teeth to chew on for the pain. "And there will always be more monsters to fight."

Petra silently nodded. She'd always known there were monsters—some that come for you in the middle of the night with their teeth bared, and others that sit at the kitchen table, smiling at you over their goulash and dumplings while their minds whir with thoughts of murder. And still others reside deep inside you, stifled and forgotten, until they rise like revenants to make you face the past you thought you'd buried.

Petra settled on the floor of the wagon beside Josef, who'd finally relaxed enough to nod off. Fastened to his hip was one of Karl's wooden stakes with the verbena symbols carved into the base. She gently slid it loose and held it up to study in the moonlight. She'd never pictured herself as a monster hunter. Or a young widow either. But as she flew home, soaring above the caravan of wounded soldiers, untethered from both the earth and her past, the shape of a promising future came into focus as she turned the stake over in her hands and Josef leaned his head gently against her shoulder.

ACKNOWLEDGMENTS

Once again, I've had the good fortune of working with the same team of people at 47North during the production of this novel as I had with my first book, *The Vine Witch*. What a gift to be able to rely on those same relationships when it's time for the hard work of making the words ready for publication. Thanks, as always, to Marlene Stringer and Adrienne Procaccini. The brilliant alchemy at work between them is the reason I'm able to continue writing books. Thanks also to Clarence Haynes, who, as my developmental editor, has become something of a therapist for me, always making me dig deeper into my characters' emotions and reactions, which any writer knows really means *my* emotions and reactions. Much appreciation goes out to Jon as well, whose eye for grammatical and historical detail has saved me from probable public ruin as a writer more times than I care to count. And much deserved thanks to Kellie, Lauren, and the rest of the team at 47North and Amazon Publishing—all those who work behind the scenes as midwives helping to birth the books in their final form. A shout of thanks also goes out to Kimberly Glyder for her stunning cover design for *The Witch's Lens*. And finally, a huge thank-you to the people of Prague, Czech Republic, for their hospitality while I visited their beautiful city as part of the research for this novel. You have my heart.

ABOUT THE AUTHOR

Photo © 2018 Bob Carmichael

Luanne G. Smith is the Amazon Charts and *Washington Post* bestselling author of *The Raven Spell*, *The Vine Witch*, *The Glamourist*, and *The Conjurer*. She lives in Colorado at the base of the beautiful Rocky Mountains, where she enjoys hiking, gardening, and a glass of wine at the end of the day. For more information, visit www.luannegsmith.com.